Broken Lives

TERESA DEVEREUX

Matador
9 Priory Business Park,
Wistow Road, Kibworth Beauchamp,
Leicestershire, LE8 0RX
Tel: 0116 279 2299
Email: books@troubador.co.uk
Web: www.troubador.co.uk/matador
Twitter: @matadorbooks

ISBN 978 1838591 953

British Library Cataloguing in Publication Data.
A catalogue record for this book is available from the British Library.

Printed and bound in Great Britain by 4edge Limited
Typeset in 11pt Garamond by Troubador Publishing Ltd, Leicester, UK

Matador is an imprint of Troubador Publishing Ltd

To my husband, Grahame and daughter Louise for their patience and support and to all the wonderful dedicated professionals I have had the priviledge to work alongside during my career.

1

NEW START

At the end of the pedestrianised high street, just off the market square and above a charity shop, could be seen a row of symmetrical aluminium-framed windows which belonged to one of the district offices for Social Services. It would be very easy not to notice the entrance to the office if you didn't know it was there inside a deep wall recess. The only thing to distinguish it as separate to the shop was the security box by the side with a number pad, a button to press, a speaker for visitors and a very small, grubby brass sign above which read Children's Services; please ring for attention.

Although it was early morning, there was a scattering of people milling around in the dappled sunshine of the high street, some occasionally stopping to look inside the few shops which were now dedicated to various charities, pound shops, betting shops, or empty with For Sale boards leaning up against the windows. This had been a prosperous seaside town many years ago, but since holidays abroad had become affordable, once-beautiful Georgian hotels had been left to wither and fade, eventually becoming hostels for the homeless or asylum-seeking families.

Appearing from amongst the amblers, and striding rather than ambling, was a slim, petite young woman in a pale blue cotton dress, her dark brown curls bouncing over her shoulders as she walked intently. She stood out from the others as someone with a purpose and for whom time mattered. In one hand she carried a black laptop case, and a brown leather satchel style bag with straining buckles hung heavily from her opposite shoulder.

April Gardiner was a new member of the social work team, and for the first time since she'd started there a week ago, she did not walk straight past the door and have to turn around and retrace her steps. She smiled to herself as she turned into the recess and pressed the button on the keypad, which was at least one thing in her new and unfamiliar environment that she had got the hang of. The door buzzed as the lock was released and she made her way up the steep, narrow staircase, her footsteps echoing on the dusty wooden stairs. The office she had left behind was a modern, purpose-built building with wide open-plan spaces on the edge of an industrial estate. A huge contrast to this old converted Victorian home in the centre of a deprived seaside town that had seen better days.

Inside, the office was buzzing, with phones ringing, the loud hum of incoherent voices and a general cluster of noises. Hot-desking was what everyone did here, and April scanned the office for a free desk where she could sit down and set up her laptop. She still felt slightly awkward being the new person in the team, not really knowing whom she could trust or even getting to grips with anyone's name. She had chatted a few times to Paula, a senior practitioner who buzzed around the office, self-assured, confident and jolly; April always found herself drawn to people like that. but despite being a social worker and her confident manner with the families she worked with, she was generally reserved, especially when entering new and unknown territory; she always treated new acquaintances with polite but distant caution.

April located an empty desk and sat down before glancing around the office, testing her memory on the location of loos, filing cabinets etc. Extremely familiar to her was the underlying tension and buzz which were part and parcel of a busy social work office. Two middle-aged social workers whose names she could not recall were sitting opposite each other, heads down, stern faces, furiously tapping away on their keyboards, probably trying to finish reports with deadlines that had long past, a situation April was acutely familiar with. They were too engrossed in their work to acknowledge April or anything else that went on around them. On the wall beside one of them was a large red poster with a few pictures, clearly done by children; handprints in pink and purple, blobs of yellow and blue creating a background of colours, and a child's writing which read, 'love from Caitlin xxxxxx.' Between the desk and the wall were four grimy, well-used car seats, one with white streaks down the back which looked very much like baby sick. The walls of the office were yellow but badly in need of a lick of fresh paint.

Although late May is arguably one of the most beautiful times of the year in England, and outside the sun was shining, with spring flowers everywhere (tulips and magnolia, not to mention the peachy-white blossom from the apple trees), in this office it could just as easily have been mid January. The windows were set too high to see out of, and the dust on the outside and the high walls of the shops opposite blocked any sunlight. The windows could be opened but, had anyone done so, the air that came in would not be beautifully scented with flowers or blossom, but tainted with exhaust fumes and traffic noise. April would have loved to work and live in the countryside but in her job that was not very likely to happen. Social workers needed to be easily accessible to their community. The state of the office was a stark reminder of the lack of funding and low priority from successive governments, placed on disadvantaged families and the people who work with them.

Just as April had sat down and made herself comfortable, she noticed the team manager Maria beckoning from her small office in the corner. 'Have you got a minute?' Maria shouted over. 'I need to talk to you about a new case'. April followed her into her small office.

'I know it's early days for you and I don't want you to feel bombarded before you've got your bearings, but I'm afraid we're really struggling to manage the level of referrals coming in at the moment. I need to ask you to take this case which I think you will like; it shouldn't be too difficult and you might even find it interesting.'

April smiled to herself. She had been a social worker long enough to know that when a manager says a case is 'interesting', what they really mean is 'challenging'. She didn't mind a challenge, though, and her caseload was low. 'Of course I will take it,' she said, as though she had any choice in the matter.

April was a member of the long-term team which, rather than taking new cases which were in crisis and then handing them over to another team, generally handled cases that required ongoing intervention until problems were resolved, either by children being removed from the family, or circumstances improving enough for the case to be closed. April enjoyed this kind of work because she could get to know her families and build a nice relationship with the children.

'This is one of those revolving-door cases, you know the type. The case was closed last year because things seemed OK, but there's been concerns raised again by the school about six-year-old Tayla Bushell. Her attendance has been poor, various strangers collecting her from school etc. Mother has had problems with alcohol on and off and it seems like things might be going downhill again. You just need to visit really to check things out.'

Back at her desk, April started to sift through emails, marking the ones which needed replies. She was fully aware that this office would be no different to her previous one and there would be more than enough work to keep her busy and interested. It wasn't easy, though, being the new person in a team where no one appeared to have time to spare to make a new person feel welcome. She found herself feeling a bit lonely and isolated, wishing that Paula was there, who always seemed to have time for a chat. She noticed the two women had stood up and were both walking towards the tea room, one of them talking intently while the other nodded her head and laughed. This intensified April's loneliness and her feeling that she didn't belong.

She then started to think about the friends she had left behind, with whom she had worked for almost ten years. In her previous team, there were a couple of social workers she had known since university. They had qualified together and begun as newly qualified social workers in the same team. How nice it had been to have comfortable familiarity with colleagues; to be able to confide your deepest thoughts and talk about your hopes, fears and despair. People who really know who you are; with whom you can be yourself. Apart from a couple of really close friends, she had chosen to leave all this behind her. Sometimes people can know too much about you. You realise too late that the laying bare of hopes and dreams between trusted people can turn into a poisoned chalice if those dreams become nightmares. There had been no hiding from the painful memories, the agonising disappointments and feelings of failure she had endured. The only way forward seemed to be to get away from everything she knew and make a new start with her husband, Jed. Looking around her now, she began to wonder if this had been the right thing to do. Her brother had told her that you can't run away from the past. Max had always been the sensible one; something to do with him being born first perhaps, although it was only a matter of twenty minutes.

Having read her final email, she leant back in her chair and, feeling stiff from sitting in the same position, stretched her arms above her head and pushed her legs out straight in front of her. Just as a yawn was starting to develop, she noticed a tall, blond man, aged about forty, heading in her direction, smiling.

'Hiya, I'm Miles; welcome to our team. I've been out of county doing a transfer conference, only back Friday, but it's nice to meet you. I guess you're April?' His smile was broad and friendly with two little dimples at each side of his mouth.

She quickly repositioned herself in a normal sitting position and, stifling the yawn, swivelled her chair in his direction. 'It's nice to meet you too,' she said, as she shook his hand.

April couldn't help thinking how attractive Miles was. She was married, though, and so, probably, was he, but that didn't mean she couldn't enjoy being his colleague, and being in the company of such an attractive man could add quite a bit of spice to her working day. He pulled up a chair and in no time at all the two were chatting as though they had known each other for years. He had it all – charm, wit and a warm and friendly persona – and most importantly, for the first time since she'd started her new job, April felt the loneliness gradually lifting.

Monday over, April returned to her lovely Georgian semi where she cooked herself some pasta and a side salad, poured a glass of Pinot Grigio from the fridge, plumped up some cushions and sank into her comfy sofa ready to watch whatever happened to come on the television. Jed wasn't due home that night because of work commitments, so she planned to have a long soak in the bath and an early night with her favourite novel, The Mayor of Casterbridge, which she was reading for the third time. This was what she loved: her new home, her novels and her comfy bed. She loved her husband too, but there was something nice about just having oneself to think about sometimes. Jed worked away more often these days after being made a partner in his firm of accountants. It wasn't a big firm, but it was expanding and more work was coming in from further afield. He wasn't due back until Thursday and she knew that by then she would be really missing him and pleased to have him home.

They had been lucky to find a house which, although it was on the edge of the town and close enough for April to walk to work, was at the end of a quiet cul-de-sac; and with nothing much between their garden and the estuary, where they could see a glimpse of blue in the distance, they could have been living in the middle of the countryside. The peace and tranquillity of their own little garden was a stark and welcoming contrast to the frantic atmosphere of work, the location of the office and the chaotic lives of the families she worked with.

2

OUT AND ABOUT

It was the following Wednesday before April found the time to visit the Bushell family regarding the case Maria had told her she would 'like'. She drove into the street where the family lived, in the heart of Coronation Estate. She was looking for Flat Number 3, Fairfield Rise, in Elder Road. She wondered how Elder Road had got its name since there was not a tree in sight. There were rows of identical semi-detached houses on either side which she drove slowly past, scanning the area for a block of flats. Although she had never been in Elder Road before, it could have been many of the places she had visited in the course of her work, with messy gardens, broken fences and a general picture of poverty and deprivation. Some of the front gardens had bits of spindly hedging where attempts to provide some privacy had been made, whilst others had scraps of broken fencing or were just open to the road, enabling passers-by to see the broken toys, clumpy grass and bits of old rubble that had been thrown out by the occupants, or thrown in by people from the street. Occasionally she would spot a neat and tidy garden with flowered borders and mowed lawn where the residents had strived to improve their surroundings, but these were almost always flanked on either side by squalor.

April had herself been raised on a council estate by a single mother, but things appeared to have deteriorated in more recent years for people who depended on social housing. There were now these deprived areas where inhabitants were routinely unemployed, often single parents and drug or alcohol dependent. They were the marginalised who had no hope or aspirations, and whom society scorned or at best ignored.

April was beginning to get frustrated as she seemed no closer to locating the flat she was seeking. She then spotted two large women standing on the pavement, smoking cigarettes and chatting. She pulled up beside them and opened the car window on the passenger side, which was closest to where they were standing. She leant over the passenger seat so that they could see her. There was a baby in a pushchair and a toddler standing quietly beside his mother, sucking noisily at the dummy in his mouth, which was almost as big as his face.

'Hi there, sorry to bother you but I wonder if you have any idea where I might find Fairfield Rise?'

One of the women exhaled smoke before stamping out her cigarette on the pavement. 'See that bit of grass?' she said, pointing further down the road. 'It's over there. You'll see the building when you get there; it looks like a big house.'

'Thank you very much,' April said as she prepared to drive away.

'No worries.' And then, 'You're not a social worker, are you? They've always got social workers going in those flats. I don't know why.'

'No, I'm not a social worker,' April said, sensing their eyes following her, full of curiosity and suspicion, as she pressed the button to close the window, changed gear and slowly pulled away from the kerb. She could see by their expressions that they didn't believe her. These people knew a social worker when they saw one. They would by now be gossiping about what went on in those flats and speculating around whose kids Social Services should be taking away.

April drove further down the road as directed until she arrived at the green, fronting a large detached Victorian house which she could see had been converted into a block of flats with three floors. She found Number 3 and rang the bell. There was no sound, so she knocked and waited. Still nothing. She knocked again before opening the letter box to peer in. Inside, she could see a dingy hallway with a buggy pushed into the space under the stairs; the paint, which probably had once been magnolia, was now a jaundiced shade of yellow. The floor was covered with old black tiling, which general wear and tear had stained with patches of grey and white. Looking further down the corridor and up to the ceiling, she could see that the paint was yellow with age, and decades of cigarette smoke. A bare light bulb hung from a dangerous-looking piece of crooked wire. A strong smell of fat frying, mingled with cigarette smoke, wafted out of the letter box. She could see that there were two flats on the ground floor, so Flat 3 must be upstairs.

After a few more minutes and still no response, she decided to phone the mobile number she had fortunately remembered to take with her from the case file. After a few short rings the phone was answered.

'Hello,' she said, 'is that Samantha Bushell?'

'Yeah, who's that?'

'It's April Gardiner, the social worker; I wrote to you, did you get my letter?'

'I thought you were coming tomorrow; you said the 8th.'

'It is the 8th today, Samantha,' April said.

'It's the 7th today; I'm just on my way down the school. Tayla's teacher wants to see me, again!'

April soon heard Samantha's footsteps coming down the creaky staircase before the door was opened and she was invited in.

April was pleasantly surprised at the bright, clean presentation of the flat, although sparse as far as furniture was concerned, but quite a contrast to the dingy, cold, unwelcoming entrance hall. Samantha had clearly made an effort with her limited resources to provide a comfortable home for her children.

9

'I'm afraid if you were supposed to go to see Tayla's teacher on the 7th, you're too late, because it's definitely the 8th today,' April told her.

'Oh shit.' Samantha was clearly very annoyed at hearing this. 'They hate me at that school anyway; they'll be back on to the Social, givin' it all the crap.'

'Is it all right if I sit down?' April asked as she perched herself on the edge of a chair, which had orange stuffing spilling out of the tears in the imitation leather. Samantha was clearing away some used crockery from the small coffee table and April was struck at first by how young she looked. Her thin, long, straight charcoal-coloured hair had an orange tint to the roots and hung over her shoulders in wisps. She was wearing tight jeans and a short, tightly fitted purple top with two thin straps across each shoulder, and, with her tiny stature and slender frame, looked more like an adolescent than a twenty-three-year-old mother of two. April, who was on the small side of average, felt quite tall beside Samantha's four feet and ten inches.

On closer scrutiny April could see many fine lines around Samantha's mouth, and her eyes, which appeared large against her dainty features, sank further into her head than one would expect for a woman of her age. Her smile revealed two quite pretty, even white teeth at the top of her mouth, but a gaping black hole to the side where a tooth was missing. Her pale skin appeared almost ghostlike against the darkness of her hair. April could see that her ears were studded with various coloured earrings from the top of the ear to the base. A spider tattoo spread from Samantha's right earlobe down to her shoulder, spindly legs stretching around her throat and the nape of her neck in the form of very fine, delicate lines. They appeared to be reaching towards the tattooed spider's web running down her left arm, where the corpse of an unfortunate insect was trapped. April was intrigued by the intricate but sinister nature of the art. Tattoos, she thought, were usually butterflies or tulips, or names of previous lovers. April wondered whether this was a visual representation of

Samantha's emotional state and somewhere deep in her psyche, she saw herself as the entrapped corpse in the spider's web, being stalked by the predatory alcohol.

April could imagine that Samantha would have been a very attractive young woman had it not been for her lifestyle and the effects of traumatic childhood experiences and abuse which had clearly taken their toll. Her appearance spoke volumes about her lifestyle and diet, as well as the poor value she placed on herself.

Tayla, six, and Lily Grace, three, were sitting together on the small two-seater settee, absorbed in Mr Tumble on CBeebies, each with a dish of chicken nuggets in front of them which they picked at slowly, their eyes glued to the television. They looked clean and tidy and their hair had been brushed and neatly styled by a mother who clearly took pride in her children's appearance. They did not look like children who were suffering or had suffered neglect. On first impressions there would not appear to be any dysfunction in this family or home.

April sat herself down on the chair opposite the girls and within minutes become the focus of interest for Tayla, who placed her dish of chicken nuggets on the settee before walking over to where April sat.

'What's your name?' she asked.

'My name's April,' April replied, smiling warmly at her.

'Are you a social worker?'

'Yes, I am.'

'We used to have a social worker called Judith but we didn't like her.'

'Oh, what a shame, why didn't you like her?'

'Because she was crap and she didn't do anything to help Mummy, and she told lies, and Mummy didn't like her either.'

'I don't think she could have been a very good social worker if she told lies. I wonder why she would have done that?' April said, amused.

'Tayla, go and play in your bedroom and take Lily Grace with you,' Samantha ordered.

Tayla huffed but did as she was told whilst bossily telling Lily Grace to come with her. April couldn't help noticing how little Lily Grace did as Tayla told her without question. Taking her sister's hand, she followed her into the bedroom. April could hear Tayla tell Lily Grace that she had to be very quiet until the lady had gone. 'You have to be a good girl and do as you're told,' she ordered, just like a mother would say to her little child.

April explained that there had been a referral to Social Services from the school expressing concerns about Tayla's poor attendance, not wearing school uniform and a variety of different people collecting her at the end of the day. Samantha replied that she hadn't been feeling very well for a few weeks and there had been days when she couldn't take Tayla to school or pick her up. She said she was better now so it would be all right from now on. Her benefits had been stopped for a few weeks because one of the neighbours had reported that she had someone living with her. That's why she couldn't afford to buy school uniform, but it had now been sorted out and she was going to get the uniform at the weekend. April pointed out that there had been concerns about the same issues in the past, and although things had improved for a while, long enough for the case to be closed, it was disappointing that these things were now happening again.

She wanted to know why a neighbour had reported that someone was living with Samantha if it wasn't true, and as she waited for her answer, she scanned the flat with her experienced eyes for any signs that a male lived or had been staying there. There wasn't anything within her limited view which suggested that, but she would wait until Samantha seemed more relaxed and trusting of her, and then she would ask for a better look around the property.

Samantha replied, 'That's just what people are like around here; they're all bitches and like to get you into trouble. I haven't got anyone living here, and I'm not going to either. I'm sick of men; they only want you for one thing. They get what they want, beat the crap out of you, then bugger off with someone else. I've just got rid of the last bastard who did that to me, and I just want it to be me and my kids now, they're all that matters.'

'That sounds very sensible to me,' April said. 'I will have to do an assessment to decide what kind of help and support you need as a family; have you got any thoughts about that, Samantha?'

Samantha was quick to reply. 'I've had loads of assessments. They keep doing assessments', almost spitting as she emphasised the word. 'They just come up with loads of crap. Last time they tried to send me to SMS. They said I was a piss artist; load of shit'. She flung her arm out as she said this. 'I'm not saying I don't ever drink, but the odd can doesn't make you an alky, does it?' she asked indignantly. 'I bet you have a can of beer sometimes; everyone does, don't they?'

April was aware that SMS stood for Substance Misuse Services. 'Well, that's fine then,' she said, unconvinced. 'We shouldn't need to keep your case open for too long if all the problems are resolved, but I will do the assessment anyway. We will then have a meeting with all the other professionals involved with your family and decide what needs to be done. It must be difficult looking after two children on your own – have you got any family you can go to for help or support if you need to?'

'There's my mum but we don't get on, she's a cow most of the time. Can I get you a cup of tea?'

'No thank you, Sam. Anyone else?'

'No. My mum comes around sometimes and we'll be all right, but it's her bloke, Wayne I can't stand; he causes most of the trouble. I wouldn't let that filthy perv anywhere near my kids.'

'Have you been assaulted by him?' April asked calmly.

'You're joking. I would knife the bastard. He used to try it on when Mum was out – I knew what he wanted though; I was only a kid; he was sick. I used to stay at my friend's most of the time 'cause I couldn't stand him.' Samantha suddenly stood up from the chair she had been sitting on, walked over to a small cupboard in the corner of the room and pulled a vape out of a drawer. She dragged the little round coffee table towards her, sat down again on the edge of the chair and started fiddling about with the vape.

'Did Wayne ever do anything to you?' April continued.

'No, I told you; he'd have got a knife in his gut. I would have got the blame if anything happened, though, 'cause Mum thought the sun shone out of his arse; she's always like that when she gets a boyfriend.'

'Has she had a lot of boyfriends, then?'

'You're joking, aren't you?' Sam gave a smirk. 'She always had some fella round. At least Wayne doesn't beat her up like Martin did. He used to punch and kick her, and once I saw him smash her head against the wall. I think I must have been about nine or ten. But he was always sorry afterwards, and he would make tears run down his face so that Mum would forgive him. They always went to bed then to make up. I would just switch the television on so I couldn't hear anything while they were at it.'

By this time, Sam had the vape set up and was inhaling deeply and blowing the exhaled steam towards the ceiling. 'You don't mind me doing this, do you?' she asked politely.

April just shook her head quickly, recognising that Sam was using distraction tactics. 'What about your dad, where is he?'

'What, that shitbag?' Sam snarled. 'He went off with someone when I was a baby. He's got other kids now; I don't know how many. Mum used to say she would make me go and live with him if I caused her any trouble, but I knew that wasn't going to happen because he didn't want me. If he had he would have kept in touch, but he didn't and I don't give a damn because I can't stand him anyway.'

These words were poignant for April and caused her stomach to turn over. Her own father had walked out on her family when she was a baby, to be with another woman. They had never heard from him since.

'Were you an only child, then?' she asked.

'No, there's my half-sister and -brother, Chloe and Braydon. Chloe was thrown out when she was sixteen, same as me. She's about twenty-six now. She couldn't stand Wayne and they used to be always fighting. He used to creep around her in a pervy way and she would tell him to fuck off. He didn't like that, so he would throw her out of the house and tell Mum she had been the one to start it all. Of course, Mum would believe Wayne, and then one day that happened and Chloe didn't come back. She lives with a smackhead now, and I think she's one as well.'

'What about Braydon?'

'He's nineteen now, I think. He's in the nick; could be out now, I'm not sure. Last time I heard he was on the streets; haven't seen him for over a year.'

From behind the bedroom door, April could hear Tayla's little voice. 'I'm your mummy now, Lily, and you've got to go to bed, otherwise that nasty man will come and take you away.'

'I am,' Lily said submissively with a hint of panic in her voice.

'Let me put the blanket over you then, darlin', or else you'll get cold. I'm just going to the shop now so you better be a good girl.'

April could see a proud smile on Sam's face as they listened to the children playing.

'Tayla gets a bit bossy with her sister. She tries to boss me about sometimes. You wouldn't believe she's only six, would you?'

April felt herself warming to Samantha, who had, during the course of their conversation, revealed herself to be a caring mother who, like most mothers, wanted to do the best for her children. April was impressed by her openness. She had admitted that she had had boyfriends, and clearly recognised that the relationships had been negative. She'd said she would never put up with what her mum put up with, and wouldn't let 'wankers' like Wayne or Martin near her children. This gave April some hope for the future, but whether Samantha would be able to keep to that intention was yet to be seen. April had heard these and similar vows made before on many occasions.

It was obvious that Samantha had experienced a difficult childhood, including at the very least chronic neglect. From what she had said about her mother's lifestyle it was very likely that physical and possibly sexual abuse as well as domestic violence had been a regular feature of her childhood. These experiences would have impacted quite dramatically on her emotional development and distorted her view of what constitutes a normal relationship. No wonder she had turned to alcohol; she would have been trying to blot out some of those awful memories. She clearly wanted very much to be a good mother to her children; specifically to be better than her own mother was. She wanted to give her two girls a better life than she had had and was trying her best, but limited inner resources and lack of support made this a difficult task. It would be interesting to see if Samantha could break the cycle of deprivation, and April felt a strong determination to do everything she could to help her achieve this.

April recalled another case she had been involved with in her previous team; the mother was called Lara. Lara's problem was drugs rather than alcohol, but each can have the same devastating effect when addiction sets in. Lara tried hard to fight the addiction, engaged with the services offered to her, and even entered rehab a number of times in a desperate attempt to hold on to her two-year-old son and baby daughter, but in the end, they were removed from her care and adopted. Lara died of a heroin overdose and it was never clear whether this was an accident or deliberate. The memory of this horrible episode made April shudder. Although she had done everything she could to help Lara, she still carried a sense of failure around with her. She hoped desperately that this Bushell case would have a happier outcome.

It was still warm and sunny when April left Samantha's flat. The street seemed to have come alive with a group of women talking at their garden gates, some children playing with a football in the street, and some adolescent boys huddled around an old quad bike in the road. There was a chip shop just down from the flats and a queue was forming outside.

As April started her engine and began to slowly move forward, three or four children aged between about five and nine came to the pavement in front of the car and started making crude gestures with their fingers, their fresh pink faces distorted with anger and hatred. Poor little things, April thought. She wondered what their parents were doing whilst their children were out in the street – or had the parents sent them out on this mission because they guessed she was a social worker?

3

TRIALS AND TRIBULATIONS

Jed wasn't due home until the following evening, so it was another evening alone for April. She had had enough of being on her own now and couldn't wait to have him home with her. She planned to prepare a nice meal with a special bottle of red, to welcome him back. She decided to spend the evening making herself beautiful so that he could see what he had been missing. She was contemplating doing something different with her long, dark curly hair. It had been in the same style for years now and she felt in need of a change. With the mirror in front of her, she lifted her hair and held it behind her head, trying to envisage how she would look with a short style. She was fortunate in that her skin was pale and clear and, with a slightly pink hue, gave her a younger appearance than her thirty-eight years. Her eyes were large in comparison with the rest of her features, and a striking sapphire blue with flecks of green. Her twin brother Max had the same eyes, and for as long as she could remember, people had commented on their unusual colour.

With her hair held back, and allowing a section of dark curls to fall forward, she moved her head from side to side to see her profile from different angles, and was happy with what she saw. She felt that a shorter style would enhance the attractiveness of her eyes. She was able to visualise her face, framed with short curls just below her ears, and the decision was made; she would have her hair cut at the weekend. She felt quite excited at the thought of a new look; new house, new job and new image.

The next day in the office was an admin day and April had a number of reports to write, including the detailed record of her visit to the Bushell family. She had not been convinced by Samantha's proclamations that she only had the odd can of beer, but having said that, everything appeared fine when she visited and there was nothing obvious to set alarm bells ringing. She hoped that was how it would continue, and that she could finish the assessment and close the case. As a social worker, April was an optimist by nature, but she was also a realist, and twelve years in the job had taught her that with the Bushell case, bearing in mind Sam's childhood experiences and the concerns that had been reoccurring since shortly after Tayla's birth, it was unlikely that this family would manage for long without Social Services' support. The best likely outcome would be that the family continued to move in and out of the Child Protection Threshold as they had been doing since Tayla was born. Sam clearly loved her girls, but addiction was a powerful dictator. The only way to overcome any addiction is to recognise there's a problem. This is difficult for any addict, but easier to ignore when you can manage for weeks or even months without indulging.

April had a few more visits to do before she could go home for the evening.

'Anyone for coffee or tea?' Paula was asking.

'Oh yes please, that would be lovely.' April found writing reports quite tedious and was always happy to be distracted.

'Have you just moved to this area?' Paula asked as she wandered over to where April was sitting.

'Yes, it was quite a long commute for my husband from where we used to live, so it was a good opportunity to exchange our boring modern semi. We found this lovely Georgian house with large bay windows and a garden which isn't overlooked by anyone; always one of my dreams.' April pressed the 'save' button on her computer, planning a much-needed break and a little light conversation. 'One of our reasons for moving was to be closer to Jed's work, but he seems to be working away more than ever. I do quite like time to myself sometimes, though.'

She swivelled around in her chair to face Paula. April had no intention of letting on about the real reason for their move, or not at this stage anyway. She judged Paula to be in her mid to late thirties. She had short hair which was bleached silvery blonde, and a plump but very pretty face which was always smiling. She seemed like a warm, open and genuine person, and it didn't take long for April to find out a great deal about her life, including that she was divorced and had two teenage children, one of whom would be off to university shortly. Paula had been looking for a man on dating websites, so far unsuccessfully.

'We must go for a drink one evening after work,' Paula said. 'I will tell you about some of my experiences with dating websites; it might give you a laugh.'

'That sounds great, I will look forward to that,' April said, smiling.

Paula told April that she had only qualified five years ago and previous to that had worked in residential homes. It had been quite tough doing her degree whilst bringing up two children as a single parent, and it was going to be many years before she paid off all the associated debts. The children's father helped out a bit but was nothing to write home about.

Miles, who had been talking to Maria the team manager, spotted the two women chatting and came over to join in their conversation. April was again struck by how gorgeous he was: tall, blond, blue eyes, and broad, strong shoulders. Looking more closely at him, she thought he was probably a bit younger than her, but she decided that if she had not been already happily married, him being a few years younger would not make the slightest difference.

'So, how's it going so far?' He pulled up another swivel chair, placing it near to where Paula and April were sitting.

20

'Good. I will be glad when I'm more familiar with the area and I've got to grips with the new cases, but it's all interesting. Cases don't vary much from one place to another, do they; same problems seem to arise wherever you go. It's just the names that change.'

There followed more general discussion about previous jobs etc., and April was struck by Miles's apparently genuine interest and attention. Was he really that interested in her? He certainly had the knack of making her feel as though he was.

She just happened to notice that Miles didn't wear a wedding ring. He could be gay, she thought, but either way it didn't really matter. She found out a number of things about him during the course of their chat, but couldn't find the opportunity to ask about marital status or relationships. She just thought how nice it would be, having a colleague who was so attractive to look at; whether he was gay or married wouldn't really matter at the end of the day.

'Miles, it's for you,' the clerk was shouting across the office whilst holding out the phone. 'It's Barbara Hollis for you.'

Miles rolled his eyes as he walked towards his desk to take the call. April didn't know who Barbara Hollis was but could guess by his response that she was probably one of the mothers he was working with; one of those who are demanding of attention. April could imagine that, being so attractive, Miles was highly likely to encounter problems with some of the mothers.

She completed her visits and then went home to wait for Jed, who finally arrived back at about 8.30pm, tired and hungry. Although April was tired too, they managed to have a lovely evening together, sitting outside on the patio watching the last embers of sunlight gradually disappear in a blaze of orange stripes. It had been remarkably warm for early May, but the temperature was cooling rapidly as the sun went down, and the air became increasingly damp.

April looked at Jed, who was relaxing in the chair opposite, in tracksuit bottoms, a black T-shirt, and with strong arms folded against the chill of the air. He was a lovely man and she wouldn't change much about him; kind, warm and dependable. He could also be quite funny at times, but she sometimes wished he would be more open. It was never easy to know what he was thinking, and twelve years of marriage had made it no easier. In the early days, this had been one of the things she found attractive, but as with most relationships, the things one likes initially can often become infuriating as the years go by.

Their experience of trying for a family had been a real trial for them both and April felt sure that many relationships would not have survived the intense pressure and strain they had endured. When they married, they had both dearly wanted children, but like the sensible people they were, they had planned to wait until they were established in their careers and financially secure. They agreed to give it four years. Then the trials began. Since she was young April's menstrual cycle had been all over the place, which made it even more difficult; raising hopes, followed by disappointment, devastation and ultimately despair. After another four years of trying and having unsuccessful and humiliating medical interventions, they started to realise that they had to either come to terms and accept that they would probably never have children; or try IVF, which they were aware was often unsuccessful and could cause them even more pain and disappointment. There was much soul-searching and questioning about their emotional resilience and the strength of their relationship before making the decision to embark on the IVF treatment. They were both sensible enough to realise there were going to be difficult times ahead, but April was very much a glass-is-half-full person and optimism prevailed.

Their first appointment was with a gynaecologist who coldly and clinically explained the risks of the treatment and the likelihood of success in percentage terms. Despite herself, April continued to feel optimistic; she wanted to believe it could happen, knowing that she and Jed had a lot to offer and would be great parents. They had both been lucky enough to be brought up in loving, supportive families, and they would be able to provide a child with the same. It would be too unimaginably unfair if they were to fail. She was aware that they would only receive one treatment on the NHS and any further cycles would have to be funded by themselves. She was not going to think about that, though, because she was unable to contemplate failure; she wanted it so much. They were both healthy and in their prime, so why would they not be able to conceive by using this method? It had worked for millions of others, so why would it not work for them?

Somehow, once they had made the decision to go ahead with IVF, everywhere they went they seemed to be surrounded by babies. The world was full of babies and baby things. As hard as she tried not to, April would find herself looking into pushchairs as they passed, and would then take herself off to the baby clothes section in a department store, looking at the vast array of beautiful things. Jed was less optimistic and tried his best to keep her feet on the ground, for fear of more disappointment.

The IVF treatment was just as gruelling as they had anticipated: multiple scans, injections, medication. The worst thing was the emotional exhaustion, which was so difficult that at times April could not face going to work. Then there was the humiliation of colleagues knowing, or making a calculated guess about what was going on. Some of them would make a pretence that they didn't know anything and make polite general conversation, but the pity in their eyes and the obvious sympathy in their voices when they spoke to her caused a pain so severe it felt like a screwdriver twisting in her stomach.

Following the second IVF treatment, much to their overwhelming joy, April had a positive pregnancy test. Her head reeling and blood surging through her veins in happiness, it was all she could do not to go straight out and buy some of those tiny baby suits with teddy bears on the front that she had admired in the past. Common sense told her that it was far too early for that, but she couldn't help herself. For the first time in ages, she could look at babies in pushchairs, waving their little legs and clutching toys, and instead of bitter resentment, she could give a genuine smile to the mother and comment with all sincerity on her lovely baby.

One night, April had gone to bed early to read whilst Jed stayed up to watch a documentary on the First World War. She had felt unusually tired all day, but instead of snuggling into the comfort of her mattress and relaxing her body like she usually would, she tossed and turned and could not find a comfortable position. She felt tense and anxious without knowing why. After some time, the tiredness began to overwhelm her, and just as she started to drift into sleep, she thought she could feel a trickle of something wet and sticky between her legs.

She sat up with a start. During the day she had felt a slight ache in the lower part of her stomach, a bit like pre-period pain, but it was only light so she disregarded it, thinking it to be a normal symptom of early pregnancy. Now a feeling of utter dread overwhelmed her as she shifted in the bed, and there on the sheet was a large patch of red. Almost instantaneously she felt a sharp stabbing pain in her abdomen as she cried out to Jed. She had heard of women bleeding during pregnancy, but somehow she knew what this meant; she was losing the longed-for baby, along with all her hopes and dreams of being a mother and having a child of her own. She was admitted to hospital and tests confirmed her worst fears.

This experience was devastating for both of them, but there is nothing like shared grief to bond people together. They didn't have to talk about their feelings; they both knew how it felt. They both knew without words that their hopes for a child of their own were behind them and looking to the future was the key to getting through. April could not face another cycle of IVF or any more medical intervention, but her desire to have a child did not change. Being a social worker, she was well aware that there are many children out there just as desperate to have loving parents, and she turned her mind towards adoption. She was fully aware of the risks involved in adopting a child and the emotional roller coaster of the process itself, quite apart from the unknown entity of a potentially damaged child, but she was willing to take them on. She wanted and needed to be a mother.

April couldn't face returning to work and enduring her colleagues' pity. They meant well, but it was more than she could bear. The house they had been delighted with before became a place of sadness and April couldn't go upstairs to bed without remembering that awful night. Jed agreed to move house to appease her, as he nearly always did. He had engaged superficially in discussions involving adoption, but without any real conviction. April couldn't even contemplate that he wouldn't want to take this step, and there it was left.

Friday morning and the alarm went off as usual at 6.30am. April looked forward to the weekend, when she and Jed would have a leisurely cup of tea in bed whilst they chatted about the week gone by. To be fair, it was mostly April who did the chatting, and nobody could argue that her work made more interesting conversation than Jed's invoices and balance sheets. Jed was not generally a big talker anyway, more of a listener, and he was quite good at it too. But today being Friday, it was, as usual, jump out of bed; shower; rushed breakfast; sitting in traffic, bumper to bumper, waiting for lights to change, queuing at roundabouts; tension from bad-tempered and impatient drivers who were stressed about getting to work on time; and April's own anxiety rising about getting to the office in time to read the reports for a Child Protection Conference due to start at 9.30am.

Normally she would have read the reports the previous evening, but she hadn't done so due to Jed coming home. She would have to bumble through it as best she could and just hope the chairperson didn't ask her any difficult questions. She had presented the cases at many Child Protection Conferences over the years and this wouldn't be the first time she wasn't properly prepared.

4

SAMANTHA

Samantha was feeling very pleased with herself. The social worker had been and gone and had seemed quite happy with what she saw. She was fed up with having nosy social workers coming and going. Even when she was a child, she had had to put up with it: different people coming to her house, asking questions; her mum telling them everything was all right and then being left to get on with it. They didn't help her then when she needed it and she didn't believe they would help her now, not that she needed help now anyway.

The girls were in bed and Sam was bored. She tried to watch the TV but there wasn't much on, so she decided to give her friend Charlie a call. Her daughter was in the same school as Tayla, although a little bit older, and they usually went around to each other's houses after dropping the kids off at school. She hadn't seen her this morning at the school gates.

'Hi, Charlie, just thought I'd see if you wanted to come around to mine for a chat. I'm bored.' Charlie lived just around the corner.

'Oh, hi, Sam; sorry but I can't tonight, Dan is here.' Dan was Charlie's sort-of boyfriend. He came when he had nothing better to do, stayed the night and then disappeared for a month or more. Samantha suspected he was married but Charlie was too stupid to realise it; either that or she just didn't want to know. 'Is Curtis not around?'

'He's in the past, gone; out of my life. He tried to punch my lights out last time, in front of the kids as well. I'm not having any man do that to me, especially in front of my kids.'

'Was he pissed?'

'Out of his head.'

'Were you?'

'I've stopped drinking. All that matters now are my kids; I don't want them to go through what I went through and I don't want them taken off me. I've got Social Services on my back again, haven't I? Some old cow at the school dobbed me in just 'cause Tayla missed some days. They make me sick; I'm a good mother, I love my kids – why can't they just get off my back and leave me alone?'

'I know what you mean, I've been through all that – they used to tell me my house was filthy and my kids were neglected; snooty lot. It's all right for them, they get loads of money; they should try living on what we have to live on, see if they could buy their nice clothes and posh cars then. They had to close my case in the end; the social worker was making it out to be worse than it was, they said she'd made it all up just to try to get my kids off me.'

'Why did she do that? I would sue them if they did that to me.'

'I'm going to; I've already told them I'm going to. Anyway, I better get going; Dan's got a bit of smoke for us tonight.'

'OK, see you soon.'

'See you soon.'

Samantha felt a lonely sinking feeling as she looked around her small, sparsely furnished flat. It was only 9pm and she didn't know what she would do for the rest of the evening. She didn't feel tired enough to go to bed. The thought of a drink suddenly flooded her mind and almost overwhelmed her. There was no alcohol in the house and she would have to leave the children on their own to go and get some from Tesco's, which would take more than half an hour. She argued with herself, the sensible part of her brain saying,

No, you don't need it, but the other saying, convincingly, A few cans won't do any harm. I need it to cheer me up. I'll only have a couple of cans; I deserve it after looking after the kids all day on my own. Samantha only had ten pounds left to last her until Monday.

The arguments continued to circle in her brain until she heard Lily Grace make a sweet whimpering sound as she stirred in her bed. Sam went into the bedroom to look at her child. She was lying on her back with both arms above her head stretched out on the pillow, her eyes tight shut. She looked adorable in her soft pink princess pyjamas, her blonde curls spread out over the pillow and her long, dark eyelashes resting on her sleep-flushed cheeks. As though an angel had intervened, Sam's thoughts of leaving her children and buying drink with the little money she had left flew right out of the window. Instead, she ran a bath and had an early night, feeling very pleased with herself.

Waiting outside the school gates with Tayla and Lily Grace the next morning, Sam looked round for Charlie. She thought it was a bit strange that she couldn't see her anywhere. Charlie hadn't mentioned last night that there were any problems with the kids. Sam decided to call round to see if everything was OK.

Charlie came to the door, wrapped in a short dressing gown which looked as though it might once have been fluffy and pink, but after years of wearing and washing was now threadbare and grey. One of the sleeves had worn right through at the elbow and the material hung down from the garment in spindly threads. There were cigarette burns down the front and round one of the cuffs. Charlie clearly had not had time to do her hair, which was usually long and straight but now stuck out from various parts of her head in multiple directions. Her pallor, her baggy eyes, the overflowing ashtray and overwhelming smell of cannabis were clear evidence of the night she had had. Nine-year-old Violet and eight-year-old Indigo were still in their pyjamas on the settee, looking tired and bored.

'Where's Dan?' Samantha asked as she sat herself down.

'Had to go early to get to the Job Centre.'

'He never stays for long, does he?' Samantha pointed out. 'I suppose that'll be it now then, for a few months.'

'He said he'd try to come tonight, but he might not be able to; it depends on if he's got the money for the bus fare.'

'Are the kids not going to school today, then?'

'No, it's a bit too late now. Violet had toothache last night anyway.'

'You'll need to watch it; that's why Social Services are on my back again, just because Tayla missed a few days at school.'

'You're kidding – is that all you did?'

'Yes, honestly, that's all it was; the school reported me. They said she didn't have the right uniform, but it wasn't my fault, I didn't have the money; she's got all of it now. Once you're on their books you don't get any peace. They just keep looking for ways to catch you out. I think they're looking for kids to give to adopters; I heard that on the news, it is true,' Sam insisted.

'They're not having my kids, sneaky bitches.' Charlie handed a cigarette to Sam before lighting one herself. She placed an already-full ashtray on the small table between them.

After a few hours Samantha left Charlie's and began to make her way back to her flat. She wondered what she would do with herself for the rest of the day. Social Services were paying for Lily Grace to stay at Nursery all day now so she was on her own. She would probably watch Jeremy Kyle again. She liked Jeremy Kyle; one of her friends was on there once. Well, someone who used to be her friend; they didn't speak now because Samantha thought she didn't look after her kids properly and she told her as much.

She didn't have money to go anywhere, so all there was to do was sit in people's houses and talk and smoke cigarettes or watch television. She had thought it would be quite nice to have a job, but there was no one to take the kids to school and pick them up, and what would she do in the holidays? Samantha hadn't been to school much herself and her reading and writing skills were poor. As she wandered back towards her flat, she spotted an advertisement in the local hairdresser's asking for someone to help out with answering the phone and sweeping up the hair, with an opportunity to train as a hairdresser in the future. The idea really appealed and she became quite excited at the thought of it. She really wanted to go in and ask them to consider her.

Whilst she tried to summon the courage, she watched the stylist as she cut an elderly lady's grey hair, smiles and hand gestures indicative of friendly conversation and rapport between the two women. The salon was small and seemed like a happy place to work, with plenty of banter going on between customers and staff. Samantha began to imagine herself working there, washing hair, cutting and creating glamorous styles; people thanking her for transforming their appearance. She knew that in reality she would struggle to know what to talk to people about, and couldn't imagine that she could ever be relaxed and friendly with customers from all walks of life in the way this hairdresser obviously was. She felt sure, though, that she could enjoy working there and would love the opportunity to use the creativity she was sure she possessed. She stood watching for quite a few minutes, agonising over her dilemma, but then she caught a glimpse of her reflection in the window. She saw herself as a pitiful creature who could not possibly fit into such an environment, and, terrified of being laughed at, she turned and walked away.

Samantha had never had a job; she was pregnant with Tayla at sixteen, by Ryan, who was also sixteen and a one-night stand. Ryan was not interested in Tayla, and after Samantha told him she was pregnant she never saw or heard from him again. Her mum kicked her out when she told her, although she hadn't been living there much anyway, mostly staying at various friends' houses, sleeping on settees; sofa-surfing, the social workers called it. Her mum said she couldn't afford to look after Samantha and a baby and that if she kicked her out she would be given a flat, so she did it for them.

At least she got some help from Social Services; they put her in a hostel for young mothers and it wasn't too bad. She didn't really get on with the other girls there but at least she had a roof over her and Tayla's heads. Having a baby was not what she thought it would be. She had not been too unhappy when she found out she was pregnant; at last she would have someone of her own who loved her and whom she could love. She had thought this would be all she needed to make her happy. Like most mothers, Sam was overwhelmed with love for her baby, but she had no idea of the level of responsibility and commitment involved, and it came as an incredible shock. What she had failed to anticipate was how much you have to give to get relatively little in return. She had no concept of the huge impact Tayla was going to have on her life.

Despite the struggle she faced, having virtually no support from her family and barely enough money to live on, Samantha really wanted to be a good mother. Unfortunately,, her support networks were generally people like herself, who had experienced family dysfunction and struggled to get by. Her experience of relationships was predominantly volatile and erratic and there was literally no one in her life she could trust. These relationships were more often detrimental to her well-being as they brought their own problems. Apart from the help that Social Services provided, Samantha and her baby were in effect alone in the world.

She was in a relationship with Josh when she fell pregnant with Lily Grace, but he went off with someone else soon after the birth. He used to see Lily Grace sometimes but often said he was coming and then didn't turn up. She had warned him that if he kept letting her down, she would stop him seeing her altogether. She had recently heard, though, that he was in prison for manslaughter. He had been in a fight outside a pub and punched someone whose head hit the pavement as he fell.

By the time Samantha had paid her electricity and bought her tobacco and a lottery ticket, she only had four pounds left to buy food and wasn't due to get any more money until Monday, which was three days away. She did have a bit of food in the house because she was starting to manage her money better and buy food as soon as possible on benefits day. There had been times in the past when she found herself without money or food and had gone to a food bank. She was given a tin of tuna and a tin of tomatoes, but had no bread or milk. She had shared the tuna with the girls for their dinner and they ate the tomatoes the next morning for breakfast. She never wanted to be in that position again. She was pleased to recall that she had a large bag of sausages in the freezer, and was sure she also had a tin of beans. Sausage and beans were Tayla and Lily Grace's favourite dinner.

Instead of carrying on home to her flat, Samantha turned off her street into Best Lane and headed towards Princess Park. The park wasn't anything special. There were a few swings, a slide and an expanse of lawn with some trees and a bench, but the spring flowers looked beautiful and some of the trees were smothered with pink and white blossom. She sat herself down on a bench and inhaled deep breaths of perfumed air. Even Samantha, whose everyday existence was blighted by a persistent simmering depression, felt herself emotionally lifted by the intoxicating smells and sounds surrounding her here in the park. For a very brief moment she experienced something which almost felt like happiness. It must be amazing to have a garden, she thought. She pictured Lily Grace and Tayla running around in their own garden, chasing each other and laughing. She imagined them playing on the slide and swing she would buy for them.

As she gazed out over the empty green space, a sense of loneliness began to rise inside her. The beauty of the spring day faded from her mind as dark thoughts began to gather. She recalled her recent visit to her mother's house, which had ended in an argument. She had been feeling particularly lonely that day, and although experience told her that her mother was not the best person to help her feel better and in fact usually did the opposite, she was desperate for company and someone to talk to.

Wayne had just got out of bed and the atmosphere was tense; Sam guessed they had been rowing. She immediately recognised that this was not a good time to visit and regretted coming.

'What's she doing here?' was Wayne's unwelcoming response on seeing Sam sitting on the sofa. 'She just wants to slouch around here and eat our food instead of eating her own. She doesn't do anything to help, though, does she? Where was she when we needed her last week when we were ill; she wasn't here then, sitting on our sofa, was she?'

Her mum then joined in the tirade as usual, making sure she kept on the right side of Wayne. Sam felt annoyed with herself for thinking that coming to visit was a good idea. Even after all the years of poor treatment and abuse from her mum and Wayne, she always returned for more. When there's not much else on offer, poor treatment by family can sometimes seem better than being alone.

The sense of beauty in the spring day had faded as the old familiar feelings of anger and self-hatred resurfaced. The memories of hurtful, insensitive verbal abuse from her mother would continue to cause her pain. When she was in this mood her negative thoughts intensified and she felt worthless in every way. She felt she wasn't fit to be a mother anyway, so her children would be far better being looked after by someone else; anyone else. The only antidote to these painful feelings was oblivion, and she could achieve this with alcohol. It wasn't just by chance that she was sitting on this bench in Princess Park. This was where she had sat many times in the past until her friends appeared with their bottles of cider. With these thoughts swamping her brain, she texted Charlie to ask her to collect her children, saying she would pick them up later to give them their tea.

Samantha's drinking habits were such that she could sometimes manage for months without drinking at all, but once she started, she struggled to stop. It was the self-loathing that was the hardest to bear, and when this was reinforced by her mother's treatment of her, there was only one way she could cope. She had felt proud after resisting the temptation to drink the previous night, but now there was no turning back.

It wasn't long before a little gathering had formed around the park bench, three men and another woman, Kate, who had conveniently all brought with them large bottles of cider in plastic carrier bags. Ronnie and Steve sat down cross-legged on the grass, beside the bench where Kate and Sam were sitting. Ronnie opened one of the bottles and had a big swig before handing it round. Within half an hour quite a few bottles had been opened and the pile of empties was building up. Sam soon felt herself relaxing and starting to feel happy. It was only in this place and with these people that she ever felt she really belonged.

The bottles were passed round between the group. Each time it was Sam's turn, she swallowed as much as she could. It wasn't about the taste, it was the effect she was interested in. Slowly her mood lifted and all the anxieties, self-loathing and deep-rooted anger that were always with her gradually dissipated on the breeze. For a brief period she felt happy, likeable and fun to be with; normal. She laughed and told funny jokes, danced and sang with her drinking partners. More cider, carefree happiness, exuberance, and before too long, a slow and blissful drift into oblivion.

Samantha awoke to find herself still in the park, lying on an old grey coat which she didn't recall seeing before. It must have been very early in the morning because the sun was just rising; the street was empty and all she could hear was the loud, frenetic twittering of birds surrounding her, which intensified the throbbing in her head. Even though there was a clear blue sky and a stream of sunlight appearing over the horizon, she felt an icy chill on her skin. She pulled the dirty grey coat around her to cover her bare arms and the stench of stale vomit wafted upwards, almost causing her to heave again. She felt disgusted with herself and deeply disappointed that she had once again submitted to this degrading method of escape. There was no sign of her friends, just the debris they had left behind: empty bottles, cigarette packets and food cartons, one of which was being pecked at by starlings who were squabbling over the half-eaten burger inside.

As always after a bout of self-indulgent binge drinking, where nothing and no one mattered any more, the real world slowly began to re-emerge from somewhere deep within her brain and she started to worry about her children. It slowly dawned on her that several days must have passed whilst she was here in the park and for a brief, terrifying moment, she struggled to recall where she had left them. A rising panic had begun to overwhelm her when the vague memory of asking Charlie to collect them from school came into her mind. She dragged herself up off the ground, smoothed down her hair in an attempt to make herself appear presentable, and, head throbbing, started to make her way towards Charlie's house, desperate to see that her children were safe and OK.

5

FREDDIE

April sat down at the long oval table in the conference room, looking hot, flustered and unprepared. This was out of character for her, being usually a very organised person, in respect of her work at least. She should have read the reports from the health visitor and the nursery last night, but because of Jed coming home after being away all week, it didn't get done. They had celebrated his return with a bottle of wine instead. Then there was the heavy traffic this morning which had made her late.

The conference was due to start and all the professionals who had been involved with the little boy were sitting around the table, quietly waiting for April to present the details of the case. Only the shuffle of papers could be heard above the silence, as the conference chairman and other professionals glanced through the reports in front of them. April looked across the table at Becky Simmons, the mother, who was sitting with her new boyfriend on one side of her and her father on the other. She appeared anxious, which was not surprising considering she was surrounded by officials who had come here to scrutinise her conduct as a parent. This was almost certainly the first Child Protection Conference this woman had attended so she would have no idea what to expect. She was lucky, though, to have parents who appeared very supportive. April had been to many conferences where the mother was completely alone with no family or friends for support, during the conference or afterwards, and if they did have family, the relationship between them was often destructive rather than supportive.

April had met Becky's parents and although they were clearly very naive, showing no understanding or awareness of the dysfunctional relationship between their daughter and her boyfriend, they appeared to be very caring and it was evident that they only wanted the best for their daughter and grandson, as one would always expect and hope to see in grandparents.

The conference was for three-year-old Freddie Simmons, who lived with his mother and her boyfriend. There had been a number of reports from the nursery of injuries being found on the little boy. In their opinion the mother was not giving convincing explanations for these injuries and alarm bells were ringing. Each time a new injury was reported a duty social worker visited and the mother would provide an explanation for the bruise or cut or whatever the latest one happened to be.

Where the injury did not seem compatible with the explanation given, normal Child Protection procedures would be followed which included the child being examined by a paediatrician. Freddie had been examined three times after injuries were reported, but each time the paediatrician felt there was not enough evidence to conclude that the mother was not telling the truth. Although this did not make it impossible to go to court to ask for a Care Order and removal of the child whilst further assessments were carried out, it made it more difficult and less likely the court would agree. The court was far more likely to accept the evidence provided by the Local Authority if the paediatrician supported their case.

The calls from the nursery were becoming more frequent, reporting injuries they had noticed on little Freddie. The injuries were also, worryingly, becoming more severe. By this stage it was the number of injuries being reported that caused the most concern. The one which had finally resulted in this Child Protection Conference was a large bruise that had been observed on the side of the little boy's face. The mother's explanation was that he had fallen off his trike. The community paediatrician was asked to examine him again and give an opinion as to the likelihood of the explanation being a true account of what had happened. The paediatrician felt it unlikely that the injury had been caused in that way but was not able or willing to rule it out completely.

This was one of April's most worrying cases. The little boy was suffering frequent injuries and there didn't seem to be a way of distinguishing whether they were truly accidental or being caused deliberately by an adult. April had her suspicions but there was nothing she could do about it without evidence. The mother, Becky, was a meek and needy young woman who had recently allowed a new boyfriend, Colin Lyons, to move in with her. April did not like Colin, who was domineering, controlling and significantly older than Becky.

Becky's view was that she had been very lucky to find this man because he had a job and was generous with money. She was full of his praises, especially when he actually bought her a car. She did not think there was anything untoward when he insisted on checking the mileage every day after he came home from work, and demanded to know exactly where she had been if the mileage had increased. He would then even go as far as to check the mileage on route planner for the journey she had done, to see if it tallied with what was on the clock. Becky, and unfortunately her parents too, thought this was a clear indication of how much Colin loved her.

As April read her report, setting out the details of the case, she glanced up at Becky who was slumped in her chair, looking down at her copy of the report in front of her as though she was reading it. She had clearly made an effort to look smart today, with her face made up and her mousy hair tied back in a ponytail. Her make-up was plastered on and far too dark for her skin colour, and with the contrasting pale green eyeshadow and bright red lipstick, she looked almost comical. April was curious as to why Becky had felt the need to plaster her face with make-up when her skin underneath was much prettier; hiding behind a mask, perhaps.

The nursery manager was the next to present her report, and she read from a list of injuries observed on Freddie followed by explanations given. She then made observations about Becky's lovely relationship with her child: how he was always clean and nicely dressed. She said, 'Freddie is a lovely little boy who enjoys playing with the other children; his attendance is good and he's meeting his developmental milestones.' April noticed Becky lift her head and smile proudly as this was said. The nursery manager then went on to say that she had noticed Freddie flinch and cower following small incidents at nursery, for example, after spilling a drink on the floor, as though he expected to be chastised or punished. This statement raised further alarm bells for April as well as the other professionals in the room.

The chairman, James Roberts, a stern looking man in his late fifties, who sat at the top of the long table, peered over his glasses and turned to Becky. 'Ms Simmons, you have heard the concerns raised by the professionals involved with your son; is there anything you would like to comment on?'

Becky shifted in her chair and looked down again at the paperwork in front of her. Before she could reply, her boyfriend Colin Lyons spoke up. 'I've told Becky she needs to be more careful. I've had children of my own and I know how to look after them; Becky doesn't, but I'm helping her to get better.'

Mr Roberts thanked him for his opinion before returning to Becky to ask again if she had any comments to make.

Becky looked up, and just as she was about to speak again, Colin Lyons piped up with, 'Becky, the man is talking to you.' Then, turning to the chair, 'She's always like this, I've told her she needs to talk more.'

The chair was starting to become irritated by Colin's unwelcome interruptions, but remained calm and politely asked him to allow Ms Simmons to speak.

At last Becky actually spoke, and to everyone's surprise her voice was clear and loud with an air of confidence. She said, 'I know I should have been watching him, and the accidents wouldn't have happened if I hadn't been so stupid. I am going to make sure I supervise him better in future.'

'You are aware that there is concern about the explanation you have given for the bruising to Freddie's face, and this has been the case with a number of his injuries? That is why we are here today,' the chair explained.

Just as though he had not made those comments, Becky continued to insist that she intended to be more vigilant in future. The chair looked exasperated but patiently and politely persisted with his questioning.

'You have heard what the nursery manager has told the conference today, some of which has been positive, but I'm sure everyone in this room was concerned when they heard that little Freddie becomes anxious and afraid, cowering even, following common minor accidents such as spilling a drink.'

Colin Lyons spoke again, clearly exasperated with the chair's stupidity and ignorance. 'That's just because he's a kid, it's normal; all my kids did that because they knew right from wrong. You have to teach kids how to behave. My kids never spilt their drinks on the carpet.'

This was becoming more and more alarming.

Everyone present agreed that Freddie needed to be placed on a Child Protection Plan, and there were a few recommendations from the meeting which needed to be followed up by April. The attendees gradually filtered out of the conference room and April, taking her papers with her, went back upstairs to her office. From the first-floor window she could see Becky, her dad and Colin Lyons walking towards the car park. Becky's head was down and her shoulders hunched. She wore a whitish woollen jacket which looked far too hot for the weather. April could see that Becky's father was also looking at the ground, but Colin Lyons, walking slightly in front of them both but looking back at them as he walked, was animated with arms flying around in gestures of anger and frustration. The body language between the three presented a clear picture of domination and submission, exactly as April suspected.

If she had been able to, she would have gone to the house there and then and taken little Freddie away. She hated the thought that this helpless, sweet little boy, so dependent and vulnerable, was being exposed to this environment. April was aware that there were a number of possible scenarios to explain this case. Becky could be losing her temper with her child to try to keep him in line with Colin's expectations of how a child should behave. She could be scared Colin would leave her if Freddie was deemed to be a naughty child. April had seen that happen in other cases. Colin could be the one who was inflicting the injuries on Freddie but Becky must be allowing it; both of them could be harming him; or the injuries could be, as Becky kept insisting, unfortunate accidents due to lack of supervision.

6

WEEKEND BREAK

April and Jed had booked a small country hotel for Saturday night and planned to set off early to make the most of the weekend. It would probably take them about two hours to get to the little village where they were due to stay. By 7.30am the suitcase was in the car and they were on their way. April loved being up at this time of the morning when she didn't have to go to work. The quiet, empty streets with no cars or people, and curtains still closed to the world. It was a beautiful morning with clear blue skies and fresh, perfumed spring air. April gave out a long, blissful sigh as she sank her body into the soft leather of the passenger seat, revelling in the pleasure of being driven for a change. She felt happy and relaxed at the thought of leaving the stress of work behind, and the added advantage of not having to think about housework or cooking for a change.

Their little hotel room was on the second floor, with beautiful views overlooking the golf course. Small groups of people could be seen in the distance, hurrying along earnestly from one hole to the next, pulling their trolleys, not communicating with each other but just looking ahead as though nothing else mattered. They must be serious golfers; April had always believed the main appeal of golfing was to chat as they walked, but that didn't seem to be the case with these people. She decided golf wouldn't be for her.

Their plans for the day were to take a walk through the countryside, visit a nearby small town for lunch, relax and read in the afternoon, and then swim, sauna and dinner. This was what they both needed after a few stressful weeks of hard work. They really would have appreciated a proper holiday but that was something they could think about later in the year.

It was always difficult for April to shut her mind off from work, and however much she tried she could not stop worrying about little Freddie Simmons. She couldn't help feeling that she was missing something. She felt certain the injuries he had sustained were caused by Colin Lyons but there was not enough proof to take any action other than a Child Protection Plan, which provided some level of safeguarding. If she had her way, she would have gone around to the family home, demanded that Becky get rid of Colin Lyons, and if she didn't agree to get rid of him then April would have taken action to remove the child from her care. Unfortunately, she did not have the evidence to do that, it was just a strong gut feeling, and the family court would accept nothing less than concrete evidence, which was fair enough when a child's future was involved. The court would not be satisfied with gut feeling and it was regrettable that April would probably have to wait until the little boy was injured again before taking further action. All she could hope for was that the next injury would not be too serious.

After dinner, Jed and April relaxed in the small hotel bar, Jed with a beer and April with a gin and tonic. Apart from the work issues which were gradually fading from her mind, April had something else that was bothering her. Soon after her miscarriage she and Jed had discussed the possibility of adopting a child, but for a long time afterwards the pain of what had happened was too raw and all they wanted to do was shut it all out of their minds and get on with everyday life, which they did successfully for a while. Now more than a year had passed, and the thoughts of adoption were beginning to surface again. April had already decided that she would raise it with Jed this weekend.

They had been chatting away about trivia for most of the evening before she found the courage to approach the subject.

'Jed,' she felt an anxious bubble expanding in her stomach, 'do you remember, after I had the miscarriage, we thought about looking into the possibility of adopting a child?' she asked tentatively, her eyes on his face, nervously watching his reaction.

He had been watching a large group of noisy, middle-aged golfers who were sitting at a table opposite, but turned his head slowly towards her with a look of complete surprise in his soft brown eyes. 'I didn't realise you were still thinking about that. You haven't said anything about it for a long time now; I thought you had changed your mind,' he replied, alarmingly.

April couldn't believe this; what had happened that meant they no longer seemed to understand what each other was thinking? How could he have thought for a minute that she no longer longed for a child?

'Of course I still want to; I was just waiting for the right time to bring it up; for us to come to terms with what happened. I thought that was what you wanted too,' she said, trying to control her astonishment.

His silence was excruciating.

'Please say something,' she begged.

'I don't know, it's just a bit of a shock. I suppose I still thought there was a chance we might have our own; you're still only thirty-eight and they didn't find anything wrong with either of us.'

'Unexplained infertility' was the diagnosis, which is in some ways the worst it can be, because hope and disappointment persist relentlessly in parallel with each other. Conversely, if a problem is identified it can sometimes be rectified, but if they find nothing there's nothing to rectify. Of course, April changed her diet and they had used the monthly cycle charts, but the ongoing roller coaster of hope followed by disappointment month after month became more than they could bear. It was made even more difficult by April's periods already being irregular.

After the miscarriage April gradually came to accept that she would probably never bear a child of her own, and this acceptance became increasingly easier to manage over time. More recently she had started to think again about adoption and despite the potential problems, she wanted a child more than anything else in the world and was prepared to face whatever these might be.

'Please don't tell me you have changed your mind. We talked through what it would mean for us both, we went through everything and you seemed as keen as I was; what's changed?' April said pleadingly.

Jed moved closer to her and held both of her hands between his across the small, round table. 'I just need some time to think, April, that's all. I wasn't prepared for this, not now, not tonight.'

April tried to disguise her exasperation. She just couldn't comprehend his response, as though they hadn't both equally longed for a child.

'Why don't we just go to bed? We can talk about it more tomorrow; I need time to think,' he repeated.

April knew the choice was either to agree with him and go to bed, or have an argument which she really didn't want. She didn't want him to see how upset she was by his unexpected reaction, but would be waiting for her opportunity to bring it up again in the morning.

April walked behind Jed as they left the bar to go to their room, her eyes piercing his back, still trying to make sense of his unexpected and bewildering response. He was a bit taller than her, although smaller than average for a man. He had a head of thick, curly, mousy hair and wore spectacles; the perfect stereotypical image of an accountant. He wasn't especially handsome but he had a nice, kind and friendly face which matched his personality. His most appealing features for April were his thick, dark eyelashes, fringing his soft brown eyes which bathed her in warmth when she spoke. He had the most amazing capacity to focus his attention entirely on her while she spoke, which still had the power to make her feel incredibly interesting and important.

April struggled to sleep that night. It was very hot in their little hotel room and she tossed and turned whilst her mind raced against a stream of anxieties. Thoughts about the past, worries about the future and stress about work all seemed to compound in her brain. She just could not shut them down until the early hours of the morning when she finally drifted into a fretful and unrefreshing slumber.

Breakfast was lovely with a variety of fresh fruit, yoghurts, cereals and pastries, and/or full English. April could only manage a cup of black coffee, whilst Jed had some of everything that was on offer. She just wanted to go home. She wanted Jed to say to her, 'Of course I still want to adopt a child, why ever did you think otherwise?', but his continuing silence on this matter spoke louder than words.

On Monday morning April paid a visit to Becky. She was aware that Freddie would be at nursery and saw this as a good opportunity to find out more about her relationship with Colin Lyons.

Becky answered the door and invited April into the lounge of her little two-bedroomed semi. One of April's skills as a social worker was the ability to make sharp observations in the home which would give her important clues about the family. She was immediately struck by the tidy cleanliness of the lounge. Although the furniture was old and somewhat shabby, there was nothing out of place, not a speck of dust to be seen, and more importantly there was nothing to show that a three-year-old boy lived there; not a train set, a child's book or a toy of any kind. From where she sat on the threadbare velveteen settee, April could see through to the kitchen, which was also shabby and, although dingy, was strikingly clean. A large picture window overlooked the garden from the lounge and April could see that the garden was unkempt, with scattered broken objects poking out from the long grass, large patches of stinging nettles and bindweed being the most dominant foliage. This garden, she thought, was positively dangerous, but what a stark contrast to the painstaking orderliness of the house.

'Your house looks very neat and tidy. How do you manage that with a three-year-old boy running around?' April enquired.

She was unsettled by Becky's answer, but not a bit surprised.

'Colin likes the house to be tidy. He gets annoyed if there's toys everywhere. He says his kids weren't allowed to have toys all over the place and Freddie needs to be taught to be tidy.'

'He is allowed to play with his toys, though, I presume?'

'Oh yes, I always let him play with his toys when Colin isn't here, but I get him to put them away before he gets home because he gets annoyed and tells Freddie off.' She laughed at this but her lips didn't smile.

'Freddie shouldn't be told off for playing with his toys in his own house. Children need to play; it's how they learn.'

Becky looked uncomfortable and confused. 'I know, but he makes too much mess and then he won't put them away when he's told. Colin says I've spoilt him. He's helping me be better.'

'Becky, do you really want a man in your house who frightens you and your child? Would you not both be happier without him here?' April felt compelled to ask.

She watched Becky's face as she waited for an answer, but Becky just stared back at her blankly. She continued to wait, but Becky continued to stare. It was just as though April's comment had rendered her speechless. April couldn't work out if Becky was just trying to think of a suitable answer to give, or was actually astonished at the unspeakable suggestion that she would want to get rid of her boyfriend.

April persisted. 'Do you not think it would be better to be without Colin if he shouts at you both? Are you worried about being on your own?'

'I admit he does shout sometimes and I don't like that, but he is good to us as well; did you know he bought me a car? He gives me money sometimes too. I don't earn much and by the time I've paid the rent and bills I haven't got much left. I can buy more things for Freddie with the extra money Colin gives me. Colin doesn't really like it if I buy too much for Freddie, though; he says I'm spoiling him again so I usually hide what I buy.' Becky was saying this in a nonchalant manner, but April felt it was false. 'It's all right, though, because Mum lets me leave things at her house if Colin's at home, then I can sneak them in when he's not here.'

'What do your parents have to say about that? Do they worry about you?'

'They don't mind me leaving things there. It's only until Colin goes back to work.'

April was astonished at Becky's honesty. What was most alarming was that Becky displayed no recognition or understanding that Colin's behaviour was neither normal nor acceptable, and her parents must have been equally naive.

April left Becky's home and drove straight off to pay a visit to Freddie's father, who lived about fifteen miles away. She felt there was no time to lose, really, because one more injury to Freddie would tip things over the edge and she would have to take immediate action.

She found the street where Freddie's father lived quite easily and rang the doorbell. A short, stout blonde woman with black roots, whom she assumed to be Freddie's paternal grandmother, opened the door.

'Hello, I'm April Gardiner, Freddie's social worker; I presume you are Hayley,' she said, smiling and holding out her hand.

'Yes I am; would you like to come in?'

This must have been one of the smallest flats April had ever been in, and she had been in some small ones in her time. The lounge was just about big enough for the two-seater settee, an armchair, a small coffee table and a television in the corner. April wondered where they kept all the other things people generally have in their lounge. She looked around and there were no shelves or cabinets to put things in. There was just one small, high window which

48

didn't let in much light, so although it was still early afternoon the ceiling light was switched on. Seated in the black PVC armchair was a short, slightly built man with dark hair who looked to be about thirty.

'You must be Leon, Freddie's dad,' she said, holding her hand out to him. Leon nodded his head before standing up and taking her hand. When they sat down their knees were almost touching. April wondered where Hayley was going to fit.

Hayley was not a woman to mince her words and no sooner had April sat down than she started her tirade about Social Services and how they were sitting on their arses whilst her grandson was being battered by that bastard living with his mum. April would have loved to agree with her but could only say, 'I understand why you are upset and worried, but I can assure you we are doing everything we can.'

'Don't you realise, it's that Colin fella that's hitting Freddie and his stupid mother is sticking up for him. You must all be stupid if you can't see that. He's not the same since that bloke moved in. Are you just going to wait until something terrible happens before you get up off your arses?' She was standing over April, shouting, eyes flashing and waving her finger. Although she didn't really appreciate being shouted at like this, April could fully understand where the woman was coming from. On the surface it appeared obvious that it was Colin Lyons causing Freddie's injuries; however, April knew well from experience that the seemingly obvious was not always the case.

'Can I just explain, Hayley, that I do understand why you're angry and how it must appear to you, but I can assure you we are doing everything we can do at this stage. I am also very worried about Freddie, and although we haven't got absolute proof of what is going on, we are taking action. Freddie is now on a Child Protection Plan, which means all the professionals involved with him are aware of the concerns and information must be shared between us. If things do not improve very quickly, we will apply to the court for permission to take him away from his mum, just to keep him safe while we find out what is going on.'

Despite her anger regarding the perceived inertia of Social Services, Hayley was temporarily stunned into silence. 'What do you mean? You mean… he will go into foster care?' she managed to stutter.

'Well, this is one of the reasons I wanted to meet you and Leon, because we always try to find suitable family members to take care of children if possible, rather than put them in foster care.'

Hayley's glance took in the space around her and April could see that her mind was racing. 'We would love to have him here, wouldn't we, Leon, but where would he sleep? We only have one bedroom; Leon sleeps on the settee.'

April looked disbelievingly at the settee. It was barely large enough for two people to sit on, let alone to allow a full-grown man to stretch out and sleep. She noticed that Leon had hardly said a word since she'd arrived and his mum did all the talking. From what she knew about Leon and the notes on the file, she doubted that he would be a viable alternative carer for Freddie. He clearly had a mild learning disability and had always lived with his mum apart from the very brief period when he lived with Becky and Freddie.

Hayley soon confirmed what April was thinking. 'He can't look after himself, let alone a little boy. I'm not saying he doesn't love Freddie because he does, he's a really good father. Leon loves it when Freddie comes on a Saturday. They play Lego together and watch the telly. Leon takes him out as well sometimes; they go to the park or somewhere to eat.'

'Who cooks the meals for him, then, when he's here? I presume that's you, Hayley, is it?' April said, smiling at Leon.

Hayley laughed. 'The nearest thing to cooking Leon can do is open a bag of crisps, and even then I have to clean up after him. He's hopeless; I don't know what's going to happen to him after I've gone, and I keep telling him, I'm not a well woman.'

'Oh dear, have you got health problems?'

'Have I? You name it – arthritis, angina, emphysema, old age; is that enough for you?'

April thought she remembered reading that Hayley was only fifty years old, although she did look a lot older. Maybe the information on the file was wrong. 'So it sounds very much as though, although you and Leon would love to care for Freddie, it would be completely out of the question.'

'Yes, not that we wouldn't want to have the little darling here because we love him to bits, you know. I don't want him going into foster care, though,' she repeated vehemently.

'But I thought you were angry because he's being left in that home with his mother and Mr Lyons?' April said, confused.

'Yes, I am. I don't know what to say… I am worried about him going into foster care; can't you just get that bastard out of his home? He used to be all right with his mum when that Colin bloke wasn't there. Becky and Leon should have stayed together; I always said that to Leon. He was drinking too much at the time but he doesn't drink any more. He hasn't drunk for over a year and he won't go back to it now, will you, son?' She clipped him softly round the head and he looked up and smiled at his mum. April could sense there was a very close and loving relationship between Leon and his mum. She had probably been overprotective of him due to his learning difficulties.

'It's not as simple as that, I'm afraid. We may be able to take Freddie away to keep him safe, but we can't force Becky to get rid of Mr Lyons. What is it that worries you about Freddie going into foster care, Hayley?'

'He won't know the people; they'll be strangers; he'll be scared. How do we know they'll look after him? You hear all sorts of stories about things that happen to foster kids. I don't want him to go.'

'You really don't need to worry about that. Foster carers are very good at making children feel safe and helping them to settle in. He will be well looked after, I promise you. He will be able to see his mum and dad and probably yourself regularly. It might even be possible for him to still spend every other Saturday with you.'

Hayley looked really surprised. 'I thought we wouldn't be able to see him again if he went into foster care.'

April put a reassuring hand on Hayley's arm. 'Of course you would see him if he was in foster care. If things go badly with Becky and the worst comes to the worst, which results in Freddie not being able to return to his mum, we may have to consider looking for adopters for him, but that's not the plan at the moment. I'm hoping for the same as you: that Becky will sort herself out and Freddie can go home, so we won't worry too much about adoption at this stage.'

Hayley's face had turned ashen at the mention of the word 'adoption'.

April left the family home thinking what a lovely family they were and how much they loved Freddie. What a pity they were not in a position to care for him. As she drove away, she was also thinking that it was such a pity that Becky and Leon had not stayed together, feeling sure that if they had, none of this would have happened.

Back at the office, April seized the opportunity to talk the case through with her manager, Maria, who was always hard to pin down.

'We've just placed Freddie on a Child Protection Plan because of all the injuries he's had over the last few months which have been picked up by the nursery. Mother always seems to come up with a half-reasonable explanation but I'm not convinced by them. As well as this, the injuries are becoming more frequent. Unfortunately, the paediatrician is sitting on the fence, and without her being able to say if the injuries appear to be non-accidental, there might not be enough evidence to make an application to court. I feel as though we are just waiting for something terrible to happen and it's only a matter of time until it does. The mother has a new boyfriend who is extremely controlling, which seems to have changed the dynamics in the family. I'm not at all happy about just sitting back and waiting for something to happen; what do you think?'

Maria tapped the tip of her pen against her mouth as she pondered over April's words. The risk to the little boy was immediately evident and she could understand why April needed to talk it through. It was one of those cases which felt like a time bomb ticking. There had been five reported injuries within the last two months, which in itself was concerning to say the least. There was the cut and bruise on his toe, the explanation for which April felt could be believed after having seen the state of the garden; the bruise on his buttock, which Becky had claimed was caused by Freddie bashing himself on the taps whilst playing in the bath; a bruise to his shoulder which was supposedly caused by the car door slamming into him; and a bruise to his thigh which happened when he fell off his trike. These accounts could all possibly be genuine, although April didn't think so, and the latest and most concerning of all was the bruise to his cheek, supposedly from falling off his trike again. However hard April tried, she could not envisage how a bruise could appear on the side of his face and the top of his ear by falling off a trike. April was certain that someone was harming him.

The question was whether there was enough evidence to take the case to court. April and Maria discussed the case at length and in depth, considering the overall well-being of the child, his presentation and the past history. He had not come to the attention of the Local Authority until the first injury three months ago, and this was soon after Colin Lyons moved in with Becky. The nursery had been alarmed by the injury to Freddie's toe because it was not quite where it would have been expected to be when taking into account Becky's explanation. The staff had also noticed a marked change in Freddie's demeanour, from a happy, confident and sociable little boy to one who was quiet, anxious and withdrawn. If the paediatrician had agreed with the nursery that the injury did not seem to be compatible with the explanation, the Local Authority could have taken action there and then because a medical professional's opinion on injuries was worth far more than those of the nursery staff or the social workers.

'My opinion is that we need to take action,' April was relieved to hear Maria say. 'Arrange a Legal Planning Meeting and let's get the case into court. I think there is enough evidence to suggest Freddie's at risk, and it sounds from what you've said as if there's likely to be at least one more injury before we get a court date. Let's start the ball rolling and try to put an end to this.'

7

FUTURE PLANS SETTLED

April waited all week, hoping that Jed would raise the matter of adoption with her, but despite plenty of opportunity to do so, he continued to say nothing, just as though it had never been mentioned at all. He was away for three out of the five nights of the working week and April couldn't help wondering whether this was avoidance tactics. Being with him in his silence was agonising for her as her mind could think of nothing else. She longed to approach him again but feared that his response would completely dash all her remaining hopes. She could at times console herself with the thought that he was getting used to the idea again and that it would all be OK in the end. On the nights he didn't come home she could manage her feelings better because at least she wasn't waiting and hoping that every time he opened his mouth to speak, he would at last say what she wanted to hear.

On Thursday evening April was preparing her report for the Legal Planning Meeting the following morning when she found herself bursting into uncontrollable tears. It was the sadness of the case she was writing about, coupled with the frustration of having no power to just remove the little boy before he was hurt again. The mixed emotions she felt about this case included anger towards the mother for letting her child come to harm, but also pity for her vulnerability. Although putting these difficult facts down on paper had set her off, she knew that what was going on in her own life was what had tipped her over the edge. She was emotionally strong and able to deal with difficult situations, but they were more difficult to manage when her own emotions were running high.

By the time Jed came home that evening, she had pulled herself together and felt quite upbeat, as, despite all that was going on, she had missed him. A tuna pasta bake was cooking in the oven and she had made a large, leafy salad with toasted pine nuts and parmesan cheese. A bottle of Chablis was cooling in the fridge. They hugged each other as they always did when he came home and chatted generally about their week; or at least April did, telling him about the difficult case of Freddie and his many injuries, and the decision to take the case to court for permission to remove him from his mother.

They cleared up after their meal and April threw herself down onto her comfy sofa, exhausted and emotionally drained. She felt she was starting to come to terms with what she perceived as Jed's change of mind regarding adoption, and talked herself round to accepting the way it was going to be. She was a strong person and able to deal with disappointment; after all, her life was good in comparison to many; no one had everything and no life was perfect. She would learn to be grateful for what she had.

Jed finished off in the kitchen, dried his hands, then sat down beside her on the sofa. He had changed into a baggy T-shirt and shorts. With a serious look, he turned towards her and she waited apprehensively, instinctively aware that something vitally important was about to be said.

'I've had time to think about things this week, and to be honest, that's why I didn't come home last night.' His eyes were downcast, causing April to take a gulp of air while steeling herself for the bad news that was inevitably coming. 'I'm really sorry for being so evasive; I know I left you up in the air, and how much it means to you. It was unfair, I know, but I needed to be sure, we both need to want it. It's no good heading into something as life-changing as adopting a child unless we're sure it's the right thing for us and what we both want.'

'So you have thought about it and made up your mind,' she said with a sigh of defeat. 'What did you decide?' She closed her eyes and waited for the blow.

'I think we should do it.' He put his arm around her shoulders.

April opened her eyes again and stared at him, speechless. She had been certain he had decided against it. 'Are you saying you want to do it?' she asked in disbelief.

'Yes, I think we should do it,' he repeated, smiling.

April found herself smiling back at him whilst at the same time, tears of pent-up emotion started streaming down her face. She had convinced herself over the last few nights that he was against the idea, and had been trying her best to come to terms with it.

They sat on the sofa, hugging and kissing each other. She couldn't contain her excitement. 'I'll phone the adoption team tomorrow; I don't know how long you have to wait for an appointment. Are you sure it's what you want? You do mean it, don't you? What changed your mind?' She was still reeling from the unexpected turn of events.

He laughed. 'I didn't change my mind; I hadn't made up my mind, I just wanted to be sure. It's true I still hoped we would have our own, but by adopting, we will have the privilege of giving a child who is already born a good, loving home, and then if we do have our own one day, we'll be doubly blessed.'

'We will need to be assessed, and they will want to know about all our skeletons; if you've got anything terrible you would like to tell me about your past you should do so now, because it will all come out,' she joked.

'What, you mean everything, including my period in Broadmoor and all my other wives?'

'Well, I expect you think you know all about me but you're wrong, as you will find out.'

56

'Intriguing… you don't have to tell me, it's obvious. You were once a striptease artist; I could tell that when we spent our first night together. You were clearly a professional.'

'I was good, wasn't I, but that isn't my secret past; it's much raunchier than that. You're going to have to wait to find out, though.'

They spent the rest of the evening laughing and talking animatedly about the future, and by the time they went upstairs to bed, they were both brimming with excitement.

By Friday morning April was prepared for her meeting with the Local Authority solicitors, who advised her that in their view the evidence that Freddie was at risk of significant harm if he remained with his mother was strong enough to put before the court with a request for an Interim Care Order. A hearing would be arranged within five days of the application being made. This was good news in some ways, and although it was a relief for April, it also meant a lot of work, including the need to prepare a detailed report setting out the evidence to present to the court. She would need to give a copy of her report to Becky and tell her what they were planning to do. This part of her job was the most difficult of all. She felt confident that she had sufficiently warned Becky about what could happen if Freddie continued to sustain injuries, but unfortunately it was common for parents to think of it as an empty threat and that Social Services wouldn't really take their children away. Becky was clearly thinking along these lines; otherwise, surely she would end her relationship with Colin Lyons.

Back in the office, April settled down with her laptop and a pile of papers in front of her in readiness to start writing the court report. As usual there was quite a lot of hustle and bustle going on, with phones ringing, two social workers chatting about a case in a corner of the office, and Maria and Miles deep in conversation in the small glass-panelled manager's office. Paula was just about to make a cup of tea, and stopped by April to ask if she would like one. 'We should have a drink after work tonight to catch up; there's just not enough time to chat during the day and I've got a lot to tell you,' Paula said.

'I think that's a good idea; have there been developments in your love life that you would like to tell me about, then?'

'Oh yes.' As Paula spoke, her head turned slowly towards the manager's office, from where Miles was just emerging. 'I would gladly give up the dating websites if only he would notice me. Trouble is, he's so in love with himself he doesn't notice anyone else.'

They both laughed, which attracted his attention.

'What are you up to now, Paula?' he asked as he walked towards them. He was very aware of how attractive he was and the effect he had on most women, but there was also a slight arrogance about him which curiously enhanced his appeal.

'We're planning a drink after work; we could make it a threesome if you like?'

'Sounds good – do you want me one at a time or both together? I'm happy with either.'

'Fantasies are always better left as fantasies, so they say,' retorted Paula.

'OK, we'll settle for just a drink, then; perhaps another time.'

They all laughed.

'I've got something to celebrate, anyway,' April couldn't help blurting out.

'You're not leaving us already, are you? Have you been promoted to team manager?' Paula asked.

'No. I will tell you more about it later.'

It was nearly 6pm when the three of them reached a stage in their work where they felt they could leave the rest until Monday. When they reached the Bow & Arrow, which was just around the corner from the office, Paula said, 'Right, it's Friday and once we step over this threshold anyone who mentions work in any shape or form has to buy the drinks for the rest of the night.'

'Agreed,' Miles replied.

The three social workers sat on high stools around a small, round table and Paula insisted on getting the first round. The pub was quite busy and April noticed a few social workers whom she recognised from the duty team in the corner of the room next to the open fireplace. They seemed to be listening intently to one member of their group, and April guessed they had not reached an agreement before entering the pub to leave work behind them. The duty team dealt with all the new referrals coming in, rather than the long-term cases.

'Come on then, Paula, tell us what you've been up to, we need a good laugh,' Miles said, shaking his shoulders in mock excitement.

Paula looked indignant before launching into her rundown of recent experiences with dating. She seemed to meet quite a few men who appeared to be to her liking, but they never lasted long. She said she was very choosy and only met with them after lots of conversations.

'Jason was really nice; he was a solicitor, or so he said. We had a good laugh together and I really thought we hit it off. We met a few times and I was thinking, Oh my God, I have met The One. He seemed really keen on me too, he said I was gorgeous, he couldn't believe his luck that he'd met me and all that stuff. Being gullible, I believed all of it; that was, until he told me about his wife. He still lived with his wife and children but the marriage was over, of course! It was just for convenience. He couldn't understand what was the matter with me. Why would I be upset? I really wanted to punch him right in the middle of his brazen fizzog and knock him off his stool.'

They were all laughing, including Paula.

Paula went on to tell them about the one who almost caused her to never want to go near a dating website again, someone called Steven. 'He was great fun in the pub. He really made me laugh. Later on he said, "Why don't we go on to a restaurant? I needed to get some cash so I said, is it alright if we stop at a cash machine on the way. Just as I was collecting the notes, I heard the engine start up, turned around just in time to see his car disappearing into the night. There was me, stranded in the middle of the high street, eleven o'clock at night, rain lashing down, wondering what I'd said.'

Miles and April looked at each other and she could see that he wanted to laugh. He was trying so hard to keep his lips straight that they twitched up and down. This was too much for April, who burst into fits of laughter.

'I'm sorry, Paula, that must have been horrible. What a pig' She still wanted to laugh. It occurred to April that she was still no wiser with regard to Miles's relationship status. She had started to notice that he never discussed his private life and actively and skilfully avoided the topic being raised. This made him even more intriguing.

'So, what is the celebration then? You haven't told us yet,' Miles asked as he put the next round of drinks on the table.

'Well, I haven't told you this before but Jed and I have not been able to have children—' April began.

'Oh my God, you're pregnant!' Paula exclaimed with delighted expectation.

'No, not really.'

They both looked at her. 'Not really – what do you mean, not really?' Miles asked, his face full of curiosity.

'We're going to apply to be adopters.'

'Oh!' Paula and Miles said simultaneously before falling into mutual silence.

April told them about their struggle to conceive, including the IVF and the miscarriage. She also told them about how she had thought Jed didn't want to adopt and what she went through whilst waiting for his response. It felt really good to get it all out of her system.

'Well, I think that's fantastic,' said Paula. 'I'm sure you will be fabulous parents.'

After the third glass of wine, April was beginning to feel quite woozy and decided it was time to go home. She would have to get a taxi and collect her car in the morning. She was still in a state of excitement, and was looking forward to being with Jed to talk more about their plans.

8

HEIGHTENED RISK

It was just after 7am when Samantha staggered from the park and made her way towards Charlie's house. Although it was just a short distance to walk, a number of people passed her, not disguising their disgust at her bedraggled and dirty appearance. This didn't worry Sam, just reinforced the feelings she already had about herself.

A vague apprehension began to rise within her as she approached Charlie's front door. There was no sound coming from the house and the curtains were still shut. Samantha was churning inside, desperate to know that her children were still there and safe. She knocked on the door and waited, but there was no answer and still not a sound. She tried a few times, knocking harder and louder each time, but still there was no answer. 'What the hell's going on?' she said out loud.

She decided to go around the back of the house where she could look through the glass of the kitchen door; there was no sign of anyone. She could see a few dirty dishes in a pile on the draining board, but otherwise the kitchen appeared quite tidy. She hoped that Dan hadn't been around because she didn't trust him and wouldn't want him around her children; something she hadn't given a second thought to when she needed to drink.

Sam was starting to get worried now; the silence was ominous. Surely Charlie wouldn't have gone out at this time in the morning? She knocked on the door again before going to the side of the house and hammering on the window. She then went back to the front of the house and shouted through the letter box: still no sound. She felt a sickening panic rising from her stomach. Luckily, she still had some charge on her phone and she called Charlie's number.

'Hello, Charlie here. I'm not around; leave a message and I'll call you back.'

Sam slumped down on the step, tears of frustration and panic filling her eyes. 'Where the hell is she? I don't believe this,' she exclaimed out loud. Thoughts were flooding her head, raising various unpleasant possibilities as to what could have happened. Sam was desperate to see her kids and at a loss as to what to do. She was bitterly regretting leaving them.

After sitting on the step for some time in the vain hope that Charlie would emerge, she decided to go home and clean herself up a bit before deciding what to do next. During her short walk Sam couldn't help thinking about her children and how much she was missing them. She thought about what a cheeky madam Tayla was and how she always seemed more grown-up than her six years. On the morning before her binge, Sam had slept in a bit later than she should have done, leaving it a bit tight to get to school on time. When she came into the front room, Tayla and Lily Grace were already up and Tayla was getting Lily Grace dressed.

'Lily Grace was cold, Mummy, and I don't want to be late for school.'

Sam smiled proudly at this memory. Lily Grace had been quite happy to let Tayla dress her, and sometimes it seemed she thought Tayla was her mum. Sam carried on thinking along these lines as she made her way home. She remembered another time when she had slept late and Tayla decided to make breakfast for herself and Lily Grace. She had two slices of bread on the kitchen floor which she had tried to butter with a spoon. Sam always kept the knives out of reach of the children. She felt a little pang of guilt as she remembered shouting at her at the time because the floor was dirty; Tayla had been very upset because she was only trying to help.

When Sam opened the front door to the flats, she spotted an envelope on the floor with her name on it. With immense relief, she saw that it was a note from Charlie, and opened it quickly with trembling fingers. 'I'm at my mum's with the kids. Charlie'

Sam knew that Charlie's mum lived just a few streets away. She washed and changed her clothes, and brushed her hair before checking herself in the mirror. The self-abuse of her body and health was evident in the reflection before her and she turned away, disgusted. Sam had always despised the image she was faced with when she looked in the mirror, but it was even more hateful and difficult when the clear signs of her most recent episode of overindulgent binging were etched into her features; pasty grey pallor and deep black circles under bloodshot eyes.

By the time Sam reached Charlie's mum's house it was almost nine o'clock and she wondered whether her children had been taken to school. It was difficult to judge whether there was anyone at home from the outside as the doors and windows were all shut, even though the heat of the day was building up. She knocked on the door and sighed with relief when Charlie came to answer it. The first thing she said was, 'Where's my kids?'

Charlie stared at her for a minute without answering. 'Where the hell have you been? I've been looking everywhere for you.' She moved to let Sam into the house, where she immediately spotted Lily Grace curled up asleep in the corner of the settee, dummy in her mouth.

'Where's Tayla?' she asked in panic as her eyes searched the room.

'Still in bed. She's been sleeping with Violet and Indigo. They were playing about until late last night.'

The tiny front room was crowded with people, some of whom Sam recognised. There was Charlie's mum, her stepdad, her half-brother Lee, his partner and their toddler, another male in his late teens whom Sam didn't know, and Charlie's fifteen-year-old half-sister Kayleigh. The television was on and although it was just after 9am on a Wednesday morning, nobody appeared to be going anywhere.

On Monday morning, April was sitting at her desk when, lo and behold, a call came through from the nursery reporting that Freddie had turned up with another bruise to the side of his face. Becky had pointed it out to the staff and given the explanation that he had crashed his trike into an open door, hitting his face on the handle.

Freddie was removed from his mother's care that evening under Section 20 of the Children Act, which decrees that there is no legal order in place and the person with parental responsibility has agreed to the arrangement. Except in truth it wasn't quite like that. After agreeing that Freddie needed to be removed for his own safety, April and Maria had gone to the home to speak to Becky. April reminded her that she had explained previously that the Local Authority would remove Freddie from her care if there were any further injuries. She told Becky that they were going to place Freddie in foster care and said she must sign the paperwork agreeing for this to happen.

'If you refuse to sign the agreement,' April explained, 'we will go to court to have an order made.'

Becky, distraught, threw herself on the sofa, crying and pleading with them not to take her little boy away. April sat beside the sofa, waiting patiently for her to recover enough to sign the paperwork she held in her hand. Eventually, Becky managed to sit herself up and April passed her the pen she had been holding in readiness. The paperwork was signed and April reassured Becky that she would arrange for her to see Freddie the next day.

They needed Becky to place some clothing in a bag for Freddie, and as they were waiting for her to get herself together, Colin Lyons walked in the door.

64

'What's going on here?' His face turned a reddish purple as his voice became louder. 'What's the matter with her?' He was a tall and heavy built man who towered threateningly above April and Maria.

April began to explain, but Becky stood up and screamed, 'They're taking Freddie away from me!' April was intensely moved by Becky's tears of anguish, but at the same time was frustrated that she had allowed it to come to this. Colin responded with a barrage of intimidating threats towards April and Maria.

It was usual practice to have a police car on standby outside the house in these situations, and the shouting from Colin was loud enough to raise the alarm. Two policemen came storming in and moved towards Colin, who immediately pushed one of them against the door. The second policeman stepped in and threatened to arrest him if he didn't calm down.

'You take him over my dead body,' he thundered, including the policemen and April in his wild-eyed glare. In the meantime, Becky had sat back on the sofa and, with her head in her hands, continued to sob.

Maria took Freddie's hand and led him into his bedroom in an attempt to protect him from the drama. She explained to him that he was going to be staying with a nice lady called Kaye and her little girl for a while.

'Is Mummy coming as well?' he asked, looking a bit frightened and confused.

'No, she won't be coming with us, but you will be able to see Mummy tomorrow.'

Freddie appeared quite happy with this, and when he was taken to the car by Maria and April, wearing his pyjamas and carrying his teddy, he calmly turned to wave to his mum, who was still distraught and sobbing, and then carried on chattering as though nothing unusual had happened.

April was aware that they were on sticky ground legally and that they needed the court to grant a Care Order to give the Local Authority the right to keep Freddie in foster care, because the way it stood, Becky could demand the return of her son and there would be nothing they could do to stop him going home. They were relying on the fact that Becky did not know what her rights were and mistakenly believed social workers had the power to just remove children without a legal order. She had believed she had no choice but to sign the consent form and that she would be in more trouble if she refused. The Local Authority needed to make this legal as soon as possible.

April wrote a report detailing each of the injuries found on Freddie along with the explanations provided by Becky. A report had also been sent from the nursery which gave an overview of how Freddie was, his social interaction with other children, his general confidence and demeanour. It was blatantly evident that until Colin Lyons came on the scene, Freddie was a happy little boy who appeared well cared for and loved, and they'd had no concerns about him or his relationship with his mother. These reports were submitted to the court and the hearing took place a few days later.

Becky and Colin were already in the court building, shut in a room with their solicitor, when April arrived. Thankfully, after reading the reports and listening to the barristers present their cases, the judge felt there was enough evidence to suggest that Freddie would be at risk of significant harm if he was returned to his mother's care. This was despite Becky's barrister emphasising the positive aspects of her parenting. This was just the initial hearing but an Interim Care Order was granted and would remain in place whilst further evidence was gathered. A date was set for the next hearing, where evidence would be heard from all parties, including the social worker, an expert witness, a guardian and Becky.

The next morning April popped in to see Freddie at his foster placement. He was sitting on the carpet in the lounge with the foster carer's four-year-old daughter. There was a box of toys beside them and the two children appeared to be enjoying each other's company, chatting together and giggling at silly things they were doing with the toys.

'When is Mummy coming?' Freddie asked April.

'Kaye is going to take you to see her after you have had your lunch.'

Freddie appeared perfectly happy with that and carried on where he had left off with the toys. Kaye said he had been no trouble at all and had just gone to bed and straight to sleep. He didn't wake up until after eight o'clock and ate a good breakfast of cereal, fruit and toast. No matter how many times she saw this scenario, April remained astonished at the resilience of young children caught up in these situations. Perhaps the fact that he was now feeling safe negated the fact that he missed his mother.

9

ADOPTION PLANS BEGIN

April was keen to get the ball rolling with regard to the adoption plans and had already arranged an appointment for the following week. She was aware that their case would be dealt with by another local area due to the confidential information which needed to be shared.

On the day of the appointment, April had arranged her visits and meetings so that she could be home a bit earlier, and was already in the house waiting for Jed, who was on his way. Although she tried hard to sit and read the paperwork for potential adopters they had received through the post, she was far too jittery and found it impossible to concentrate. She had been home by five on the dot, and Jed followed soon after.

'Do you think she will like us?' April asked nervously.

'She'll probably like me but I'm not so sure you'll be all right. You might need to keep quiet about what happens to you when there's a full moon. Don't worry, though; I won't say a word.'

April laughed. She loved the way he could joke during times like this.

At 5.30pm on the dot, the adoption social worker arrived. This visit was for the social worker to determine whether the couple were potentially viable as adoptive parents, and April was keenly aware that they could be ruled out after this first visit if the social worker found some reason why they would not be suitable. It was also to discuss the process of the assessment, preparation, and to make clear what would be expected of them throughout the assessment process.

The social worker was short, plump and jolly, and her name was Jenny. They all shook hands and introduced themselves; then April brought in a tray with cafetière, coffee cups and a selection of small biscuits, which she had already set out in readiness.

'I understand you are a social worker, April, so there will be things I am going to say that you will be very well aware of. I hope you don't mind but I will still go through everything just to make sure there are no gaps; feel free to stop me if it starts to get annoying or if you need to question anything I say. I have to admit it's much easier doing this with people who are basically ignorant about it all.'

'I understand,' April said, 'and I agree that it is important to go through everything. It will be better for Jed anyway.'

They began with a general chat about how they had come to the decision to adopt, and whether they had any personal experience of adoption; this was followed by questions about their jobs and extended family.

'We will be covering these things in much more detail later down the line,' Jenny explained. 'In the meantime, we need to do some paperwork. I need to know who your family networks are.'

Jed gave the names of his parents and brother, whilst April could only give details of her mother and brother.

'What about your father?' Jenny asked, looking over her glasses at April.

'Oh, he left when I was a baby,' April explained. 'I haven't seen him since and don't even remember him.'

'Have you ever wanted to see him?'

'I have to admit I have sometimes had thoughts of trying to find him, but I never did anything about it. I was angry for a lot of years that he didn't care enough about me to get in touch, and that he walked out on us, I suppose, but I've always had the impression Mum wasn't keen for me to do it. She might be all right now, after all these years, but I'm not sure.'

'We will be discussing this subject in more detail when we get into the assessment. Is that OK with you?' Jenny said, looking from April to Jed and then back to April.

'There's not much to discuss, really, but yes, I'm fine with that.'

During the conversation Jenny had focused almost completely on the negative side of adopting. She talked about the many reasons children came into care, and the potential implications of their early experiences on their development and future; for example, those whose mothers had misused illegal substances or alcohol whilst pregnant and the impact on the foetus, including foetal alcohol syndrome. Her main focus was around attachment disorder, which many children with neglectful and abusive backgrounds are blighted with.

April, being a qualified social worker, was well aware that a child with attachment disorder could struggle to form relationships and might never be able to trust an adult to keep them safe, leading to all kinds of complications and disappointments for the adopters. She knew only too well the destructive nature of attachment disorder and the life- long problems it caused so many children who were or had been in the care system. She also knew that attachment disorder was one of the most common reasons for adoption breakdowns. Without treatment these children found it impossible to form emotional bonds, and however much love and attention they were given it might never be reciprocated, which was extremely difficult for a parent to deal with. They were also likely to struggle with friendships and this could go on throughout their adulthood, resulting in chaotic and unstable lives. These children had learned from a very early age that they couldn't rely on an adult to keep them safe or meet their needs. They might have experienced harm from the very person they would naturally go to for care and protection.

'It sounds as though you're trying to put us off the idea,' Jed said, embarrassingly.

'Absolutely not, but prospective adopters are almost always completely absorbed in the niceties. They want a child for the same reasons most people want children and most of them understand that if they are lucky enough to get a baby, there will be sleepless nights, lots of washing, terrible twos later, limited freedom, and they don't mind these things at all; they welcome them. They weigh up the pros and cons and make the choice to go ahead, because the joy of having a child is worth it. But when a child is placed through the adoption process, there is always going to be a part of their child's life which no one apart from the birth mother or father will ever know. Clearly the sooner they are taken into care the less likelihood there is of emotional damage, but it's now known that babies are affected by their environment even in the womb. This isn't to say that they won't ever be able to live a normal, happy life, and a loving, stable family is the best thing to help them achieve that, but adopters need to understand that it is not the same as giving birth to your own child. There is nothing sadder for everyone concerned than an adoption breakdown, and it is really important that prospective adopters know the worst possible scenario before making such a life-changing decision, for the sake of themselves as well the child.'

April knew this was true; she had been involved in cases where adoptions had broken down. It is devastating for the child of course, but it is devastating for the adopters too, who have planned a future with the child; and often their extended family and friends have been involved and are acutely aware of what has happened. They frequently experience many years of shame, guilt and a dreadful feeling of failure.

After Jenny had left, April put more coffee on and she and Jed sat down together on the sofa, both quietly thinking over what had been discussed.

'Jenny had to tell us the worst; that's what they do,' she said. 'There are many successful adoptive families, and we will be one of those.'

Jed put his arm around her shoulders and they hugged each other. No other words were needed.

As they climbed into bed, April said, 'Now that we've started this, I think we need to tell our families. They'll be asked to give references, and Mum would not be impressed if the first thing she knew about our plans was Jenny turning up on her doorstep.'

'What a good idea. We should go at the weekend. They must be due a visit. I think they will be pleased for us, don't you? We could go to your mum's on Saturday and then on to mine Sunday morning.'

As usual Jed was asleep within minutes of his head touching the pillow whilst April lay staring at the ceiling. This time, though, she wasn't worrying about children on her caseload; she was thinking about matters of her own. The discussion about her father had rekindled the latent desire that was dormant within her, and her need to know about him. After lying awake for some time, curiosity building up, she quietly slid out of bed so as not to disturb Jed. She took her white cotton dressing gown from its hook on the door and crept downstairs on tiptoe. She sat down at the desk in the study, pushed her hair behind her ears to stop it flopping forward, and opened up her laptop before typing Anthony Tuczemski. Disappointingly, nothing came up. Although she hadn't been able to sleep when she was in bed, she now felt so exhausted it was a struggle to keep her eyes open. She went back to bed and fell asleep within minutes.

They set off early on Saturday morning, hitting the traffic on the M1 at around 9am. It was a bright, sunny day in the middle of June, and the world and his son seemed to be on this motorway. April pressed the button to open the window but quickly shut it again after they were both nearly suffocated by the stench from the traffic fumes. She didn't like air conditioning because it was too cold but it was definitely the best option now. She and Jed had been lost in their own thoughts as someone on the radio prattled on about parallel universes.

'Did you realise that scientists now believe there could be millions of other universes, some of which would be identical to ours? This means there must be another couple identical to us on their way to visit their parents, fed up, stuck in traffic, being slowly poisoned by fumes on a beautiful stifling hot June day.'

'Yes, that's right.'

'What?'

'Yes, I agree.'

'You agree to what?'

'To what you just said.'

'What did I say?'

Jed turned quickly to look at her, eyes blank, trying to think of a way he could disguise the fact that he hadn't been listening; but he was quick to realise he had been caught out.

'You weren't listening to me, were you, Jed? I can't believe you wouldn't listen when I am talking about something so profoundly interesting and important. If the theory is correct, every possible decision we could have made, but didn't, has happened in another universe,' April exclaimed, animated by the whole idea.

'Oh, I'm sorry, that's all a bit much for me; can we just talk about what we're going to do for lunch?'

'God, you're boring sometimes,' April said, frustrated that he wasn't as taken by this idea as she was. She was no scientist but the whole idea of parallel and multiple universes fascinated her. She found herself pondering on whether she should have been an astrophysicist rather than a social worker, but in reality, she knew she wouldn't change what she did. It was hard work, stressful at times and working with the saddest of lives, but she loved what she did. She and her colleagues would laugh about the times people said to them, 'I couldn't be a social worker, I wouldn't be able to sleep at night; I don't know how you do it.'

'It's just as well some of us have no feelings,' she would reply. It would be impossible to explain how she dealt with the sadness she faced every day, but just knowing that in her position she could make a difference to people's lives, especially children, was always a joy and a privilege.

At long last, the car turned into the street where April's mum lived on the outskirts of Northampton. This used to be a street of council houses but you would hardly know that now, as every one of them had been bought under the Right to Buy scheme. Although the framework, shape and size of the houses were almost identical to those in some of the areas where many of April's families lived, the difference in their appearance was stark. Doors and windows had been replaced mostly with UPVC, but each one with different styles and colours where the owners had put their own individual mark on their homes. Every garden was uniquely designed, each with neatly trimmed hedges and colourful borders. Some had extensions at the side or in the roof. The beautiful aroma of freshly cut grass wafted through the open car window as they drove down the street. The sound of lawnmowers and hedge trimmers seemed to be coming from everywhere.

Diana, April's mum, had been looking out for them and was waiting by the door as they walked up the path. In contrast to April's petite stature and dark brown hair, Diana was tall, slender and a natural blonde. April clearly took after her father. Coming home to her birthplace was always a joy for April. The familiar sights and smells, and knowing that many of the families she had been brought up living around had remained in the area, some of them still living in the same houses. This still seemed more like home to April than anywhere else.

The house was totally different to how it had been when April was a child, when it belonged to the council. Back then, there was no central heating, just a little gas fire with four bars, and a few night storage heaters upstairs. Almost everything in the house had been changed; the kitchen now had fully fitted units, the tiled bathroom a walk-in shower – a complete transformation. Having been built in the 1930s, the house was spacious with large rooms and a dining room. April's mum would not have been able to dream of owning a house of this size, had she not been able to buy her council house.

'Hello, darling,' Diana said, hugging her daughter first, then Jed. 'How was your journey?'

'Terrible,' answered April, 'but it's nice to be here and to see you, Mum. It seems ages.'

'It's OK, I understand, April, you're both very busy people. I will come to you next time, then I can make your dinners while you're both at work.'

'Sounds good,' Jed said, 'and I'm sure there would be plenty of other things you could find to fill your time whilst you're there – ironing, bit of vacuuming perhaps, windows haven't been cleaned for months. When do you think you can come?'

'I would be happy to do that if you wanted me to.'

'Take no notice of him, Mum; we would love you to come but not if you think you're doing all that. Jed said he was going to start doing all those things because he loves doing them, especially the ironing.'

'When did I say that?'

'I'm sure I heard you say that.'

'I'm sure you didn't.'

They looked at each other, smiling as they walked into the house, where the welcoming aroma of home cooking embraced them.

Following a lovely lunch of smoked salmon salad, cheese scones straight from the oven and lemon drizzle cake eaten outside on the tiny rose-scented patio, April and her mum walked into the nearby small town centre to do some window shopping whilst Jed stayed at home to read the paper, in order to give April and Diana some time on their own. The two women enjoyed each other's company, chattering away, making up for the months they hadn't seen each other.

'I think we need a cappuccino to set us on our way,' April said as they approached Diana's favourite little coffee shop.

'Yes, I will treat us. You go and get yourself a seat in the window over there.' She pointed to a corner of the room where a little round table was set in an alcove in front of a bay window which was draped with white lace and had a potted fresh lilac in the middle.

'You sit down, Mum, I'm going to get these,' April insisted.

'If you say so.' Diana sat down as she was told. As she did, she noticed someone she recognised, although she couldn't think who it was for a minute. The woman appeared to be leaving; she had a pushchair which she turned full circle towards the door. Diana saw the woman look at April, who was approaching with the coffees, when it dawned on her who she was.

'April, hi, how lovely to see you. I haven't seen you for years, how are you?'

April turned around sharply, and before her was her old friend Catherine from her schooldays. 'Catherine, hello, it's lovely to see you too. I'm absolutely fine.' She immediately noticed the pushchair and the very new baby inside. 'I didn't know you had had a baby,' she said, poking her head under the hood which was raised to keep the sun off. The baby was dressed in a white cotton dress with a silk collar and a little matching hat. Her feet were bare and the tiniest of perfect little toes wriggled and stretched as she stirred in her sleep. 'She's gorgeous, what's her name?'

'Melody,' answered Catherine. 'She's an angel – feeds and sleeps, hardly ever cries. It's not like people said it would be; you know, the usual stuff: "No more sleep for you for a few years; you think you're tired now, you wait – you don't know what tired is." I don't know why people are always so negative; it's wonderful being a mother. Have you not got any children yet? I would highly recommend it, and on top of all that you get to take a year off work.'

April felt the familiar pang of jealousy rising from deep within her stomach, although she managed to smile and look pleased for her friend. 'No, not yet.'

Whilst she spoke to Catherine, she became acutely aware that her mother was staring at her, scrutinising her responses, and knew instantly that she had been wondering about their childlessness and drawing conclusions. Diana would be too sensitive and polite to ask her directly, even though she was probably desperate to know. This was the first time April had considered her mother in all of this,

76

and it was now dawning on her that whilst her and Jed were going through their trials, her mother had probably also been worrying about their childless state.

'We are thinking about starting a family, but nothing in the pipeline yet,' April replied.

'You and Jed must come around one evening when you're home next; it would be great to get together.'

'We definitely will, that would be lovely.'

They said their goodbyes, with April promising to get in touch next time she was home.

After dinner that evening, April, Diana and Jed sat together in the bright but cosy front room, Diana and April sipping a gin and tonic and Jed with a glass of beer. It had been a really hot day but the sun was now making its rapid descent towards the horizon, leaving a fiery red blaze in its wake. The air was turning cooler, although still pleasant enough to leave the wide front window slightly ajar. It was a still night and the traffic noise from the road had subsided; all they could hear now was a delightfully rich, crisp and varied sound of a lone bird chirping from somewhere out in the bushes. They listened for a while, enthralled, until April decided this was the right time to break the silence.

'Mum, we have some news for you.' Just in case her mum should jump to the wrong conclusion, she quickly added, 'It's not that I'm pregnant, but we are hoping to have a baby.' She paused again. 'We're hoping to adopt one.'

Diana stared at her daughter and then at Jed, then back to April with a look of bewilderment. April could tell that she was trying to read their emotions. She was keen to understand how this felt for them. She had no idea about the IVF or the miscarriage. April had not told her anything, knowing that it would have worried her, and she hadn't wanted her mum to share their pain.

'I…' Diana seemed to stumble on her words. 'I just don't know what to say. I want to say I'm happy for you but I don't know how I feel.' She took a deep breath and stood up from her chair. 'I think I need to know how this came about; have you been trying for a baby? I always wanted to ask you but didn't feel I should. I should have asked you; why didn't you tell me?' Diana was pacing the room as she spoke, and April could see she had tears in her eyes. She wanted to hug her mum and say she was sorry for keeping her in the dark.

It was not for herself Diana worried, although she desperately wanted to be a grandmother; she couldn't bear to think that her daughter was enduring the pain of longing for a baby and not succeeding in becoming pregnant. She had wondered for quite some time whether they were trying for a family, but the sadness in April's eyes when she looked at Catherine's baby confirmed everything she had feared.

April explained what had happened and said she was sorry for not letting her know what was going on. She explained her reasons for not telling her and Diana seemed to understand, but the tears poured down her face, shedding pent-up emotions that had finally been shared. April cried too, and the two women hugged each other.

Jed made a cup of tea. 'We've come to terms with it now, Diana, and we are looking to the future. We've already had our first meeting with the adoption social worker and she hasn't ruled us out yet; she's even made an appointment to come and see us again so we must be reasonably OK. We are hoping to get a young baby and the social worker seems to think we should have a good chance, being quite young ourselves. We don't mind if it's a girl or a boy and he or she will be just as much our child as if we were birth parents, and we hope you will be just as much a grandmother.'

Diana's face began to lift and the colour returned to her cheeks. 'Of course they'll want you, don't be silly, they'll be banging your door down, especially when they realise I'm going to be the granny. I'm starting to get excited now – how long do we have to wait?'

They all laughed.

'Once they've found the right child for us, it shouldn't take too long, but we don't know yet how long it will take for them to find what they call "the right match",' April explained.

Diana had qualified as a midwife in her mid forties and often attended Social Services meetings when there were worries about a pregnant or new mother. She had seen situations where new babies had been removed from their mother soon after birth by social workers because of the high possibility of serious risk to the baby if left in the care of the mother. This was always hard to witness but she was fully aware that thorough assessments would have been carried out and the risks to the baby were real and severe; the evidence would have been put before the court and an order granted for the removal of the child. Although she would not have been involved after the birth and removal, Diana understood that these babies would normally be placed for adoption and this would be likely to happen very quickly because babies who are removed early are in high demand from adopters.

The next morning Diana waved Jed and April off as they went on their way to Jed's parents' house. 'So we will see you in a few weeks then?' Jed shouted back.

'Yes, I'll phone you when I get to the station.'

They waved and blew kisses as they climbed into the car.

Jed's parents were much more matter-of-fact and practical than Diana had been in their response to the news. Sally and David had both been teachers in Milton Keynes, where they still lived in a sprawling, spacious bungalow. They had two sons, Jed, and Richard who was a late baby, born just before Sally reached menopause and a baby was the last thing on earth she expected. After the initial shock both Sally and David were absolutely delighted and Richard was the sun and the moon in their lives. Jed was nearly fifteen when Richard came along, and not too pleased to say the least. Suddenly his world was turned upside down by this tiny being whom everybody adored more than life itself. As Richard grew, he became more revered; he was the cleverest little boy that had ever been born, he was the funniest, the handsomest – everything about him was amazing. Sally and David had not lost interest in Jed but he clearly wasn't any match for the wondrous Richard. Richard was currently in the Gambia saving turtles. He had completed a degree in medicine and intended to become a GP eventually, but at the moment was just enjoying doing what he liked to do, mostly funded by his adoring parents.

Despite all of this, Jed loved his little brother. His parents had come to their senses in later years and realised that Jed was also a son to be proud of. Whether it was due to his character or his parents not being quite as biased as he remembered, there was no resentment on Jed's part and the family were all very close.

When they were told the news, Sally and David hugged April and then Jed. They told them they were looking forward to being grandparents to the child and that it would make no difference that they were not grandparents by birth. David opened a bottle of cava, saying that they would leave the champagne until their grandchild arrived.

10

TAYLA AND LILY GRACE

April was soon back at work and absorbed again in other people's problems, which was what she got paid for, but more importantly what kept her inspired. It was time to visit Sam again and she had been made aware by the school that there had been further unauthorised absences and no explanation from Sam.

It was about four o'clock in the afternoon when April pulled up beside the pavement alongside Fairfield Rise and walked across the green toward the flats. As she walked, she raised her eyes to the window on the first floor where Sam lived, and could see Lily Grace standing on the inside windowsill looking out. Although the window was shut, this looked quite a precarious position for a small child to be in.

As usual there was no response to the doorbell, so April rang Sam's mobile.

'I didn't know you were coming today.' Sam never seemed to know what day of the week it was.

'I sent you a letter to confirm the day and time; did you not get it again?'

'No, I told you – post goes missing here.'

April wasn't sure whether to believe this but decided to give her the benefit of the doubt. 'I won't keep you long, I just have a couple of things I need to check with you and I would like to say hello to the children if that's OK with you.'

Sam came to the door. 'I was just going out. Lily Grace has got a temperature and I was taking her to the doctor's.'

'What time is your appointment?'

Sam clearly didn't know what the time was, and looked at April blankly. 'I was just going to turn up.'

'That's fine, then; as I said, I won't keep you long.'

Sam reluctantly moved aside to let April in the door, recognising that she wasn't going to be got rid of that easily.

When April walked through the door, it became immediately obvious why Sam had not wanted her to come in. She was faced with a very different picture than the last time she had visited. There were another two young children in the flat, and all four of them looked grubby and bored. One of them was lying on the floor behind the settee, playing on a Games Console. There was a large woman dressed in a tight pink strappy top slouched in the armchair, and two young men, one standing up and the other sitting on the sofa. The living room was cluttered and stank of tobacco smoke. An ashtray on the floor overflowed with cigarette butts. April looked through to the kitchen and could see that, as well as dirty dishes by the sink and a pile of dirty clothes on the floor, the pale grey tiles were covered in grime. Lily Grace had climbed down from the windowsill but April could see streaks of greasy fingermarks which she had left all over the window.

'Are you going to introduce me to your friends?' April asked.

'Oh, OK then; this is Curtis, he's my ex.'

April remembered Curtis was the one who'd beat Sam up, and whom she'd said she was never going to see again.

'This is Charlie, my friend, and this is Danny, Charlie's boyfriend. They just popped in for a chat.'

As she said this, Danny stood up and beckoned to Charlie. 'We have to get home; come on, kids.'

The two children seemed too bored to move.

'Come on, move,' Danny said with a hint of impatience.

Tayla walked up to April and said, 'Hello, April, I haven't been to school today. Mummy said I was too late.' She looked downcast and was clearly unhappy about not attending school.

Sam looked at Tayla, clearly annoyed, then at April, wondering how to get around the fact that she had been caught out. 'Tayla had a temperature this morning.'

'What have you been doing today then, Tayla?' April asked.

'Watching CBeebies.'

April asked Sam to come into the kitchen for a private word.

'Sam, what's going on? I thought your relationship with Curtis was over? Didn't you tell me he beat you up and you weren't going to put up with that from anyone ever again?'

'I'm not going back out with him; he's just a friend now.'

'So he's not staying here, then?'

'Well… yes, he is, but…' It was obvious to April that Sam was trying hard to think of an excuse. 'He hasn't got anywhere else to live because his dad's kicked him out. He's only staying until he can get a flat.'

'You do realise that is a concern for me, Sam? If he was to hit you again in front of the children it would be really upsetting for them.'

'He doesn't hit me any more; anyway, it was only when they were in bed. He never did it in front of the kids, he wouldn't do that.'

April felt exasperated; she had lost count of the times she had heard that one. 'It's not all right even if they are in bed, because, believe me, they will hear and they will know what is going on. They will be just as emotionally damaged by hearing it as they would be by seeing it. My advice is don't let him stay, tell him to go; put your kids first.'

Sam looked blankly at April and didn't answer. By her silence April assumed she had no intention of heeding her advice.

'Sam, things seem to have taken a turn for the worse. I need to ask, have you been drinking again?'

'No, I'm not going down that road again,' she replied indignantly.

April didn't believe this for a minute, although after a brief scan of the flat she could see no evidence of alcohol. 'The parenting group starts next Monday and you need to attend. I am also going to arrange an appointment for you to speak to a domestic violence worker. Sam, believe me, I am trying to help you. I'm not here to make your life miserable but you need to accept the support I'm offering you. Tayla needs to be in school regularly; have you got everything she needs to go tomorrow?'

'Yes, course I have,' Sam said defensively.

'I need to make it clear before I go that this visit has raised the concerns for your children. I am concerned that Curtis is back in your life, that you appear to have been entertaining friends instead of seeing to your children, that your home is dirty and unkempt, and that you've allowed people to smoke heavily around your children and in their home. I will be visiting again shortly and I want to see a big improvement.'

April left the flat feeling a mixture of emotions. She felt angry that Lily Grace and Tayla had been exposed to the environment she had found them in. It was clear that their needs had been put aside whilst Sam and her friends sat around chatting and smoking. She also felt sad and disappointed because she had hoped things were going to improve for this family and Sam was going to find her feet. She was fully aware of how much Sam loved her children, but the dysfunctional family life she had endured herself as a child had impacted badly on her, leaving her dreadfully lacking in capacity to be an effective parent, and struggling to meet her children's needs. April felt the familiar sense of foreboding. She had been in this situation before when, however much support was offered to the mother or parents, they were just unable to turn themselves around and the children ended up being removed from the family, which was distressing for everyone concerned. April had a soft spot for Sam. In many ways she was still a child herself and her vulnerability brought out the protective instinct in April, although she never lost sight of the fact that her priority was the well-being and safety of the children.

When April had left, Sam threw herself on the settee next to Curtis.

'Nosy cow. Who does she think she is, telling me who I can have staying in my fucking flat?' Sam then mimicked April's voice. '"I need to make myself clear. This has raised my concerns",' she mocked.

They both laughed.

'I love my kids and nobody can say I don't; she can fuck off.'

'I don't care what they say, you're a really good mother, and I'll tell them that if they ask me,' Curtis assured her.

Despite this bravado, inside Sam was feeling distraught at being caught out, as well as petrified of what April could do. She made a decision that she was going to tell Curtis he had to go. She would let him stay tonight but then he would have to leave. Her feelings towards April were complex and hard to define. Although her natural instinct was to defy her, like a naughty child defies a parent, there was also a strong desire to please. Although she was angered at being told what she could and couldn't do, deep down she understood that April really did want the best for her and her children.

Curtis spread himself out on the sofa. 'Now that snotty social worker's been and gone, we can get some booze in; I got my money yesterday.'

'No, I'm off the booze. I went a bit crazy last week and I'm not doing that again,' Sam insisted.

April returned to the office to catch up with the pile of paperwork which had accumulated over the last few days. She always felt she could do a much better job as a social worker, helping families to improve and manage their lives better, if she didn't have to spend so much time at the computer, writing reports and recording everything she did in word-for-word detail. It was a general feeling amongst social workers that they spent more time recording what they had done to show that the boxes had been ticked, than actually doing the

85

work. She had hundreds of emails waiting for a response, from foster carers, education professionals, other social workers, managers, which all needed dealing with as a matter of urgency. Also, the deadline was approaching for the final statement for little Freddie. April wondered when she was going to get the time to do that, since all her working hours over the next few weeks were already taken up.

The office was quite quiet when she arrived the next morning, with a number of empty desks and a scattering of social workers typing away, absorbed in their work. She sat down at one of the empty desks, pleased that nobody seemed to notice her, and set about the tasks in hand. An email from a fostering social worker reported that the foster carers had given notice on a young boy who was on April's caseload. He was only six and this was already his third placement since coming into care. Her heart sank as she thought about having to go and explain to the little boy, whose name was Nathan, that he was going to have to go to yet another family. It was hard for a social worker to hear that a boy of six could be so difficult to care for, that three sets of foster carers were unable to manage him as this raised a high level of foreboding for his future. April's first thought was how they might be able to keep this placement going, and if there would be a possibility of the carers changing their minds if they were offered more support, such as respite care. She decided to put that to the top of her priority list.

Sifting through the rest of the emails, she came across one from the foster carer of two little boys aged four and two, who were about to move from foster care to live with their adoptive family. They were going to have their goodbye visit with their mother in the morning and the foster carer wanted to know what time to bring them to the Family Centre. These were two little boys who had been extremely difficult to care for initially due to their chaotic life with their birth family, where there were no boundaries. Their mother was always leaving them with various people, whoever she could find to look after them as long as it wasn't herself. It took the foster carer a year to settle them into a routine but she had done an amazing job and against all the odds they became adoptable. It occurred to April that these carers could be the right ones to have Nathan.

The next day in the Family Centre, April set up a table with a few cupcakes, some crisps in a bowl, grapes and orange juice in preparation for the goodbye party for Josh and Luke, the two little boys who were going to be adopted. The boys arrived with their foster carer carrying little parcels which had been wrapped up for them to give to their mother. Justine, the boys' mother, arrived five minutes later. She nodded hello to her boys before walking over to the table where the food was laid out and helping herself to a plateful. Josh asked his mother if he could have some too, and she nodded to him before walking over to April, who was sitting on a chair on the other side of the room. She had wanted to remain as inconspicuous as possible to give the family time together. Justine started chatting to April about how she had fallen out with her sister because she had 'grassed her up' to her boyfriend about talking to an ex on social media. April listened for a few minutes, then suggested Justine go and play with the boys. There were plenty of activities available and the boys were busying themselves with a play kitchen. They did not expect any attention from their mother and they weren't disappointed.

At the end when it was time for them to say goodbye to each other, Justine surprised April by grabbing both boys and hugging them as though she would never let them go. She didn't cry until they had left, which was what she had been advised, but as soon as they had gone, she sobbed uncontrollably. April thought she was going to cry herself, and although a final contact between a mother and her child is always going to be an emotional situation, she was not expecting this response from Justine, who had always appeared so wrapped up in her own issues that she hardly acknowledged her children. April should have learnt by now that people are nearly always far from predictable, particularly the ones she came across in her line of work.

Despite Sam's protests Curtis had been out and bought some cans of lager. Sam was putting the girls to bed whilst he sat on the floor with his back against the settee watching the television, lager can in one hand and cigarette in the other. When the children were in bed Sam started to sort out their school clothes for the next morning. She was going to make sure they didn't miss another day; she didn't want April banging on her door again.

'How much money have you got, Sam? You could go and get us a pizza.'

'Don't be stupid, I've only got twelve quid and it's got to last till Monday.'

'Have you got any pizzas in the freezer?'

'No, I haven't, and if I did, I wouldn't give it to you. I buy them for the kids.'

'Can you get me something to eat, then?'

'Get yourself something, you lazy fat-arse.'

Curtis leant over and handed her a can of lager. 'There you are, I got some for you as well.'

'I told you I didn't want any,' Sam said as she took the lager out of his hand, curled her legs beneath her and pulled the ring from the top of the can, which made an appealing fizzing sound.

There was nothing much on the television and the two of them sat drinking, smoking and playing music. Sam must have dozed off because when she woke up, she could see Curtis still held a drink in his hand, which was tipping on its side. She jumped up to grab it, and before she knew what was happening, she found herself suddenly flung hard against the wall, then strong hands around her throat, choking her.

She tried to pull Curtis's hands off her neck, screaming at him to let go, but he just increased the pressure, squeezing harder, his face screwed up in anger; she thought she was going to die.

'You stupid slag,' he bellowed. 'You scared the shit out of me, what the fuck?'

Sam felt the blood pounding in her head and she welled up with rage. Self-preservation overwhelmed her, and without thinking of the possible consequences, she raised her right knee and thrust it between his legs, causing him to recoil from her, releasing her neck to clutch at his groin. As he did this she ran out of the flat, down the stairs and onto the road. She was running so fast her pulse raced and her heart pounded, but sheer terror kept her going. As well as her natural instinct to escape from this violent man, from somewhere deep in her mind the words of the social worker came back to her, telling her how damaging it is for children to hear their mum being physically assaulted, and she wanted to protect them from this by getting away from her flat.

She was running so fast, her feet were hardly touching the ground, but Curtis was not far behind her and was shouting, 'Get back here, you fucking slag, or you're gonna be sorry.'

Sam carried on running; she was heading towards Charlie's house without really knowing why. Being the early hours of the morning, the streets were quiet with most people tucked up safely in their beds. Sam's heart was pounding so loudly she could feel it throbbing in her ears. This wasn't the first time she had been on the wrong side of Curtis's unprovoked, violent attacks and she was keenly aware it was not a good place to be. She soon became out of breath, the pace she had been running coupled with the evening's heavy smoking taking their toll. She stopped running and panted loudly, leaning against a parked car, gasping to get air into her lungs. She knew he would catch her up but there was nothing she could do about it now; she had run out of steam. Her legs had given in and her lungs were about to burst.

He was shouting something incomprehensible when he grabbed her by her hair and punched her hard in the face, sending her head reeling backwards. A snapping sensation in her neck, followed by a sharp burning pain down her spine, and for one horrible moment she thought he had broken her neck. He then, to her surprise and relief, stopped, as though coming to his senses, and said softly, 'You shouldn't have done that, Sam. I didn't want to do this again but you made me do it. You always make me do it.' He seemed completely exasperated.

Sam knew from experience that there was no point in arguing or questioning what it was she had done, because there was no reasoning with Curtis. He was always in the right.

'Shall we go back home?' Curtis said.

'Yes,' Sam said meekly, and they walked side by side in silence back to the flat.

When they got into bed, Sam sobbed quietly as Curtis slept. She was crying because she was hurt physically, but more so because his violence had confirmed once again that she was a worthless and unlovable human being who deserved to be treated this way; and also because, once again, she had let her children down.

She was woken in the morning by Tayla pulling at her arm. 'Mummy, I've made breakfast; can we go to school now?'

Sam was forced into consciousness long before she was ready and it took her some time to grasp the situation. She half-opened her eyes and the pain down the side of her face, and her throbbing eye socket, thrust her mind back to the ghastly memories of the previous night. Her first instinct was to hide the mark of violence on her face from her child, and her second was to get Tayla out of the bedroom where Curtis still slept in case he should wake up in a foul mood and start on her again.

She took Tayla's arm and pulled her out of the bedroom into the lounge where she saw Lily Grace sitting on the floor eating a slice of bread with a lump of chocolate spread in the middle. On the floor beside her was an open jar of chocolate spread and a spoon. Sam looked at the clock and her heart sank when she saw that it was ten minutes past nine. 'Quickly, girls, we need to get ready; we're going to be late for school.' She was pleased that their uniforms were clean and ready, although the children had not been bathed before going to bed so were not particularly clean. Lily Grace had baked beans down her pyjamas and parts of her leg, and both her daughters had dirt on the bottom of their feet from walking barefoot on the dirty kitchen tiles. Sam, in a panic, wiped the chocolate spread from their faces with a wet towel and put their clothes on over yesterday's dirt.

She had already thought up a story about why she was late before reaching the school gates. 'Lily Grace was up all night being sick,' she told the receptionist, whilst Lily Grace, holding her mother's hand, looked up at her in bewilderment. Tayla just kept her head down and waited to be allowed to go to her class. She knew full well what the procedure was when they were late or when they hadn't got to school. Either her mum would have told her what she had to say, or she would have been told not to say anything at all.

11

TOO MUCH WORK

Jenny was due to make her second visit that evening and April was rushing to try to make a dent in her outstanding workload. One of her mothers had been sectioned by the mental health crisis team and her children placed with foster carers by Out of Hours. This was quite a regular occurrence for these children – Martha, four, and Ben, three – but it meant a huge amount of paperwork to complete and a statutory visit to the children. This was of course additional to the packed schedule already arranged for the day, including a still-outstanding addendum report for the court, for Freddie's case.

Paula, who was sitting opposite April, ended a telephone conversation which appeared to be quite heated. Somebody was shouting at her from the other end of the line. She stood up and marched up and down the office before stopping at April's desk. 'Do you know what, I get fed up sometimes; people seem to think they can talk to us as though we're pieces of shit. Oh, but we're still expected to be nice, polite and caring. We're not human beings though are we? We're just social workers'. The strutting began again as she continued to rant. 'Just wait till I retire – I'm going to knock on all the doors of those rude people and tell them exactly what I think of them. Looking forward to that day is the only thing that keeps me going.'

April laughed. She knew what Paula meant, having been on the other end of abusive telephone calls many times during her career. You had to remind yourself that it wasn't personal and you were representing the organisation so were expected to listen with a sympathetic ear, but it still had an impact.

Paula began to rant about the abusive father who had just been on the phone. 'He's got borderline personality disorder and I'm not supposed to visit without someone with me, but it's all right for him to abuse me on the phone, I suppose. Funnily enough, he's usually OK when I visit the family. I'm always a bit nervous because he has a violent history. He's put Tia, his wife, in hospital a few times. The children are sweet but not properly looked after. I sometimes wonder whether I should be taking steps to remove them.'

As Paula spoke, April thought back to her previous post and a father with bipolar disorder. She had dreaded visiting even with a colleague because she could never tell what mood he would be in. He had been in the army and his experiences had changed his personality, which may have already been frail bearing in mind his childhood experiences. The trouble was, there were children in the household and they had to be seen by the social worker regularly because they were on a Child Protection Plan. The police didn't like going there and if they did, they would be armed with truncheons and wearing bulletproof vests.

'He's telling me I'm crap at my job, I don't know what I'm doing and he wants to know why I lie all the time; stupid pratt.'

April was beginning to become agitated at the work that wasn't getting done, and Paula noticed that she seemed preoccupied. She knew exactly what it felt like to be snowed under with work and have someone keep talking to you.

'Oh, I'm sorry, April, I can see you're really busy. I'll leave you to it.'

'If you wouldn't mind, Paula, sorry but I am a bit pushed at the moment. I need to get quite a lot done today. I want to be home before six to prepare for the adoption social worker; she's coming for her second visit this evening.'

Just as Paula walked away, April's own phone rang. She was very tempted to ignore it and get on with her report, but she knew the call would go back to admin, who would direct it back again to her. She would just try to get rid of whoever it was as quickly as possible.

'Good morning, April Gardiner speaking.'

'Hello, April, it's Lynn Speakman from Middlefield Primary School.'

'Oh, hello, Lynn,' April said with a sinking heart. She knew this was going to be bad news as Middlefield Primary was where Tayla Bushell went to school.

'I need to report to you what has happened this morning.' It was just before 11am. The teacher went on to tell April what had happened, including details of the large purple-and-red bruise to the side of Sam's face.

'How was Tayla, did she seem OK?'

'I haven't had a lot of time to observe her as she has not long settled in class, but I would say she appears a bit withdrawn and she doesn't look particularly clean. I thought I ought to let you know as soon as I had the chance to come out of the classroom.'

'Thank you for reporting this to me. I'll follow it up and let you know what happens. I think we will need to arrange another Core Group Meeting as a matter of urgency; get everyone together again, including Sam.'

April said goodbye and put the phone down. She put her elbows on the table and thrust her head into her hands. This was typical: when there was more work than could possibly be managed within the given timescales, this was when all the other cases were bound to blow up.

April's diary was chock-a-block busy all day and the only time she was going to be able to fit in a visit to the Bushell family was after 5pm, and this was a visit she could not put off until tomorrow. With a heavy heart she reached the conclusion that she was not going to be able to get home in time to make the appointment with Jenny, so would have to cancel. She would suggest Jenny did her session with Jed as she knew that they would each be meeting with her individually at some stage in the assessment. April phoned Jenny's number but was greeted by her voicemail asking her to leave a message. April explained the situation and said she would wait to hear from her. She hoped that it could still go ahead with Jed as she would hate to have to delay the assessment.

April completed the paperwork for Martha and Ben, then gathered her things together to go out to the foster home to see the children and pass on the paperwork to the carers. She had an avocado sandwich in her drawer which she had been hoping to enjoy peacefully in the little office kitchen with a cup of coffee, but instead it would now be gulped down whilst she was driving, along with a swig of water from her thermos bottle which she always kept in the car.

Ben and Martha were out in the garden, jumping up and down on the trampoline, when April arrived. She could hear their lively chatter and giggles as she walked up the garden path towards the front door. She had bought them a comic each. She always felt terribly sad that at their young age they were having to deal with frequent disruption in their lives. Their mother suffered from bipolar disorder and although when well was a very good mother to them both, her dark moods and depression, which came upon her periodically, left her unable to cope or even care. Luckily the children were usually able to come to the same carer when this happened, which helped to reduce the trauma for them, but like all young children they just wanted to be with their mum. Martha, at four had taught herself coping mechanisms through which she would become the adult. This stemmed from her experiences of her mother not being available emotionally as she slowly sank into depression. Even at this young age, Martha could see it coming and would decide she wasn't going to go to Nursery. She would kick and scream and refuse to leave the house. At first her mother worried thinking that something bad had happened to her at Nursery, but she started to realise that it was none of these things; it was because Martha thought she needed to be at home to look after her. It was painful for her mother to accept that Martha was taking on responsibility for her, at such a young age.

April knew the children would be pleased to see her, and after being let in by Gwen the foster carer, and a quick hello to Gwen, she went straight into the garden to see them. She watched as the children jumped, twisting and turning, falling over and getting back up again, until Martha spotted her standing there.

'April!' she called, with a beam of delight on her little cherub face. 'Watch me, I can do a roly-poly.' She proceeded to put her head down on the canvas and turn herself over, kicking Ben as she did so. Ben started to cry and, holding his arm out in front of him, tumbled towards April looking for comfort.

April rubbed his arm and lifted him down from the trampoline. She took his hand and led him into the conservatory, with Martha following close behind, chattering away.

'Mummy had to go to the 'ospital again,' Martha told April.

'I know,' April said as she sat down on the wicker settee. 'They are going to make her all better again and you will soon be able to see her.'

Ben had found a toy car in the large plastic box, which was brimming over with every kind of toy imaginable. He busied himself pushing the car around on the parquet floor whilst at the same time making hissing and buzzing noises, which to his own ears probably sounded exactly the same as the real thing.

Gwen told April that the children had been brought to her in the early hours of the morning. They apparently hadn't been to bed before coming and were still in their day clothes when they arrived. A neighbour had called the mental health crisis team, and Gwen wasn't sure how the neighbour had got involved. Gwen was a lovely foster carer and April was confident the children were happy in her care; the trouble was, she loved a natter and it was always difficult to get away. Much as April would have loved to sit down, drink coffee and chat, she was feeling really stressed about all the things she needed to fit in, and was desperate to get going.

Finally, she was able to get away, though this was after politely listening as Gwen talked to her at the door for what seemed like hours about the plans she had for her garden that summer and how her tulips just hadn't appeared. April managed to gradually edge herself away whilst Gwen continued to prattle, then as soon as Gwen stopped for breath, she shouted goodbye and waved as she got into the car. Just as she was pulling the seat belt around her body, her phone started ringing; she searched through the scrunched-up old papers and debris that lined the bottom of her huge bag and located it just in time to catch Jenny.

'Hello, April; I do apologise but I'm not able to do a session with just Jed this evening. I need to see you both together to begin with. Shall we arrange another appointment?'

April's heart sank. 'I suppose we will have to, then. I'm sorry to be a nuisance; I've just had so much happening lately.'

'Don't worry, I know what it's like; don't forget I used to do the same as you once. I can come at the end of next week if that's any good for you.'

April had hoped it could have been sooner, but the date was agreed and put in her diary.

Before doing anything else she needed to let Jed know what was happening. She sensed an element of disappointment in his voice, but there was also a touch of annoyance. April was fully aware that the reason for this would be more to do with the fact that this was yet another occasion when their plans had to change due to April's ever-demanding job, rather than missing the session with Jenny in itself.

Back at the office, she finished off the report for the court before setting out again to visit the Bushell family. Her heart was heavy as she turned the corner into Elder Road. She had already decided to initiate PLO (Public Law Outline) procedures. This entailed the parents of children the Local Authority had concerns about being told, in detail, by letter, what the concerns were and what they needed to do to reduce the risks for their children. The parents in these circumstances were entitled to seek legal advice and find a solicitor to support them through the process. They would be given a period of time to make the changes required. In many cases this worked for the parents because it set out clearly what they needed to change, but it also shook them into realising how serious things had become and that they really could end up losing their children.

12

ALTERCATION

After Sam had dropped the children off at school and nursery, she made the decision to call in to see Charlie. She didn't really want to go home knowing Curtis was there, although she was sure he wouldn't even be awake yet.

Unusually for Charlie, she was on her own in the house. She usually had various visitors.

'Where's Dan today, then?' Sam asked.

'I don't know,' Charlie said, shrugging her shoulders. 'I'm getting rid of him anyway. I've got a feeling he's seeing someone else behind my back.'

'I wouldn't be surprised,' Sam replied. 'I told you what I think, anyway; I think he's taking you for a mug.'

It was then that Charlie noticed the bruise. 'What the hell's that, or need I ask?' she said, pointing at Sam's face with a look of horror.

'We had a row, that's all. We had a few drinks; he got pissed. He was sorry afterwards.'

'That's no excuse for him to smash you in the face. You're not going to let him get away with that, are you?'

'I've told him he's not staying; he's got nowhere to go at the moment but as soon as he finds somewhere else, he's out.'

'You're mad; I'd have kicked his arse out the door years ago. You must be stupid, keep letting him back and—'

'You can't talk,' Sam interrupted angrily. 'Dan comes and goes as he pleases and you just let him in – "Oh, hello, Dan, where've you been? Come on, let's go to bed",' she mocked.

'That's none of your business.' Charlie's large, flabby face was growing red with anger as she stood up and moved towards the chair where Sam had seated herself. 'He doesn't hit me,' she shouted down at her, 'and if he did, he'd be straight out of that door. I wouldn't have that in front of my kids.'

Sam was now raging; Charlie's confrontational manner had roused her temper, but the reference to her kids struck a fragile nerve. 'Dan doesn't care about you; he just comes when he wants a shag – that's obvious to everyone else but you're too stupid to realise it. I'm surprised he wants that with you anyway, you ugly, fat bitch.'

'Piss off out of my house, you wasted old alky.'

'I'm off; don't worry,' Sam said, storming out of the house and slamming the door.

Although she could hold her own and give as good as she got in any argument, underneath Sam was as fragile as tissue paper. She had gone to Charlie's because she desperately needed comfort from someone. She didn't want to be told that she was an idiot for putting up with it; she sort of already knew that anyway. She had no one else to turn to; Charlie was her only friend.

Her emotions were in turmoil. The anger burned inside like a furnace and, not knowing which way to turn, she found herself heading towards the park. This was the one place she could come which offered her the chance to sweep away all the miseries of her life for a brief period. She could feel a knot developing in her stomach as she wrestled with the familiar voice that tried to warn her not to do it. The voice wasn't strong enough and she continued to walk towards the park at a quickening pace.

To add to her troubles, Sam had received a letter from her landlord that morning threatening her with eviction if she didn't pay the outstanding rent she owed. As she walked towards the park bench, she was thinking about how unfair it was. Some anonymous person had reported her to the council when Curtis was staying before, and they'd stopped her benefits. It was quite some time before they started again, and by that time she was in significant arrears. At the time she was given a crisis loan to help out, but then they refused to give her any more. She borrowed from a moneylender to get by and had been struggling to pay that debt ever since. It seemed to be going up rather than down.

Sam sat down on the bench where she knew she would soon be joined by others similar to her who came for exactly the same reasons. As she sat there looking around, she started to think about what she was about to do and tried again to talk herself out of it. An intense altercation was taking place in her brain.

Go home, the voice was saying. If you have a drink you'll be here all night, and what about the kids?

Another voice piped up to override the first: I only want a couple of drinks; I'll be back to pick them up from school.

Then the first voice again: You know you won't be. Don't be stupid; go home.

As this argument was taking place in her head, she was distracted by a young woman with her toddler, and another woman who looked as though she was probably the young woman's mother. This was confirmed when she heard the young woman say to the toddler, 'Do you want Nanny to put you in the swing?'

The little girl ran to her nanny, who swept her up, squeezed her, and kissed her head as she put her in the swing. Nanny was chanting, 'Wheeeeee!' in synchrony with the movement of the swing, and the little girl squealed with delight.

'Higher, Nanny, push me higher,' she shouted.

Nanny was laughing. 'You'll fall out if I push you higher.'

The toddler's mother stood looking on, smiling proudly.

'Shall we go and get an ice cream?' Nanny said.

'Mum, you shouldn't spoil her, she's already had lunch.'

'What else are we for if it's not to spoil our grandchildren? That's our main purpose, isn't it?'

They both laughed as Nanny took hold of the little girl's hand and the three of them walked towards the town to get an ice cream, smiling and chatting happily.

It suddenly seemed deathly quiet in the park. There was no one else around, just Sam sitting alone on the bench. The only sound was the gentle rustling of leaves as they were caught in the soft, warm breeze. Observing the family had made her think about her own mother and how wonderful it would have been if she had been at all bothered about her grandchildren. Sam couldn't even remember being taken to the park herself when she was a child. For some reason she didn't seem to have many memories from her childhood but the ones she had were mostly bleak to say the least, and she relived these through frequent and vivid flashbacks. She remembered being slapped hard across the face by her mother after losing a plimsoll at school once. She also remembered being forced to go outside and play with her brother Braydon, who was only three at the time, so that her mother could entertain a new boyfriend. It was January and bitterly cold. They had thin nylon jackets on and no gloves or hats. They were both so cold they stood in the corner of the next-door neighbour's shed, shivering. She remembered trying to comfort Braydon, who was crying and asking to go back in the house. This put her in mind of how Tayla was with Lily Grace. She had thought about going to her mum's after leaving Charlie's, but she knew she would only be likely to get even more grief. She couldn't really go to her mum's anyway because after the last row they had, Wayne had told her not to come back because she always caused trouble.

Sam waited patiently, confident that it wouldn't be long before her friends came, bringing plenty of cans with them. She had resolved the argument in her brain by deciding that she would just have one or two drinks and only stay until it was time to pick the children up.

She texted Curtis to ask him to collect the children from school if she wasn't back in time, just as a precaution. He had collected them before and she could trust him to do that. She told him she was going to get some shopping and might be a bit late back.

She had a fleeting thought about April and what she would say if she knew Curtis was collecting the children. She didn't worry too much, though, because she wasn't due to visit. It hadn't occurred to her that the school would contact April to tell her about the bruise.

Curtis had been playing on his Games Console since getting out of bed at around 1pm and wasn't particularly happy at the prospect of having to go out, but he agreed to do it. He had made himself a Pot Noodle for lunch and was just thinking about what to eat now as he was getting hungry again. Sam had been shopping recently so there was food in the cupboards and fridge. He didn't want to have to cook anything, but luckily after pushing aside a pile of old papers, some dirty tee-cloths, empty cereal packets and a half used tin of beans from the kitchen worktop, he found some crisps and a jumbo pack of chocolate buttons which Sam had bought for the children. He was really starving by now, so devoured three bags of crisps and all of the chocolate buttons whilst continuing his game, which completely absorbed him.

At about 3pm Sam hadn't returned, so he swung his legs over the arm of the chair, put his shoes on and left the flat to make his way to the school. Tayla was not pleased to see him waiting for her. 'Where's Mummy?' she asked with a clear tone of apprehension in her voice and demeanour.

'I dunno,' he replied, with total disinterest and no concept of the little girl's anxiety.

They collected Lily Grace from nursery, who followed behind Curtis as they walked home, holding on to her big sister's hand.

When they arrived back at the flat, Curtis immediately sat himself down, threw his legs back over the arm of the chair, and resumed the game he had been playing. Tayla pulled a chair up to the sink and made herself and Lily Grace a drink of water. They sat on the settee and Curtis turned the television on for them so they could watch CBeebies whilst he got on with his game.

It was nearing 6pm when April rang the bell at Fairfield Rise. As usual there was no response and after three attempts, she rang Sam's mobile number. There was no answer, which was unusual. April rang the bell and knocked at the door really hard, but there was still no answer. She was just about to leave when a young man in a hooded jacket walked towards the flats and let himself in via the main door.

'Oh, excuse me,' April said, rushing back to the building, 'I wonder if you would mind letting me in? I can't get an answer from my friend; I think her buzzer must be out of order.'

He looked her up and down, grunted and then stood aside as April walked in. The young man followed but then walked straight on, heading for the ground-floor flat at the end of the corridor. April wondered whether Sam knew this person.

As April approached the door of Sam's flat, she could hear the theme tune from a children's television programme blasting out. She knocked on the door. After a short time, Curtis opened it and gawped at her in astonishment. With the door only slightly open, he said, 'What do you want? Sam's not in.' He purposely positioned himself to ensure April could not cross the threshold or see into the flat.

Tayla then appeared and stood behind Curtis.

'I really need to speak to her. What time will she be back?'

April noticed Tayla was uncharacteristically quiet and staring at the floor. 'Are you all right, Tayla; did you have a nice day at school today?' she asked, bending her head around Curtis so that she could get a better look at her.

'She's all right, aren't you, Tayla?'

'Yes,' Tayla said meekly, still looking down at the floor.

April wasn't happy to leave. It was very obvious that something wasn't right. 'Can I just come in for a few minutes to see Lily Grace and have a little chat with them both? I have to chat with them when I visit, otherwise I'll be in trouble with my boss.'

Curtis reluctantly moved aside and let her in.

'I got a new reading book today and Miss Prior said I have to get Mummy to read it with me. Will you read it with me, April?' Tayla said as she followed April into the front room.

'Of course I will, Tayla, do you want to show it to me?'

The thick smoke in the room almost made her choke. She noticed two lager cans on the floor beside the armchair, some empty crisp packets, an empty Pot Noodle container and some screwed-up sweet wrappers scattered on and around the coffee table. Lily Grace was nearly asleep on the settee in front of the television.

'What did you have for your tea?' April asked Tayla.

'I was just about to make their tea when you came,' Curtis lied.

April, noticing the Games Console on the chair and the debris surrounding it, including an overflowing ashtray, guessed that he had hardly moved off the chair all day and thought to herself that it was most unlikely the children had been given anything to eat.

'I'm hungry.' Tayla focused large, pleading blue eyes on April, which melted her heart.

'I think Curtis is about to make you something to eat, aren't you, Curtis? What were you going to make?'

He didn't answer, knowing he had been caught out but at least having the decency to be embarrassed about it.

'What time is Sam due home?' April asked.

'All right, I'm not going to lie, I don't know where she is,' he declared, looking April directly in the eye.

April was alarmed by this but not entirely surprised. 'Have you had a row?' she asked, knowing full well that they had.

'No, she just does this sometimes; she'll come back when she's ready.'

'Why don't we have a look in the cupboard to see what we can give the children to eat, then? I'll give you a hand. I get the impression cooking isn't your favourite pastime.' She was trying to get him on board with feigned joviality.

'I'll be honest, I don't ever cook. I can make beans on toast but that's about it.'

April carried on her show of jollity, although she was appalled. She laughed as she stood up and went into the kitchen. 'Well, it's a good job the social worker turned up, isn't it?'

Lily Grace, Tayla and Curtis were all served up with a plateful of steaming hot beans and buttered toast. April had even found some ketchup for them, and they were all tucking in as though they hadn't been fed for a week. The small table in the kitchen had needed clearing before the meal could be served. It had been piled up with debris, and had to be scrubbed down with a wet cloth as there was no detergent or cleaning liquid in any of the cupboards. At least there was food in the cupboard, April thought to herself.

She was just starting to clear up the plates when the door to the flat suddenly flew open, and standing in the space where the door had been was Sam, her eyes glazed, swaying gently forward and back, clearly intoxicated. She almost tripped as she stumbled in, then, with both feet placed firmly on the ground, she tried hard to steady herself. Her feet remained in the same spot but she continued to sway back and forward, which made her giggle stupidly. They all watched as she tried to place one foot in front of the other in an attempt to walk into the kitchen, but she only managed a couple of steps before having to steady herself again by leaning sideways against the kitchen door. The purple and red swelling to the right-hand side of her face stood out like a beacon.

Tayla immediately got down from the table and ran up to her mother, helping to hold her steady as she began staggering towards the kitchen table. Sam would not have managed without Tayla's help. As she reached the table, Tayla let go of her expecting that she would sit down. Instead she continued to stand, still swaying whilst looking at the chair as though she was trying to work out how to get herself into a sitting position without toppling.

Then with glassy eyes focussed on April, she slurred, 'what the fuck's going on?'

106

By this time Tayla had walked back to the table and was staring at her beans on toast rather than eating it, distracted and anxious about the unpredictability of the situation.

April was now in a dilemma. This was a situation where she needed to take action; a highly inebriated mother and her violent partner caring for two very young children. She could see that there was not going to be any rational conversation with Sam about whether she could think of someone who might be able to look after the children for the night, but she also knew that the only family Sam had was her mother, who could not be considered due to the things Sam had disclosed about her own childhood experiences.

April attempted to talk to Sam but her responses were incomprehensible. Sam, meanwhile, decided she had had enough of standing, managed to get herself into the front room and, just like a rag doll, slumped down on the sofa and placed her hands on either side of her face as though she was trying to steady herself, before shutting her eyes and letting go of all consciousness.

April tried to explain that she was going to make some phone calls and would come back to let them know what was going to happen. 'I'm going to my car. Curtis, you must let me in when I'm ready to come back,' she ordered.

Curtis grunted in response, looking quite bored with the situation. He was clearly not happy about being kept from his Games Console.

April spoke to the Out of Hours manager first to get consent to accommodate the two children in the short term. Only the police would have the power to remove them without a court order so she needed to contact them. She would then have forty-eight hours to decide what to do next. The manager approved of her plan and April phoned the police, who said they would be with her within half an hour. The next phone call was to Jed to let him know what was happening. He told her he had a mixed bean chilli waiting in the oven, which set her stomach rumbling. She hadn't eaten since the sandwich she had gulped in the car at lunchtime, which seemed like weeks ago.

April was let back into the flat by Curtis and could see that Sam had fallen into a deep sleep on the sofa. She lay on her back with her mouth wide open, oblivious to the events taking place around her.

'Would you be able to get some clothes together, Curtis? Tayla and Lily Grace will be going into foster care for the night. They will need pyjamas, toothbrushes and some clean clothes to wear tomorrow. They will probably have a day off school so they won't be needing school uniforms yet.' It was very near the end of term and she just hoped they weren't going to miss any end-of-term treats. Treats in their lives were already too rare.

She quickly realised how pointless it was to expect Curtis to be of any use in this matter. She found a chest of drawers in the bedroom which was packed with clothes; there were also piles of clothes on the floor. She began by going through the drawers but it soon became clear that these clothes were outgrown and the ones they still wore were in the piles on the floor. She managed to find just about enough items to last for a couple of days. Finding toothbrushes was more problematic as there didn't appear to be any in the bathroom. The next thing April did was to sit with the children and try to explain to them what was about to happen. She explained that Mummy wasn't well and couldn't look after them tonight.

'I know, it's because she's pissed again,' Tayla offered.

'She's having a nice sleep now so I'm sure she'll be all right by tomorrow. I will bring her to see you tomorrow, is that all right?'

'What is the lady called who will be looking after us?' Tayla asked.

'I don't know who it will be yet but I know that she will be very nice and she likes looking after children. She will have a warm, comfy bed for you both to sleep in. Would you like to sleep in the same room as Lily Grace?'

Tayla's expression was a strange blend of trepidation, confusion and stoical determination. 'I will need to sleep with Lily Grace so that I can look after her. She might be scared if I'm not there.'

'You're a good girl, Tayla; Lily Grace is lucky to have you for a sister.'

Tayla trusted April and, although only six years old, she completely understood that her mother was not in a fit state to look after her and her sister. By this time Lily Grace had fallen asleep on the chair, her chubby little arms folded around her tummy, just as though she was giving herself a cuddle.

The police arrived, and April picked Lily Grace up from the chair and wrapped her in a blanket. It was now 7.30pm and there was a chill in the night air. April asked Curtis to carry their belongings down the stairs, to which he obliged.

As they opened the front door, the young man who had let April into the building came out of his flat accompanied by a small, youngish woman with orange hair and various imaginative piercings on her face. 'About bloody time an' all, we keep telling the Social about those poor kids but nobody bothered to do anything about it,' the woman was saying. A distinctive smell which April recognised as cannabis wafted from the open door of their flat.

'They don't care about kids, those social workers; look at that baby what's just been killed by its dad. It's lucky these kids weren't killed before, things what go on up there.'

April ignored the comments and focused on trying to get the children into the waiting police car in an attempt to shield them from any further distress.

13

FREDDIE'S INITIAL HEARING

At last the children were safe and settled with their foster carers and April could go home to her husband, who was patiently waiting for her so that they could enjoy their evening meal together. By the time she arrived home she was absolutely exhausted mentally and physically.

Jed placed dishes of spicy chilli and steaming hot rice on the table, where he had already put condiments and various chutneys.

'I'm so sorry that we had to cancel Jenny today,' April said after settling herself down at the table. 'I have arranged another appointment and I'm not letting anything get in the way of that one.'

Jed looked at her and smiled. 'Yes, April,' he said sardonically, sitting down next to her.

April was reminded again of how lucky she was to have Jed. He was so laid-back, and understood the trials and uncertainties she faced in her job. He would have been disappointed about missing the appointment but would not let her know that.

'It's a huge responsibility, bringing up children, isn't it? I sometimes wonder why we want to bring it on ourselves. Perhaps we should just carry on as we are, enjoying ourselves with no one else to worry about. We can have lovely holidays, just the two of us. Maybe we just weren't meant to be parents.'

'What on earth has brought this on?' Jed replied, a look of sheer bewilderment on his face.

'Oh, I probably don't really mean it, it's just sometimes when I see how some of these children are so damaged by what their parents do, it makes me scared. What if I got it wrong, or we didn't like being parents once we had the child with us; what if we didn't like the child?'

They cleared up the dishes together before throwing themselves down on the settee. Jed just sat back and let April talk while he listened; he knew from experience that this was her way of releasing her pent-up emotions from the day, and that whatever she said during these times usually didn't count for a lot.

'We can talk about it more tomorrow if you like. In the meantime, how about a nice glass of wine?'

'No thank you!' she said indignantly. 'When we have our own child, we won't be able to just have a glass of wine whenever we feel like it. We'll need to think about their needs, not our own any more.' She was clearly thinking about Tayla and Lily Grace, irrationally confusing the very moderate quantities of alcohol they generally drank, with Sam's binge drinking that had led to the distressing events she had just been a part of. Jed filled the cafetière with freshly boiled water from the kettle and placed it on the coffee table in front of where April was sitting, along with two Emma Bridgewater coffee cups and a jug of milk.

April was fully aware that she should never discuss her cases with anyone who was not professionally involved, but she needed to offload and was confident that Jed would never discuss anything concerning her work with anyone else. She wasn't sure how much he really took in but he always made a good show of being totally absorbed and interested, and this was therapeutic enough. Ideally she would have had regular supervision so she could debrief, but in the real world this didn't happen. It was more usual that social workers were left to find their own way of dealing with the high emotions evoked by some of the situations they faced in their daily work, and talking about it to Jed helped to get it out of her system, even if he wasn't really paying her his full attention.

'I have to go to court tomorrow for Freddie's case, so let's hope it doesn't take all day because I also really need to go and see Sam. The duty social worker will have to take her to see Tayla and Lily Grace because I can't be everywhere at once. If the court case goes on all day it's likely to be another seven o'clock finish for me.'

Jed nodded sympathetically. He was fully aware that there was no point in him remarking about her long hours. He had tried that many times in the past and it had had no effect, so there was no reason to believe it would be any different this time.

Whilst April verbally plotted her itinerary for the next day, Jed was thinking about her earlier remarks and found himself wondering how she would manage if and when they had a child. As things stood, she could prioritise the needs of the children she worked with, but it would be very different if they had one of their own. April being the type of person who would not be happy with any job not well done. He wondered if she would continue to be so dedicated to her work, or whether having a child would change her priorities. He couldn't imagine that she would not always do her best for the children she worked with, but she would also want to be the best mother she could be.

Later, April immersed her body in the warm bath she had run for herself, feeling completely relaxed as she breathed in the intoxicating scent of the camomile bath soak Jed had bought her for her thirty-eighth birthday. She felt utterly exhausted and drifted in and out of consciousness. Unfortunately, the blissful relaxed feelings quickly dispersed after she climbed into bed. Whilst Jed was asleep in seconds, April tossed and turned, throwing back the sheets against the warmth of the night. The bedroom window was wide open and, although the curtains moved in the gentle breeze, it was only warm air coming in, which made the room feel even hotter. She was thinking about Freddie and the court hearing she would be attending in the morning. She might have to give evidence, be cross-examined on her statement which she had not been able to perfect as much as she would have liked. Becky's barrister would have scrutinised every word she had written, and would be trying to trip her up with every opportunity.

April had mixed feelings about this case; it was not as clear-cut as most of those she had encountered. Becky was a devoted mother to Freddie and there was a clear and positive attachment between them. Freddie showed no signs of being scared or anxious in his mother's presence. Becky had been diligent in attending contact, which had taken place every day. The foster carer had allowed it to happen in her home and had been asked to report on the sessions. Her reports were full of positive descriptions of the fun Freddie had with his mum. Freddie was always delighted to see his mum and Becky would hug and kiss him, and spend every second of the contact engaged and enjoying her son.

April had come across many vulnerable women in the course of her work who were so fearful of being on their own that they would cling on to a man at any cost, and she wondered if this was what was happening. Colin was in work and although the work was low-skilled and poorly paid, the money he brought home would be more than Becky had ever had before. She was pregnant with Freddie at eighteen and had been living on benefits when she met Colin. Since he had moved into her council property, he had bought new things for the house, including a new carpet for the front room which Becky was really proud of. He seemed to be quite practical and had built a shed in the garden. Becky had told April during one of her visits that he had bought a second-hand trike for Freddie and done it up so that it looked new. April wondered if it was the material aspects of his presence which Becky did not want to forfeit, in order to have a life where she wasn't having to walk on eggshells and constantly cover up for Freddie to prevent him from being physically chastised. April still believed Colin was the perpetrator of Freddie's injuries.

The next morning, April was up and about early, brushing down her dark grey suit jacket which she hadn't worn for a few months, getting herself ready for the initial hearing which was taking place that day for little Freddie. Jed had already left for Cardiff where he would be for the next few days, completing an audit for a large company. The case was being heard in the magistrates' court, in the middle of town where there was no convenient parking. She hurriedly searched through her bag for loose change to put in the parking meter. April couldn't stand rushing into court late; she needed time to get herself together and settled in with her papers all organised in front of her.

Unfortunately, the traffic was heavy and by the time she arrived at the court car park there were no spaces left. She drove around the area until thankfully finding a space by the side of the road. She took her bags from the back seat, slammed the door shut and hurried towards the court, already stressed before the day had even started.

It was impossible to know how long they would have to be at the court. Although the case was listed for 10am she knew from experience that this could mean anything and depended on what other cases were listed for that morning. She needed to be there by 9.30 to meet the Local Authority's barrister and discuss the case before going in front of the magistrates to present their case. She just about managed to rush through the main doors into the court building a minute or two before 9.30. She walked around the building and then up the stairs, searching for Shiva, the barrister who would be representing the Local Authority. As she rushed through the corridor towards the main waiting area, she passed a little room where she saw Becky ensconced with her own barrister, who would have been advising her of the Local Authority's plan for Freddie to remain in foster care whilst further assessments were carried out. The Local Authority's barrister had also recommended that an expert witness was appointed to report on the injuries which had been found on the little boy.

They were finally called into court at 11.15am. The evidence was presented and, as she expected, April was cross-examined by Becky's advocate, which didn't turn out to be as difficult as she had anticipated. She was honest with her answers as always and as she had been in her statement of evidence, agreeing with the advocate that up until recently Becky had been considered to be a good and devoted mother. The advocate questioned April on the relationship she had observed between Ms Simmons and her son, to which April responded candidly that she had not seen anything of concern and it was true there appeared to be a close and loving relationship between them. The advocate asked if April had seen Freddie with Mr Lyons at all. April had to admit that she had not. Mr Lyons was always at work when she visited.

The evidence she had given was bizarrely positive considering she was asking for the child to remain in foster care. At the same time April made sure she had the opportunity to raise the important point that if, as everything would seem to suggest, it was Mr Lyons causing the injuries to Freddie, then Ms Simmons must be just as culpable as this would mean that she was covering up for him.

The expert witness took a methodical approach, addressing each injury in chronological order. He was in possession of colour photographs of all seven of the injuries reported. For each one, the specialist concluded that the explanation given by Freddie's mother was not compatible with the injury. At least two of the injuries, in his opinion, could not have been accidents, including the final one where the bruise spread across his cheek to the side of his face and the top of his ear. He concluded his evidence by telling the magistrates that it would be impossible for this kind of injury to happen accidentally and it was almost definitely caused by a hard slap with an adult hand. He went so far as to pass this photograph around the courtroom so that everyone could have the opportunity to observe the fingermarks he had identified. April, along with the other people in the room, was shocked when looking at the vivid detail before them. There in the image, as clear as day, were dark bruises in the shape of two smallish, flat circles and four long lines across Freddie's face; the shape of a hand.

Becky was the last one called to give evidence, and she was asked by the Local Authority barrister, Shiva, to give her opinion to the court on what the expert witness had said. Becky looked like a rabbit caught in the headlights, her usually pale face, despite the thick make-up, glowed red as a beacon. Although she appeared timid and scared, Becky was a master at astonishing people with her assertive responses, and she did exactly that. Her voice surprisingly loud and clear, she retorted, 'I know I should have been more careful. Freddie's a proper boy, he gets himself into pickles. Colin says I should be stricter with him. I shouldn't let him go out in the garden when I'm not there. I am going to be more careful and keep a closer eye on him in future.'

'Pardon me, Ms Simmons, but I'm not sure you have quite understood the question I asked you. I will ask you again. You have heard what the expert has said, haven't you? Would you now be so kind as to tell me your opinion on this matter? The evidence given by the expert clearly suggests that Freddie was deliberately harmed by you or someone else whilst in your care.'

Most unexpectedly, Becky's next move was to look up at the barrister, and smiling, answered, 'Yes,' .

'You're clear that the expert is saying that at least two of Freddie's injuries could not have been accidents?'

'Yes,' she said again, smiling at everyone from the witness box.

'Then can you tell me, Ms Simmons, how you think these injuries might have occurred?' Shiva was starting to become noticeably agitated.

'I shouldn't have let him go out in the garden on his own. I know I was stupid; Colin told me I shouldn't let him have his own way all the time,' she repeated. 'Colin has had children of his own so he knows how to bring them up.'

'Ms Simmons, let me be clear: I put it to you that someone has physically assaulted your child, and that you have either done that yourself or have allowed someone else to do it. What is your answer to that?'

Becky promptly burst into floods of tears. Some tissues and a glass of water were brought for her but she could not be consoled. She had been putting on a brave face and had managed it for a while, but it had obviously become too much for her when she started to realise that she was not going to fool anyone that a lack of adequate supervision was the problem here.

It was about 3pm when the magistrates conferred with their advisor and came back with their decision to grant an Interim Care Order to the Local Authority. What happened to little Freddie now would depend on the outcome of further assessments, which would have to include Colin Lyons. Becky would be expected to continue to attend domestic violence counselling services. She had attended a couple of sessions already but it was difficult because she wanted to keep it a secret from Colin. She thought he would get angry if he knew she was going somewhere like that. At the same time as the assessments were being carried out, April would be investigating alternative carers within the family networks so that if Freddie was unable to return home to his mother, which was looking very likely, at least he would continue to be cared for within his birth family, which is always considered to be the best option. Should Freddie not be able to return to his mother, and no viable alternative carers within the family be identified, an adoptive family would be found for him. This would probably be quite easy as he was only three years old, very sweet and attractive with curly blond hair and a cheeky smile. He was bright and intelligent and had no health issues. April worried about adoption for Freddie, though, because of the very obvious positive attachment he had with his mother. Even with all the work that would inevitably take place to prepare him for the change, April wasn't sure it would be easy for Freddie to settle with another family. She was of course relieved that an Interim Care Order had been granted because it meant Freddie would remain in foster care for the time being where he would be safe from harm.

She was just getting her papers together, ready to head off, when Shiva gave her some news that left her reeling: Ms Simmons had just disclosed that she was three months pregnant. Another court date was set and the unborn baby would be adjoined to the proceedings.

The impact of this news on April was disturbing for two separate reasons. Firstly, she had retained some hope that Becky would suddenly come to her senses and realise what a fool she had been, prioritise her child's needs above her own and get rid of Colin Lyons. This seemed even less likely now and increased the possibility that Freddie would never return home to his mum. Secondly, April felt a strong and overwhelming sense of injustice. She couldn't help thinking how unfair life was, when a woman like Becky could get pregnant, probably without intending to or even thinking about it, when she couldn't even manage to look after the child she already had. Life seemed very unfair sometimes.

14

A NARROW ESCAPE

It was the end of another exhausting week for April and she was closing down her laptop ready to head off home when Miles approached her desk.

'Don't know about you but I need a cold beer. I don't know where Paula is but I'll text her to let her know we're in the pub.'

'I haven't said I'm coming yet, Miles; I thought I was just going home to stretch out in front of the television.' The thought of the pub was tempting and Jed was not due home until late.

'Are you telling me you can resist my exhilarating company? You can have me all to yourself for once; all your dreams come true.'

April laughed. 'Is it that obvious?'

'It's fine, don't be embarrassed; happens all the time.'

'Well, I must say I am truly grateful to be given the honour of being in the company of one so desirable as you obviously think you are.'

It was a perfect summer evening and the heat from the blistering July day still hung in the air as they walked together to the pub. April told Miles to find a nice table in the garden whilst she went to the bar to buy drinks. He chose a wooden bench set which was placed aside from the rest of the garden, under a weeping willow and facing the small stream which ran alongside the pub garden. There were only a few other people in the garden. A middle-aged couple with a dog who, with their sunburnt faces, looked as though they had been sitting there all day, their dog sprawled out under the table, looking perfectly comfortable. There was a small group of young men and one young woman who may have been colleagues having an after-work drink, whose periodic laughter pierced the otherwise tranquil surroundings.

April, drinks in hand, stepped out of the back door of the pub onto the concrete steps which led into the garden. She was surrounded by a magnificent array of colourful hanging baskets and pots full of various brightly coloured summer flowers. She stood there for a moment, delighting in the delicately scented air. Her pale-yellow dress seemed to blend imperceptibly with the yellow flowers in the baskets. From his bench over by the stream, Miles could see her expression of bewilderment as she looked around the garden for him whilst trying to concentrate on not spilling the drinks. He stood up and waved both arms vigorously, finally catching her attention.

'I wish I had brought my camera,' he said as she put the drinks on the table. 'You looked a picture of beauty and elegance stood there amongst the flowers. I shall call you Titania from now on.'

Much to her annoyance, April flushed at the compliment. 'And what shall I call you, then, sitting under the willow tree spouting Shakespeare?'

'Uhm, Mark Antony, I would suggest, is the obvious answer to that; Cleopatra's brave and handsome lover.'

'Yes, that would be perfect; I believe he was his own biggest fan as well.'

'Humph, I'm glad you don't mean that.'

'Did you text Paula?' April suddenly asked.

'Yes, no reply yet; I hope everything's all right.'

April looked at her watch. 'It's twenty to seven.'

'I'm getting a bit worried now. This just isn't like her. She would have let us know by now if she wasn't coming,' Miles said.

'I don't know where her last visit was but I do know she has a violent father on her caseload, Larry Fuller. She's not supposed to visit on her own but we all know about that, don't we? His children are on a Child Protection Plan and there's not always someone around to go on regular visits with her,' April told Miles. 'I believe he suffers from borderline personality disorder.'

'I know the one you mean; surely she wouldn't have gone there without at least letting someone know, especially on a Friday evening?' Miles said. 'Do you think we should try to get hold of Maria?'

April was also beginning to worry. She had no reason to believe Paula had gone to visit this family but it was unlike her to not respond to messages and texts; she was obsessed with checking her phone, always hoping it would be somebody nice from the dating site.

Maria was able to get into Paula's electronic calendar, and sure enough she had put in there that she was due to visit the family with the violent father. She had also written that the Social Worker Assistant, Sarah was accompanying her. Maria told Miles that she would call Sarah and see what happened. Five minutes later she called back to say that there was no answer from Sarah's work or home phone. The next thing was to go around to Paula's house to check she wasn't in and just not answering her phone for some reason or another.

Miles and April sat quietly, watching the phone which was lying on the table in front of them, waiting for Maria to ring again. Even though they were waiting, they both jumped out of their skin when it rang. Maria informed them that Paula was not at home. Her daughter had answered the door and was also worried as she had been expecting her home before now. There was a discussion about what to do next; whether to phone the police or go around to the house she was visiting. In the end they decided to do both.

Paula sat waiting in the car outside the home of the Fuller family. There were four children in this family and a lot of concerns about them. Larry Fuller had been in prison a number of times for GBH and once for manslaughter. His wife, Tia, had been in hospital twice following physical assaults perpetrated by him. Tia suffered from bipolar disorder and depression, unsurprisingly.

Most visits Paula carried out were absolutely fine and everything appeared calm and settled, but there had been times when tension was high and she felt the need to leave before things became potentially dangerous for her. She felt that she had developed some insight into Larry's moods and could tell when he was becoming agitated. Always evident, though, was the nervousness of the children, who appeared frightened of their own shadows. Although they were all under the age of eight, Paula had never witnessed them playing imaginary games or with any toys. They were always sitting quietly, either watching television or just sitting. All four children had sweet, angelic faces, but their skin was grubby and their hair lank and matted. Paula always felt an urge to offer to run a warm bath for them, fill it with bubbles, and shampoo and condition their hair. She could picture them dressed in clean, cosy pyjamas, their little faces shiny and pink, and their hair glossy and thick. This would make her so happy, if only she was allowed to do it.

After about fifteen minutes Sarah had still not arrived. Paula was beginning to get impatient; it was Friday evening and she was supposed to be at the pub. She didn't want to leave without checking the children were OK though, so she decided to knock on the door and do a quick visit, just long enough to say hello to the children and put her mind at ease. That way she would not have to worry about them over the weekend. She had visited alone many times before when there hadn't been anyone to go with her and it had always been fine.

Paula walked up the short garden path, squeezing her body between two overflowing wheelie bins and an old fridge with its door hanging off, holding her dress close to her body to protect it from the green mould that seemed to be oozing from the fridge. She could see that the curtains at the small lounge window were almost closed and one of them was hanging down from one corner where it had become detached from the rail. It was always dark in this house due to the small windows and smoke-stained walls.

She knocked on the door, which was soon opened by Larry, looking unkempt in baggy tracksuit trousers and a black T-shirt with white stains down the front. His face hadn't seen a razor for weeks. Paula was relieved to see that he appeared congenial as he stood aside to let her in. She walked across the narrow hallway into the tiny lounge and although it was quite dark inside, it became immediately evident that there was no one else in. 'Are Tia and the children not at home?' she said, asking the obvious.

'They won't be long,' he answered; 'they've just gone around the corner to Shelby's. She's got problems with her old man again.'

Paula looked furtively around the room, vainly hoping to find someone else present. She quickly realised the dangerous situation she had got herself into. She cursed herself for being so stupid, allowing herself to get into a situation where she was alone in the house with a man of this nature. She couldn't believe she had been stupid enough to walk into the house without checking first that the others were at home. Not only was she on her own with this man, she was on the far side of the room, whilst he had quickly and stealthily positioned himself in front of the only exit: the door which led from the lounge to the hall.

Paula asked herself angrily how many training courses she had attended which stressed the importance of always having access to the door in situations which may be unsafe. She tried to convince herself that she was exaggerating the risk, and to keep calm, managing to make small talk; but it was becoming increasingly obvious that Larry's position in front of the door was no accident. Whilst he was not doing or saying anything untoward or openly threatening her, he was blatantly blocking her way out and seemed to be getting some kind of thrill from the power he had over her. She wanted to leave but although nothing had been said, by his mannerisms and gestures and the way he seemed to be enjoying the situation, she could guess that he had no intention of allowing that to happen, and asking him to let her go had the potential to escalate the situation. She deemed that the best approach would be to try to keep him talking, show a friendly interest in him. This way the situation could be managed until Tia returned with the children.

Trying hard to appear calm, she asked, 'Is Alicia looking forward to starting school in September?'

'I dunno. Our Keith don't like it, and I 'ated school, used to skive off all the time. Teachers 'ated me.'

Paula was relieved that she had got him talking about himself, which should help to take his mind off any intentions of harm to her he might have had, stalling him for a while.

'What school did you go to, Larry?'

'I can't remember all of them; used to change a lot. Got kicked out; teachers were shit scared of me. Ended up in a school for young offenders; that was a laugh, best thing I learnt there was how to roll a spliff. Got my arm broke by a warden once 'cause he caught me shooting up.' He paused but then quickly added, 'I don't do that now, though, so you needn't start thinking I'm a smackhead 'cause I ain't. I've got kids now, got to be responsible.'

He was pacing up and down a bit as he spoke but not once did he stray far from the door. He was clearly fired up by the memories of his school experiences and for a fleeting moment he seemed to forget that he was guarding the door and started moving towards the window. A flash of hope soared through Paula's veins, but the involuntary darting of her eyes towards the open space drew him hurriedly back to his position in front of the door. Paula had thought for a second that she might be able to make a run for it, but before she was able to even take a step in that direction, Larry had jumped back, dispelling any illusion she might have had that she was overestimating the dangerous situation she was in.

She didn't know how she was managing to appear so calm when inside her stomach churned. She felt sure that if he had the slightest indication that she was scared of him he would relish it, and God only knew what he might do then. The way things stood, Paula felt that even he didn't know what he was going to do. He just seemed to be enjoying having the power to detain her. She noticed that as he positioned himself in front of the door again, his eyes seemed to glaze over as he stared at her. He didn't have to speak or move; his whole demeanour was enough to make her shudder. In some ways it was more alarming because she recognised there was a threat to her but she had no idea what it might be.

When he spoke again his tone of voice had changed from congenial to confrontational and mildly aggressive. 'Why do you want to know what school I went to; what the shit has it got to do with you? You think I'm a thicko, don't you? Well, I'm not a thicko; you shouldn't laugh at me, it's not funny. Why are you laughing at me?' His voice was getting louder and shriller as he spoke, and the flashing in his eyes suggested a mania was building.

'I'm not laughing at you, Larry; why would I laugh?' She was struggling to hide the tremor in her voice. Her fear was turning to terror and was becoming increasingly difficult to hide. She was thinking to herself, Please let Tia come home; how much longer will she be?

'You're a liar, I saw you sniggering. You think I'm stupid, don't you?' His lips were twisting into a sinister half-smile but his eyes were flashing with rage.

To her absolute horror, he suddenly started striding towards her. Before she knew what was happening, he had grabbed her by the arm and pushed her onto the settee. Oh my God, she thought to herself, I'm going to be raped. All the time she continued to curse silently for getting herself into this dangerous situation.

He stood over her, looking down, suddenly calmer and appearing congenial once again, but with the alarming look of madness still shining in his eyes.

'I think I had better be going now.' Paula tried to disguise the quiver in her voice as she spoke.

'You can't go yet; you've got to wait until Tia gets back with the kids. You've got to say hello to the kids, that's what you always tell us.'

125

'I will come again on Monday to see them; they might be quite a long time, mightn't they?' she asked, hoping for a positive answer.

To her horror, he started laughing loudly, rocking back and forth in mirth. 'They won't be coming back,' he said, laughing and rocking, holding his stomach, 'they're staying with Tia's stepdad. They might come back tomorrow; that's why I want you to stay with me. I get frightened on my own.' He suddenly stopped laughing and looked seriously at her. Then after a pause he was laughing again, clearly finding the situation hilariously funny.

Paula was at a loss as to what to say next, but before she could answer he was sitting on the settee next to her. He immediately put his arm around her while continuing to talk and laugh, becoming increasingly manic and excited. With horror she noticed him moving his face towards hers, and all she was aware of was the sight of his hideous broken, yellow-and-brown teeth, and the stench of his rancid breath which made her retch. She tried to stand up but nausea overwhelmed her and she found herself frozen in fear.

'You like me, don't you?' he was saying.

Paula's head was pounding. She tried to speak but no sound came from her mouth. She was struggling to think straight but realised that whatever she said could trigger a dangerous response. One minute she was being told she was negative towards him, and now he seemed to be suggesting that she liked him in a sexual way. She was aware that this was typical of personality disorders, in which sufferers construct their own reality according to how they want things to be. There was no rationality in his thinking and whatever she said he was going to put his own interpretation on it. There was no possible way she could anticipate his response.

He started moving his hand up and down her arm and she felt as though she was drowning in fear. She was unable to move or speak, until out of the blue, she heard her own voice speaking as though it was coming from underwater. 'Shall I make us a nice cup of tea?'

Just like a clockwork figure which had unwound, Larry stopped with his arm in mid-air. He looked into Paula's eyes, making her skin crawl with disgust, but to her surprise and great relief, he said, 'Yes, you can make me a cup of tea. That's what you women are for.' He gave a sinister laugh.

Paula stood up slowly, praying that he wouldn't change his mind. She continued to move slowly as she walked towards the door, her mind racing with the thought that a few steps away from that door was the one which led to the street. She took a deep breath and tried to move calmly, to disguise her rising excitement as the lure of the door beckoned. She managed to reach it, but as she put out her hand to grasp the handle he was off the settee and in front of her, leaning against the door with a lurid smirk on his face.

'You were going to leave me, weren't you? You thought you could get away.' He moved his head from side to side as he mimicked her voice. '"Shall I make you a nice cup of tea?" You thought you were going to escape, didn't you? I'll come with you.'

He led her by the arm into the kitchen, positioned himself in front of the door and watched as she proceeded to fill the kettle. Whilst he leant against the door, rolling a cigarette, she looked through the cupboards and found two cups which she placed on the worktop, her trembling hand causing one of them to tumble onto its side. Larry suddenly lurched towards her and, his face close to hers, bellowed, 'You stupid cow.' His tone changing again, and with an eerie smile, he continued, 'You're going to have to be nice to me now for trying to break my cups.'

All the while Paula was frantically searching her brain for what to do next, but her brain was more jittery than her stomach and she couldn't string two comprehensible thoughts together, let alone think of a plan, however hard she tried. As she poured the boiling water into the cups it occurred to her that she could throw it over him. The thought of this made her shake even more, but she slowed the pouring by gradually reducing the tilt of the kettle, whilst at the same time trying to muster the courage to turn around and scald him with the water.

All of a sudden there was a loud knock at the door. Larry promptly jumped in front of her, and hissed, spitting as he spoke, 'don't answer; they've come to take you away from me. You're staying with me tonight, aren't you?' He looked pleadingly at her, almost like a little boy asking his mother for sweets. There was another knock and she tried to move towards the door, but in a flash he leapt forwards and pulled her back, roughly covering her mouth with his hand. He was behind her and she could feel his arm pressing into her thigh, pushing her forward whilst the hand around her face was pulling her back. Her mind was racing and the blood pounded in her brain as she tried hard to calm herself enough to think of some way to let them know she was in there. An involuntary groan escaped her stifled mouth.

The next thing she heard was a voice shouting through the letter box, and she breathed a sigh of relief as she heard the words, 'Police; open the door or we will break it down.' Thankfully Larry did as he was told and two police officers stormed into the kitchen where Paula stood, still in shock, hot tears streaming down her face. The female officer put her arm around her shoulders and led her, still trembling, out of the house.

Larry was asking them what they wanted and seemed to be genuinely confused about the need for them to be there. Paula could hear the other officer telling him that he was arresting him on a charge of abduction. She didn't care; she just wanted to be outside and breathe the fresh air, enjoy being free and alive. She stood on the pavement, shielding her eyes against the bright sun, which was in stark contrast to the dingy house she had been in for hours. As her eyes began to adjust, she could see a group of people on the pavement, walking towards her with their arms outstretched. She quickly realised that it was April, Miles and her daughter Natasha, and simultaneously they all threw their arms around her. The feeling of warmth and love after the horror of the last few hours was too much for her and she sobbed uncontrollably.

April had been intending to tell Paula off for visiting this particular family on her own, but all she could do now was hug her.

128

'Thank goodness your car was parked outside,' she said. 'That's how we knew you were definitely in there.'

'I wouldn't mind, Paula, but we were waiting for you at the pub,' Miles said. 'And it was your turn to buy the drinks.'

Paula's swollen, tear-stained face broke into a crooked, watery smile.

15

REALITY KICKS IN

It was after midnight when Sam began her slow recovery. As she gradually opened her eyes, she felt the sofa moving beneath her as though she was being tossed about on a wave. She thought the ceiling was moving from side to side and held tightly to the cushion, trying hard to make it stay still. 'Get me a drink,' she groaned, almost incomprehensibly.

'Get it yourself. Look at you, you fucking alky,' Curtis snarled. 'You've done it good and proper now, you stupid cow; you've lost yer kids and it serves you right. You can't just have a few drinks like everyone else, can you; gotta get smashed out of your brain.'

Just as though she had been injected with adrenaline, Sam sat bolt upright, her eyes trying hard to focus on the room around her. 'Where are they? Where are my kids?' Somewhere inside her head was a vague memory of something happening which had been upsetting, something significant which she had been unable to do anything about. She could vaguely remember seeing Tayla following April, who had Lily Grace in her arms, out of the door of the flat. She couldn't quite work out if it was a dream she had had, but what did Curtis mean, she had lost her kids?

'What was April doing here last night? Did you call Social Services?' By this time, she was on her feet, confronting Curtis with a fearless aggression she hadn't known she possessed.

'No I didn't, you stupid bitch; she came around when you were in the park getting pissed. What could I do about it?'

Sam wasn't focusing on his answer; instead she was heading for the girls' bedroom. She pulled back one of the duvet covers as though she might find them underneath. She stared for a moment at the empty bed before returning to the front room, sitting down on the settee and, with her elbows on her knees and her head in her hands, repeating, 'Oh no, I don't believe this; no, she can't take my kids; oh no, no. I'm not letting that cow get away with this – what am I going to do?' She was asking herself this rather than Curtis. 'I'm gonna get them back,' she told herself out loud. She was now standing up and pacing the floor, still repeating, 'Oh no, I don't believe she's done this', hands gripping either side of her face. 'Why did you let her take them? You should have stopped her, you could have woken me up – why did you let her?' She was screaming at him, her face turning red and purple with rage and frustration. 'You let her walk out of the door with my kids; you helped her, didn't you? You helped her, I saw you; I remember now, I saw you with their bags going out of the door.'

She moved towards him aggressively as though she was going to lash out, but he took hold of her arms and threw her back against the wall. She was shaken by this and brought to her senses, realising what she was up against. There was not going to be any sympathy or understanding from Curtis which, although it was a strange way of going about it, was what she was craving. Suddenly it all became too much. Still where she had been thrown with her back against the wall, she put her face in her hands, sank to the floor and sobbed her heart out. Curtis had never experienced empathy in his own life and had no idea how to deal with this kind of situation, so he responded by walking out of the door and slamming it behind him, leaving her alone, still crouching against the wall.

Sam had never felt more alone and was beside herself with grief and anger. She had always known she had a problem with alcohol but she wasn't always drunk. She never really believed that it was so bad they would actually take her children away from her, and still couldn't accept that it had been necessary. She paced the flat, going from one room to the next, thinking about how unfair it was, drifting from anger to despair. Once she started to think along the lines of injustice, a sudden surge of strength seemed to rise from somewhere deep inside her. She decided that she was not going to sit back and cry; she would go down to the Social Services office and demand her children back; that's what she would do. They had no right to do this. She decided to try to get some sleep, and then first thing in the morning be at the door as soon as the office opened.

Sam lay on her bed but she didn't sleep. The hours dragged like she had never known before. She watched the shadows in her room slowly disappear as night turned to day, until rays of sunshine came in streaks through the pale, ill-fitted curtains. With her heart feeling like a lead weight, she dragged herself off the bed to look at the time; it was still only 4.50am. Curtis had not returned, which caused her to fret. Perhaps he wouldn't come back at all. She needed him to; he was no good but she couldn't be on her own, she wouldn't be able to cope. At the same time, she was wondering where the children had been taken, what was happening to them, were they frightened? Lily Grace would be crying for her mummy, Sam was sure.

Around 7am Sam got up off the bed, made herself a piece of toast and put on some jeans and a baggy, sleeveless black top. She pulled her long, thin hair back from her face and, without brushing it, tied it back with one of Tayla's hair bobbles. She picked up her bag and checked her purse to make sure she had enough money for the bus into town. She could walk there but was not in the mood for wasting time, apart from the dread that she might bump into someone she knew and have to admit what had happened.

By 8.30 she was standing outside of Social Services office, ringing the intercom bell at the side of the door. She had to ring it a few times and cursed under her breath until someone finally spoke.

'Good morning, can I help you?' the voice asked.

'I want to see April Gardiner,' Sam demanded.

'Can you tell me who you are, please? Have you got a meeting with April?'

'It's Samantha Bushell.'

Sam heard a click as the lock was released.

'Would you like to come upstairs? I will check if April is available.'

Sam walked up the narrow staircase and into the reception area where a couple of other people were waiting. She had been here before many times so was not surprised by the dinginess of the surroundings. She sat down on one of the soft benches which were set out in the waiting area, and after only a few minutes she noticed a young woman heading towards her.

'Hello, I understand you are here to see April. Unfortunately, she isn't in the office yet. I am the duty social worker today and I know what has happened. We can go into the meeting room and have a chat, or would you rather wait for April?'

'I want my kids back. I don't care who gives them to me but I want them back now,' Sam demanded.

The duty social worker walked towards the meeting room and held the door open, gesturing to Sam to enter. 'Your children are with foster carers and April will be arranging for you to see them today at some point. They were removed under police protection due to them being at risk of harm.'

'What do you mean, I can see them today?!' Sam said, exasperated. 'I want them back with me. They need to be with me, I'm their mother; who the hell do you think you are, telling me when I can see my own kids?' She was shouting with a trace of hysteria.

In the end, feeling completely powerless, Sam realised she had no choice but to leave the office and wait for April to phone her. She was going to be able to see the children for an hour, supervised by a social work assistant in the Family Centre. She had been told by the duty social worker that she needed to find a solicitor because she would have to go to court next week. She couldn't face doing anything until she had seen the children, and all she could do was wait for the call.

April phoned soon after 10am. She arranged to come and collect Sam to take her to the Family Centre for 3.30pm. This was apparently the only time the social work assistant was free to supervise the contact. Sam would not be allowed to see her own children unsupervised. Dispirited, she agreed; what else could she do? It was going to be a long day. She tried to pass the time away by watching the television. The emotional exhaustion catching up with her, she drifted in and out of a restless, unrefreshing slumber. The ache in her head was unbearable.

Through all of this she remained acutely aware of the time, and at long last it was coming up for three o'clock. Time to get ready. April arrived as she said she would at ten past three and drove Sam to the Family Centre, which was about half an hour's drive away. During the journey, April explained the reasons she had felt it necessary to do what she had done. She told Sam that she was disappointed and upset that it had come to this but her job was to make sure the children were safe. April explained about the court procedure and that the Local Authority would ask for an Interim Care Order so that the children could stay in care whilst decisions were made about their future. Sam sat quietly, staring ahead, stunned into silence and disbelief by what she was hearing.

April took periodic glimpses at Sam as she drove. From her perspective in the driver's seat, Sam, with her long hair and tiny stature, almost looked like a child. She had come into the office with all guns blazing but now, was staring ahead in frustrated submission.

'When can they come back to me?' Sam asked meekly.

'The court will make that decision. I will be recommending that they stay in care while you get help. You will need to attend alcohol services regularly to address your problems, and have regular sessions with a domestic violence counsellor. You are going to have to prove that you can change your lifestyle. It won't be easy, Sam, it will need strong commitment from you and you will have to be strong, but I know you love your kids and I know how much you want them to be with you. I know you can be a good mother to them and these services can help you to do that. If there's anything else anyone can do for you, let me know and I will do what I can to help. Believe me, I want you to have the girls back with you as much as you do, but without huge change on your part it's more than likely that it won't happen.'

'I'm not an alcoholic, only alcoholics go to those places; I've seen them outside, sitting on the wall getting pissed with their cans of beer. They go to their meetings, then as soon as they're out they get pissed with the mates they've met there; it's disgusting.'

'I will be recommending that you have regular hair strand and liver function tests so that we can be sure what's going on. Don't think for a minute that we won't know if you're drinking because when a problem is as serious as this is, we need to be sure we have our facts right, and that is what the court will expect.'

'I will do what you want me to do. I can stop drinking easily because as I keep telling you, I'm not an alcoholic,' Sam said defiantly.

'I really hope you can.'

As they pulled into the Family Centre car park April and Sam both noticed the dark blue Volvo four-by-four. The foster carer was just lifting Lily Grace from her car seat. They sat watching as Lily Grace and Tayla each took one of the carer's hands and the three of them walked into the building together.

'The foster carer is called Karen. She's very experienced and Lily Grace and Tayla are the only children she has with her.'

Sam made no reply. It seemed to her that April was expecting her to be grateful for offering to help, but all she felt was a tumultuous anger and bewilderment that, because of April, someone else was looking after her children. April told her to go into the building where the children and the social work assistant would be waiting for her.

The automatic doors swung open as Sam approached and she walked into the large reception area, full of apprehension. She couldn't wait to see the children but the situation felt so unnatural and strange that she wasn't quite sure how to behave. She could see the foster carer giving the girls a little hug and handing them a small paper bag which she thought might have a snack inside. This intensified her feelings of inadequacy as the thought of buying them sweets or a treat had not crossed her mind.

She stood in the doorway for a minute, looking at her girls, whilst they in turn stood looking back at her, equally bemused. The social work assistant approached her and tried to make her feel at ease by pointing out toys and games she could use to occupy the children, but instead of getting down to play with them, Sam walked over to the nearest chair and sat down. She asked Tayla if she was all right, and Tayla replied that she was.

'I slept with Lily Grace last night and Karen said I can tonight as well if I want to. Lily Grace was frightened so I looked after her.'

Sam gave her daughter a tearful smile. 'Is it nice at the foster carer's?' she asked.

'Yes, we've got new pyjamas; Lily Grace has got pink and I've got yellow. Hers has got Elsa and I've got Belle. Mine are nicer than hers because they're lovely and cosy. We got some more new things today as well. Karen got me and Lily Grace a toothbrush each and we cleaned our teeth last night.' Tayla opened her mouth wide to show her mum her newly cleaned teeth.

Sam watched as the girls played with the toys that were provided and was relieved to see that they seemed happy. When they left with Karen, she felt a little bit more at ease, seeing that they were happy enough to be taken and seemed relaxed with Karen. It hadn't occurred to her to hug and kiss them; it just wasn't something she did. She waved to them as they left and they waved back to her before being lifted into the car and driven away.

After dropping Sam off at the Family Centre, April popped in to see Freddie. The first thing he said to her was, 'When is Mummy coming?'

'You will see her again tomorrow,' she answered.

Freddie appeared quite settled and relaxed in his foster placement but his attachment to his mother remained strong. Although this was positive with regard to the quality of parenting he had enjoyed, it was a worry for April because if he wasn't able to return to Becky's care the plan would be for him to be adopted and she could not see him settling very easily into a new family. The attachment was strong and the quality of the contact which took place daily and was attended diligently by his mother was enjoyable for Freddie, enhancing their already healthy and secure attachment. If things continued as they were with Becky and Colin Lyons, April would have to start reducing Freddie's contact with his mother to start preparing him for adoption.

Later as she pulled up outside Becky's house, she noticed Colin's grimy white van parked on the grass. The memory of how violently he had protested when they removed Freddie, and how it had taken two police officers to contain him, almost made her think twice about going in. However, it would be useful to see both of them together and it was going to be necessary in any case considering there was a new baby on the way.

Colin opened the door and, strangely, appeared happy to see April standing there, greeting her as though she were an old friend. 'Hiya, April, come in,' he said, standing aside to allow her to enter.

April was struck by the stark tidiness of the observable space, which included the front room, hallway and some of the kitchen. There was not a thing out of place and although the shabby old furniture was still there, everything around it was precise and immaculately in place. She could see into the kitchen, where the cream-coloured floor tiles, which previously had been just about OK, almost sparkled, drawing her attention to them as soon as she walked in. The tiles had been scrubbed and polished to such a high standard, April thought at first that they might be new. The stainless-steel draining board shone and there was not so much as a teaspoon in sight. April couldn't help noticing that the garden hadn't changed, and if anything, it was worse than before, with the handlebars of an old rusty bike poking through the long grass, a broken swing with the plastic seat hanging from one piece of rope and piles of rubbish, including old carpet and broken fencing. On the far side of the garden next to the fence, April noticed an upside-down shopping trolley. She couldn't help being amused by the complete contrast between inside and out. Outside clearly didn't matter.

'Can I get you a drink?' Colin asked.

'I'm fine, thank you,' she replied. 'I just thought I would pop in to tell you how Freddie is and catch up on how the pregnancy is going.'

'Everything is good,' Colin answered.

April made a very obvious turn of her head towards Becky, deliberately excluding him. 'And how are you, Becky? Have you got over your morning sickness?'

'She's OK, she's only three months gone. My wife worked until she was nearly ready to drop when she was pregnant with my boys. She didn't complain. All she's got to do is keep the house clean,' Colin said disdainfully, looking towards Becky as he spoke.

April looked at Becky and wondered how she could help this woman to understand she was being savagely dominated. 'Thanks for that, Colin, but I would like Becky to tell me how she feels herself now, if you don't mind,' she said with as much politeness as she could muster.

She couldn't help noticing a look of trepidation in Becky's eyes as she looked at Colin, as though she was scared she might give the wrong answer. Becky then did as she always seemed to do when she didn't know what to say; just stared into space.

'So tell me how you're feeling with the pregnancy, Becky. Do you feel tired at all, do you sleep OK?' April tried again.

'I do feel tired a lot of the time to be honest with you, but it's OK, I can manage.'

'She always says she's tired; she can be a bit lazy, though, can't you, Becky? I always have to remind her to do things around the house. You would think she would know by now how to keep a house clean, wouldn't you, April?'

'I can be a bit lazy sometimes,' Becky said submissively.

'What do you mean by lazy, Becky?' April asked.

'I caught her watching telly the other day and there was a sink full of dishes. You should have seen it, it was disgusting. I shouldn't have to come home from work to that mess, should I, April? She's at home most of the day and I'm slogging my guts out and she can't even be bothered to clear up dishes. She used to do that when she had her friends around. I had to put a stop to that; they don't come around any more.'

April just looked despairingly at them both as Colin continued with his chauvinistic mental bullying of Becky, whilst Becky sat meekly in her chair, with seemingly no concept or recognition of what was happening to her.

After a brief discussion about the court process and options for Freddie, April got up to leave.

'Don't just sit there on your fat arse, get up and see the lady out. She can be so rude at times,' Colin snarled.

Becky meekly did as she was told and got up to see April to the door.

At the door, April seized the opportunity to talk to Becky alone. 'Would you come to the office to see me, Becky? I would like to talk to you about a few matters regarding Freddie.'

Becky agreed and an appointment was arranged, surprisingly without any interference from Colin who had remained in the front room.

As April drove off, she felt relieved that there hadn't been any confrontation, but she started to realise that although it was very clear that Colin Lyons was a controlling bully who exploited vulnerable women like Becky, he believed that he was a good man. He was fully convinced that what he was doing and the way he treated Becky were for her own good and would benefit her in the end. April could see a link between the way he genuinely believed he was helping Becky to be a better person and a better mother, and poor little Freddie being physically chastised for his own sake, so that he would learn how to behave.

During the drive home, April found herself thrust into melancholy thoughts about her own lost child. He or she would have been nearly a year old now. Her child would have been born to loving, protective parents and given all the advantages and opportunities a child could be given. She tried to snap out of this mood as she pulled up outside her home.

16

SECOND ADOPTION VISIT

April was at home preparing for Jenny's second visit. She had arranged her appointments and visits to make sure she could be home in plenty of time to prepare herself and to ensure the house looked cosy and welcoming. Luckily, for once nothing out of the ordinary happened to keep her working longer, and Jed had texted to say he was already on his way home.

April changed out of her work clothes, which were sweaty after rushing around in the heat. She wanted to look reasonably smart but not too formal, and selected a colourful hip-length top and white cotton leggings. After checking herself in the mirror and tweaking her lustrous dark curls, she turned her attention to where they would sit: in the lounge, or outside on their courtyard patio? Being evening, the sun had passed over the house, leaving the patio in the shade. April decided it would be more appropriate to sit in their comfortable lounge and let the fresh air in through open windows. She had placed a vase of flowers in the bay window but removed them quickly when it occurred to her that vases of flowers are not particularly child friendly.

April was relieved when Jed arrived home at 6.15pm, just in time for Jenny, who was due to be there by 6.30. He had been stuck in traffic. She had been fretting about who should sit where and whether they would need nibbles on the table.

'Calm down, April; Jenny won't be making her decision about us based on what biscuits we provide. If she turns us down it's more likely to be due to you flapping so much about it.'

'You obviously don't know anything about us social workers if you think biscuits don't matter. Biscuits will be the key to whether she likes us or hates us, believe me. I just wish I had bought them from Waitrose instead of Aldi.'

Jed was relieved to see she was smiling as she said this. 'She will be too busy being dazzled by the top you're wearing to worry about what she's given to eat. It's nice and bright.'

April spotted signs of a snigger. 'Oh my God, don't you like it?' she said, rushing over to the full-length mirror in the hall.

'I'm only joking, you look gorgeous. You just need to calm down a bit and everything will be fine.'

April selected a variety of biscuits to put out and filled the cafetière in readiness. Jed sat himself down on the sofa with the paper, looking completely relaxed and self-assured.

It was just after 6.40 when Jenny arrived, and by this time April had almost worn the carpet out as she walked back and forward to the window and out into the kitchen, then back to the window in repetitive sequence. She checked her diary a couple of times, thinking she might have got the date wrong, but at last the doorbell rang and Jenny arrived, full of apologies for being late.

Once again it was not too long before Jenny had them both feeling perfectly at ease. She radiated warmth, which drew people to trust her. At the last meeting she had given them some paperwork to complete, with questions to self-analyse their personality traits. They had been asked to complete the questionnaire without consulting each other, and April in particular had found this hard. The first question asked for a brief paragraph detailing the following: Other than gender, race and religion, how would you describe your identity? Another was Whom do you most admire and why? Both Jed and

April struggled with these as they couldn't quite understand why they were necessary or how they related to the assessment. They were both scared of getting it wrong.

Jenny asked for the paperwork, which April had ready to give her, and after reaching over to take the questionnaires from April's outstretched hand, Jenny skimmed over them quickly before laying them down beside her, as though she had no real interest in their answers, which was very irritating considering the time they had spent agonising over what to put.

'So how did you find answering these questions?' Jenny asked, addressing them both.

'I don't mind admitting I found it really difficult. Analysing one's own personality is not something you do every day,' Jed offered.

'I found it really difficult too,' April agreed. 'I tried to answer as honestly as I could but I felt it would have been a lot easier if I could have consulted with Jed. I think he knows me better than I know myself.'

'You will probably be pleased to know that most people say the same thing. We are rarely called to question ourselves about our own personalities, but believe me it is a very useful exercise and enormously helpful for the assessment. I don't want to form opinions about you myself because they will largely just be assumptions, whereas you ought to know yourselves; don't you agree? It is also useful for you to consider yourselves more deeply because it helps you think about what you may be able to deal with in the future and what you might find more difficult. We may come back to those questions at a later stage in the process.'

They both nodded, but April was thinking, This woman is going to end up knowing more about me than anyone ever has before, and that is quite scary.

The discussion which followed was relaxed and seemingly informal and April found herself almost enjoying the chat. She had never before sat and talked about herself or her relationships and it wasn't something she ever really gave a second thought to. She also noticed with surprise that Jed had become unusually chatty and appeared to be enjoying himself too.

After about an hour of this, Jenny sat back on the sofa and, putting down her pen and writing pad, looked directly at April. 'So,' she said, looking quizzically at them both, 'I have heard and gleaned quite a lot about you and it appears that you have both had a relatively easy ride through your first thirty-odd years. Apart from the usual upsets like grandparents dying, there has been a distinct lack of real trauma or hardship. You were both popular at school and clever enough to achieve your goals, and had happy childhoods with happy memories all round, and loving parents who provided stable, secure homes for you. I would now like you to tell me, excluding the obvious ordeal concerning your infertility, what is the most difficult thing you have had to deal with so far in your lives? You can go first, Jed.'

Jed had a look of complete bewilderment on his face as he looked towards April, then back at Jenny, who for some reason was smiling broadly as she waited for his answer.

'Don't worry too much if you can't think of anything at this point. I have put you on the spot a bit, I can tell. What about you, April; what has been the most difficult thing you have ever had to deal with, excluding infertility?'

April surprised herself by opening up about the past she had buried for years. 'I was in a relationship when I was young. We were together from our early teens until our twenties. We argued a lot but still kept getting back together, and this went on for years. I treated him badly, took him for granted, and the more he loved me the worse I treated him. He died in an accident, and it was only after he died that I realised how horrible I had been to him. The guilt was difficult to cope with. For a few years after, I frequented spiritualist gatherings. I wanted him to know that I was sorry.' April felt the tears welling up and was taken by surprise at the powerful emotions reliving this memory evoked in her. Jed was looking at her with bemusement; he had known about this relationship but had no idea that it was still so poignant and painful for her.

144

'Are you over it now, April?' Jenny asked, looking from Jed to April and from April to Jed, who was still staring at April.

'Of course; I still think about it sometimes but it doesn't have the effect it did have. I am lucky to have met Jed, and although I can be horrible to him sometimes, he still seems to love me regardless.'

'That is very true, she can be horrible at times – oh, and also that I do still love her regardless.'

'Why do you think you treated this previous boyfriend so badly, April?'

'I have asked myself this a lot over the years. I often ask myself why I sometimes say cruel things to Jed when he really doesn't deserve it. I have no idea why, but I do know that I get a constant niggling feeling inside when somebody seems to love me. It's almost as if I think there must be something wrong with them, they must be a bit weird. Why would they love me?'

'You're not that horrible to me; most of the time anyway,' Jed said jokingly.

'This is something I am going to throw into the pot for you to stew over, April; do you think this may be something to do with your father? I have to admit that I have been surprised that he has not yet been mentioned in any conversation we have had so far. I am intrigued that the answer to my question, "What was the most difficult thing you have had to deal with?" was about a previous boyfriend, and the father who abandoned you at a very young age was not even mentioned.'

'He left us when my brother and I were babies. I don't remember anything about him. Mum never talks about him, I suppose because it's upsetting for her or she doesn't want to upset me, I'm not sure which. I have never seen a photo of him so don't even know what he looks like. Mum never spoke badly about him or anything like that, but I just always knew she didn't want him mentioned. All I know is that he went off with another woman and that was that. Would you like some more coffee?' April asked, hoping to end this topic of conversation.

'Have you or your brother ever thought about trying to find him?'

April didn't want to admit that she had, but felt there was no use in lying. Jenny appeared to have the capacity to see directly into her soul, and would be sure to guess that she wasn't telling the truth.

'Yes. I have to admit; I have thought about it.' She hesitated before adding, 'Max and I have never spoken about him. I have no idea if he has tried to find him, or even if he has ever given him a second thought. It's as though there never was a father, I suppose, as far as Max is concerned.'

'Could you tell me a bit more about your thoughts of tracing him, April?'

Jed was staring at April again, but this time with astonishment. He'd had no idea that she had thought about trying to find her father; she had never spoken about him. At the same time he was thinking about their jokes before Jenny came about dark secrets being revealed.

'I have done a bit of investigating but haven't really got anywhere. I haven't found the courage to take it any further. I would think it's highly unlikely he would welcome me into the life he now has with his new wife, family, whatever.'

'Jed, I can't help thinking that what April has just disclosed has shocked you; had she not told you that she has thought about contacting her father?'

'No, I have to be honest, Jenny; I am as surprised as you are.' He turned his head slowly back to look at April. 'April, why didn't you tell me; why didn't you tell me that you wanted to contact your father? I had no idea.'

'I'm sorry, Jed, I just felt stupid about it. He wouldn't want to know me anyway so it wasn't really going to get me anywhere.'

'Another coffee would be very welcome, April, thank you,' Jenny said suddenly.

April was relieved to have a reprieve from the highly unwelcome subject of her father. She was quite stunned by the emotions this discussion had evoked in her. As she walked into the kitchen, she sensed Jenny behind her.

'This is a lovely house, April; it hasn't taken long to make it seem homely. I lived in my house for years before it felt like home.'

'I know, it's unusual, isn't it, but we felt at home here within a few months. It's exactly the type of house we had dreamed of; we were so lucky to find it.'

April found herself chattering about anything she could think of, including the stoneware flowerpots in the hallway which she had chosen to match the ivory curtains. She was stalling, and Jenny knew this. They continued the light conversation whilst they drank their coffee and then, to April's relief, Jenny said she was drawing the session to a close.

'Thank you both for being so frank and open with me this evening. It has been a very productive start to the assessment process. April, I would like to discuss your father with you again next time because although you may not think he is or has been important in your life, you may be surprised to realise the impact his non-presence has had on you as a person. I wonder whether you might be able to bring yourself to ask your mum some questions when you next see her? You never know, it might do her some good to open up.'

'Oh... I don't think so; I don't think she would like me asking.'

'Think about it, April. I don't want to push you into anything, but promise me you will think about it.'

'OK, I promise I will give it some thought.'

After Jenny had left, although there were a number of important things they needed to discuss, they both felt completely drained and so just spent the rest of the evening slumped in front of the television, hardly even engaging in small talk. If they had been asked, neither Jed nor April would have been able to say what the programme they were slumped in front of was about, as their minds were swamped by going over the discussions and revelations of the evening.

A long time after they had gone to bed, April lay awake, looking into the darkness of the room. She was thinking about her father, something she rarely gave herself the luxury of doing. In the quiet stillness of the night, April started to realise something quite significant about herself. She had always longed to know about her father but had never been brave enough to ask her mum. It had been an unspoken rule in their house for as long as she could remember; it had always been April, her brother and her mum, and her father had had no part to play in their lives.

Being a social worker, she was expected to analyse and assess the emotional impact of life events on the parents and children she worked with and she was very skilled at doing so; however, she had never stopped to analyse herself. She wondered if this had been a deliberate omission on her part; perhaps she was scared of uncovering feelings she would rather keep buried? Whatever the reason she had not followed through with her plans to locate her father, she was coming to realise that what Jenny had said may have been true: the way she'd treated her first serious boyfriend could very likely have been something to do with her father's desertion of the family.

Lying there beside the sleeping Jed, she slowly started to acknowledge that she did feel a sense of rejection and abandonment which had possibly impacted more significantly on her life and relationships than she'd realised. She made the decision that she would talk to her mum about her father and would be proactive in providing a setting for the discussion to take place. She resolved to do this as soon as possible. This decision made, April was able to drift off into a deep and satisfying sleep.

17

SKELETONS IN THE CUPBOARD

It was Saturday morning and April and Jed were getting ready for their planned break in northern France where they would be staying in a chateau hotel for four days. Jed had received a sizeable end-of-year bonus and they were planning to treat themselves. They were both of the view that this was well deserved. Jed's job wasn't an easy one, with constant pressure from clients, deadlines and charge-out fees, and with everything that had been going on, April felt quite drained. They were really looking forward to just relaxing beside the outdoor pool, reading their books and eating nice food. April's mum had been invited; partly because they wanted her there and partly so that April could take the opportunity to raise the matter of her father in a relaxed setting. They had invited Jed's parents just so that they wouldn't feel left out, but they were preparing to go and help Richard with the turtles.

After taking the ferry from Dover and a drive of just under an hour, they arrived at the little French village where they were staying. Jed turned the car off the quiet narrow road and drove through pillared gates, down a long winding gravel drive, and through wooded landscaped gardens with an abundance of colourful plants, until the imposing facade of the chateau loomed in front of them. As Jed drove slowly through this beautiful, tranquil parkland, April could already feel the pent-up tensions of the last few months begin to drain away.

Inside, the seventeenth-century building was furnished throughout with lavishly thick green-and-gold carpets which swept through the long hallway, into the reception area and up the winding marble staircase. Their rooms were equally plush, with wall-to-wall carpeting, large sash bay windows overlooking the extensive grounds, and a river to the side with ducks and geese gliding gracefully and turning their heads from side to side as if admiring the view as they swam. The bathrooms were decked in colourful ceramic tiles with a huge bath on forked metal legs, a walk-in shower and plenty of large, fluffy white towels. At the bottom of Jed and April's bed were two neatly folded white cotton dressing gowns.

'I think we're going to like it here,' April said to Jed as they parted from her mother to go into their own room.

'This is exactly what we both need. Shall we just retire and stay here for good?'

'It's a nice idea, but I'm needed in court next week and I can't get out of it. They'll come looking for me if I don't turn up, otherwise I wouldn't hesitate.'

'Oh well, maybe another time then. You will keep getting yourself into these situations where you end up in court.'

'Yes, I must learn to behave myself.'

They both laughed before throwing themselves onto the huge, soft bed, exhausted after all the travelling.

That evening they spoiled themselves with a three-course meal in the Michelin starred restaurant which was a separate building in the grounds of the hotel. All along one side of the restaurant were bifold doors which overlooked the grounds and swimming pool, which were made visible through the darkness by shady blue lanterns. April and

Diana had Helford crab with white mooli, followed by extra virgin olive oil ice cream, figs and yoghurt, whilst Jed had the honey-glazed duck breast followed by a selection of cheeses, home-made digestive biscuits, seasonal chutney and fig-and-hazelnut bread, which they all shared. They drank nearly two bottles of Sancerre between them, and as they were already tired this went to their heads, causing all three of them to become quite tipsy and giggly as they made their way back to their rooms in the dark, warm calmness of the evening.

It was late afternoon on their first whole day at the chateau, when they were relaxing beside the pool, enjoying the peaceful atmosphere and warm sunshine, that April decided was the right time to raise the issue of her father. Jed had swum a few lengths and was on his way back to the room for a break from the sun. This was an ideal opportunity.

April looked at her mum, who was resting her head on the back of her sunbed with her eyes half-shut and the corners of her mouth forming the trace of a smile. April was apprehensive about raising the matter, and took a deep breath to summon her courage before speaking. She didn't really want to disrupt the lovely time they were having, but this was the best opportunity she was likely to have.

'Mum?'

Diana raised her head drowsily. 'Yes, what is it, dear?'

'I need to talk to you about something.' Once she'd started the conversation a strange determination took hold and all her initial apprehension disappeared. 'It's to do with our plans to adopt a child. The social worker has asked about my father. I know you don't like talking about him, and that's never bothered me at all before,' she was quick to explain. The last thing she wanted was to hurt her mum's feelings, or to make her feel bad. 'It's come up in a session with Jenny, though; she thinks I should find out more about him.' She braced herself, entirely unsure how her mum would respond. All the years that had passed without a mention of him had rendered the subject completely unmentionable.

A stark and dramatic change in Diana's complexion took place before April's eyes. The pink glow from bathing in the sunshine drained from her in a flash and a stunned expression stared out from an alarmingly pale grey face.

'If you don't want to talk about it, Mum, don't worry,' April said hurriedly. 'It would be useful, but it's not the end of the world. Jenny didn't say it was absolutely essential for the application, she just suggested that it would be helpful to have some information about him. I think she might have been thinking about any child placed with us. They might be curious in years to come, I suppose.'

'There isn't anything to say about it,' was Diana's terse reply.

'OK, Mum.' April did her best to hide the bitter disappointment she felt. 'I won't mention it again.'

They sat together for a few more hours, reading, relaxing, and April having the odd dip in the pool to cool off, before going back to their rooms to prepare for the evening, when they planned to go into the village where the local farmers would bring along their produce for people to taste. This was a monthly event, and one of the reasons Jed had chosen this destination. There would be live music and local families all getting together to dance, share food and enjoy the lovely atmosphere.

Although April had managed to appear calm during her very brief conversation with her mum, inside she felt churned up and sick. It had taken quite a lot of courage to broach the subject and she desperately wanted to know about her father, now more than ever. Why, she wondered, did her mum find it so hard, even after all these years, to talk about her dad? Since the issue had been raised during the session with Jenny, April's curiosity was brimming over. It would be incorrect to say that the session had caused her curiosity to surface, because although she hadn't really admitted it to herself, she had come to realise that it had always been there, buried so deep within that it bubbled persistently below the surface of her consciousness. It had now bubbled over, and she was intensely curious and desperate to know about him.

Jed was disappointed when she told him about her mother's response, but his advice was not to pursue it further with Diana. They agreed that there must be more to the past than they were aware of, and that, whatever it happened to be, Diana was still feeling the pain.

'Maybe when we get home you could continue with the enquiries you started to make. You could find out for yourself then.'

April agreed that she would do this. She decided that was going to be her next step; she didn't want to upset her mum by persisting.

18

BRADLEY TRAVERS

April didn't have much chance to settle back into work before her action-packed schedule kicked in. Paula was back in the office after a few weeks off to recover from her ordeal with Larry Fuller, and, sitting at the desk opposite April, she was in the mood for chatting. Her daughter Natasha was due to go to university in September. She was going to Manchester to study history of art, which Paula was not very happy about. 'It's going to cost a fortune, and what do you do with a history of art degree, for Pete's sake?'

Unfortunately, April couldn't think what Natasha would do with a degree in history of art either, so wasn't much use in offering suggestions apart from the obvious. 'She could work in an art gallery, I suppose, or she could become an academic, or...' She had run out of ideas. 'I'm sure there are lots of opportunities,' she said unconvincingly.

Conveniently, April's phone rang.

'Hello, April Gardiner speaking, how can I help you?'

'It's Jackie Dixon here, Bradley Travers' foster carer. I wanted to let you know that Bradley has gone missing again. Police were out last night looking for him. He wasn't at his mum's or with any of the usual friends. This is the third time this week we've been up all night and had to get the police and I don't think I can cope with it any longer. I didn't want to give up on Bradley but to be honest, April, it's a constant worry; I've just about had enough.'

April felt that familiar sinking sensation in the pit of her stomach. 'Oh dear, are you saying you're giving notice on Bradley, Jackie?'

'We've tried our best, but he's been with us for six months and it's getting harder, not easier. I have to say yes, I am giving up on him, April, I'm sorry. I really wanted to help him, and at first I thought I was going to succeed, but it's just gone from bad to worse. If I could see I was getting somewhere with him, even in a small way, I might be able to carry on but unfortunately I can't. It's as though he doesn't want to be helped. Whatever we do for him he seems to throw it back in our faces. I think he hates us.'

This was fifteen-year-old Bradley's ninth placement since coming into care three years ago.

'I presume the police have checked his family home?' April said. 'I will pop round there anyway later to find out if his mum knows anything, then I will come to see you. I can't say what time exactly but it will be late afternoon, will that be OK with you?'

April was in the process of trying to write her statement of evidence for Tayla and Lily Grace's court case, which was due to be filed within two days. By the time she put the phone down Paula had thankfully left the office, so she was able to get her head down and crack on with the report. There was a list of emails which had come in that morning but she was ignoring them for the time being, knowing full well that most of them would require an action of some sort.

By 1.30pm, April had finished the draft report and emailed it to the Local Authority legal team to be edited. She fully expected it to come back with some amendments but for the time being she felt happy that she had done as much as she could. She could now concentrate on the next matter of urgency on her list, which was Bradley. She picked up her sandwich box, which had been in her drawer, threw it in her bag, left the office and set off to visit Bradley's family. There was a possibility that he had gone there after the police had been, or maybe the family would just be able to shed some light on where he might be.

Social Services had been involved with Bradley's family since he was about eleven years old, mostly because his mum Stacey was unable to cope with him. He was the oldest of five siblings, soon to be six as another baby was due in just over a month. The family lived on the appropriately named Grimsfield Estate, which was inhabited predominantly by the poorest and most deprived families. The majority were either not in work and dependent on state benefits, or employed on zero-hours contracts. Many of them were single parents who themselves or their children were into drugs, alcohol abuse or crime. Most of the houses were owned by the Housing Association, but many had been bought by private landlords and rented out to families, and these private tenants were the most deprived and disadvantaged of them all. Whilst the rent for the Housing Association properties was generally covered by housing benefits, the rent for the private properties was too high and had to be subsidised out of pitiful benefit allowances. Although the residents paid substantially higher rents to live in the privately rented properties, they had no security of tenure; being on six-month contracts, they were never sure how long they would have a home for. The Local Authority tenants complained about waiting for months to have essential repairs carried out, such as leaking taps or a boiler not working, but compared to the private tenants they were relatively well provided for and a basic standard was maintained. The private landlords of Grimsfield Estate were always on schedule with their rent collection, but when it came to fixing the boiler, electrical faults or damp patches in the bedrooms they were very difficult to get hold of.

April hadn't been in this area long but she had already picked up on the problems these families faced through discussions in the office involving other families on this estate. It appeared that there was one landlord who seemed to own most of the private houses. He had conveniently set up a company called Style Properties; this misleading name gave a falsely positive impression of the type of properties available, whilst also helping to remove from the landlord direct responsibility for his tenants by disguising his business as a company.

April drove quite a way down Honey Pot Lane, a wide, busy road with a few shops and mainly modern houses, until she almost reached the end where she turned into the Grimsfield Estate. The change in surroundings from Honey Pot Lane, which was colourful and vibrant, to the estate, which was dark, dismal and depressing, was stark and forbidding. Deprivation seeped from the dilapidated buildings, the grey-mottled window frames which had once been white, and the wide cracks in the dark grey tarmac which fronted the houses. This street was eerily devoid of people, considering it was a lovely sunny day and the schools were still on holiday. April drove past a small children's play area on the opposite side of the road which had various apparatus to play on, including the usual swings, roundabout and see-saw. The apparatus was painted in bright colours, mostly red and yellow, and was clearly quite new. Unfortunately, the area around it had been badly neglected, with patches of bare mud and long grass almost as high as the apparatus in some parts. To the side of the play area were a little shed and a bench, both of which were covered in graffitied obscenities. It wasn't the most appealing play park she had seen by any means, but it was still surprising that there was not a single child to be seen.

With a strange irony, the streets were all named after lakes in the beautiful, picturesque Lake District, and April soon found Windermere Road where Bradley's family lived. She parked her car at the end of the tarmac which was just a few feet from the brown front door. Being sensibly cautious, before leaving her car she looked about her, then double-checked that the car doors were locked. She rang the Travers family's doorbell, which sparked a series of loud, extremely ferocious-sounding barks, suggesting there were at least two dogs on the premises. April didn't mind dogs generally but this particular barking sounded alarmingly deep and aggressive.

It wasn't long before the door was opened a crack by a girl of about ten, who peered through the small space between the door and its frame. 'Who are you?' she asked.

April's attention was drawn to a huge black canine who was baring his teeth and snarling as if impatient to rip her apart. The girl was pulling the dog back by his collar in an attempt to stop him hurtling towards April, but this didn't fill her with confidence as the dog was huge, powerful and determined. For a moment she felt her life was in the hands of a petite adolescent girl whom she had never met before, and she found herself temporarily speechless and unable to answer the girl's question.

After a short time, which to April seemed much longer, a large man joined the little girl, took hold of the dog's collar and dragged him back, shouting, 'Cut it, Dave, cut it, do you hear?' For a moment April was confused and looked behind the man to see who Dave was, before it dawned on her that Dave was the dog. Dave took no notice of the man and barked even louder, increasing his belligerence by including a piercing howl in between barks in clear frustration at not being allowed to get at his victim.

April held out a trembling hand to the man, who was nearly six feet tall and almost as wide, especially around his stomach area. He wore a T-shirt that used to be white, and seemed to only cover half of his belly. She wondered if he had put a lot of weight on and hadn't yet realised that his clothes didn't fit him any more. 'Hello, I'm April Gardiner, social worker. Is Stacey at home?'

'Yes,' the man answered. 'Stacey, someone to see you,' he called, turning back towards the front room.

The door remained only slightly ajar. 'Who is it?' was the answer.

'Social worker,' he shouted back. 'I can't remember her name.'

'It's April, April Gardiner,' April said, trying to peer through the small space in the doorway.

'Oh, I bet I know what she wants. Tell her to come in, then.'

The door was held open and, much to April's relief and the dog's frustration, Dave was led out of the room and shut in the kitchen.

Stacey sat on a two-seater sofa which was covered by a dirty white blanket. Shannon, who was two, sat beside her mother, watching CBeebies and adding more stains to the grimy blanket and her face as she tucked into a packet of chocolate buttons. Underneath the chocolate and grime, Shannon was the sweetest-looking little girl, with chubby pink cheeks, dimples and masses of curly red hair. April could never look at a pretty young child without wanting to pick them up and cuddle them, but that was not something she should do as a visiting professional.

April sat herself down on the chair opposite Stacey, who was the first to speak.

'I suppose you've come to see if I know where Bradley is. The police have already been here and I told them the same as I'll tell you: I don't know where he is and I don't give a damn either. I don't want him near me or my kids. He just causes trouble and I don't want it any more.'

Hearing a mother talk about her own son in this way made April grimace, which she tried unsuccessfully to conceal.

'I know what you think of me; you think I'm a bad mother, but you don't know half of it. He's been a little shit since the day he was born. I gave him everything he wanted to try to get him to be good but it didn't matter; he still caused trouble. He's spoilt, that's the trouble; I spoilt him. He used to kick and punch his sister all the time, you should see the bruises he put on her; and he's threatened me in the past. I'm just not having it any more. You can look after him now; he's not coming back 'ere.'

April was aware that the family had been offered support to help them accept Bradley back into the home, but all the help had been refused. Stacey couldn't see beyond his behaviour; to her he had always been troublesome and she fully believed that he came out of the womb a demon. As far as she was concerned, her parenting had nothing to do with it whatsoever.

Whilst this conversation was taking place the dog continued to bark from the kitchen. Dave was not one to give up easily. April noticed the girl had gone into the tiny garden and was calling the dog to come out.

'I presume that's Scarlett, is it? I haven't met her before because she was at school last time I called.'

'Yes, she's excluded now. That school is crap, they're always excluding my kids. I'm going to have to find another school for her in September. She's being assessed for ADHD because the school say she won't stay in class. She gets up and walks out if she doesn't like the lesson, and she doesn't like any of the lessons so she spends most of the time walking around the playground. I don't know why they don't just tell her to come back and sit down, but they don't. They just let her do it, then they blame her – or me! We've got ADHD in the family; I had it when I was a kid, my brother had it and the two boys have got it as well.'

April had heard this said many times by parents who lived in a cycle of poor parenting.

She was curious about the man who had opened the door because, although Stacey was pregnant, she had told April that she was not in a relationship with the baby's father. Curiosity got the better of her.

'I know it's not really any of my business, but who is the man who opened the door; is he a neighbour?' April didn't know where he had gone to.

'That's Damien, he's just a friend; he comes around sometimes, I've known him for months. He gets on well with the kids, they all adore him.'

Alarm bells rang loudly in April's head. 'You don't know him very well, then, by the sound of it. Do you know where he lives, or anything about his past?'

'Of course I do. I wouldn't have him in my house if I didn't know anything about him,' Stacey said, clearly annoyed by the inference. 'I'm careful who I have around my kids. He's told me loads about himself. He told me he was in a relationship for a few years but his girlfriend turned out to be a right cow; she kicked him out because she met someone else. She's even stopped him seeing his kid. I think that's why he likes to be around my kids.'

'Stacey, I must warn you, Damien might be a very nice man, but there are a lot of men out there who can seem perfectly nice but turn out to be bad. You need to spend a lot more time getting to know him properly before you let him be around your kids. He doesn't stay here, does he?'

Stacey gave a humourless laugh. 'I don't think so, do you? He'd have to sleep on the floor. I've only got two bedrooms so the boys sleep in one room and I sleep in the other one with Shannon and Scarlett. I've had my name down for a three-bedroom house for years but they won't give me one because I'm in rent arrears.'

'How did you get into arrears; is it much?'

'Five hundred pounds. It was Shannon's dad; I couldn't claim benefits when he was here because he was working. He was on a zero-hours contract so sometimes he didn't have any wages coming in. He wouldn't claim anything, and then by the time I made a claim he would have work again. It just built up. I'm paying off five pounds a month but on top of that I have to pay three pounds a month for a crisis loan I had, and another five pounds a month for the washing machine, so sometimes I can't pay the extra rent because I wouldn't be able to buy enough food. I have to pay for the washing machine because the money is from a loan company and they come to your door to get it. He's scarpered now and doesn't pay me a penny.'

April found herself staring blankly at Stacey, trying to work out why she had let herself get into this situation. She couldn't begin to imagine how hard life must be for her, especially with another baby on the way. Stacey was in her early thirties but, being grossly obese with short, straight, greasy brown hair, she could have easily been taken for someone of middle age. She didn't seem to get off the sofa very often but the one time she had got up whilst April was there, her excess weight caused her to sway from side to side, her large,

161

unsupported breasts moving in one direction whilst her pregnant belly went in the other, and April couldn't help but be reminded of a camel with its underbelly swaying in one direction whilst its hump swayed in the other. She tried to erase these thoughts from her mind.

The one time that Stacey moved from the sofa during April's visit was when she got up to fetch Shannon another packet of chocolate buttons. She had finished the packet she had been eating and was complaining of feeling hungry. April could see the unfortunate future for Shannon, who without intervention would be heading the same way as her mother if she continued with the pattern of sitting watching television and scoffing chocolates. The prognosis for her future health was not looking good.

'Do you ever go to that play area down the road, Stacey?' April asked.

'You're kidding me, aren't you? The druggies go there every night and leave used needles all over the place. You never know what you might come across in the long grass. There was a boy stabbed last year; he didn't die, but only because someone from across the road saw it and called an ambulance. I wouldn't go anywhere near there with my kids.'

'That's such a shame; don't the police move them on?'

'Sometimes, but we don't see many police around here. Can't think where they might be needed more than here, but we don't see them. Scarlett wanted to go to after-school football but she can't go out after dark, not around here.'

It was clear to April that she wasn't going to make any progress on finding Bradley but as she left, her 'nanny state' training got the better of her and she couldn't help but look back as she walked down the path and say, 'Don't forget, Stacey, don't let Damien be alone with your children; don't trust anyone because you never know. Sometimes the nicer men are to children, the more worried you should be.'

Stacey stared at her in absolute bemusement.

'You need to be taking the children out somewhere while the weather is good, and you also need to stop feeding Shannon chocolate buttons; try giving her fruit instead.' With this, she got in her car and drove off.

April left the Travers household feeling quite depressed. It was the helplessness of the family she had just visited, which she knew was prevalent amongst many families like them. What hope had they got of ever improving their lives, which threw one hurdle after another at them? OK, some people might say they brought it on themselves, especially with regard to the number of children they chose to have, but how could anyone who had never been in that situation judge them? People who had no idea what it was like to have anything to look forward to, who owned nothing and could see no way of escaping their dismal existence. Just like Sam, Stacey could barely read and write; she'd spent her childhood looking after her mother, who'd suffered from chronic depression. She'd taken an overdose and died when Stacey was fourteen, leaving her with an alcoholic father. Not surprisingly, these experiences had a major effect on her ability to function in any area of life, and just like Sam, Stacey had no meaningful, positive support networks.

April had one more visit to make before finishing for the day. Martha and Ben's mum had been discharged from hospital and they had returned home. She needed to pay them a visit to ensure they had everything they needed and things were OK. It had been a short stay this time for their mum, Tina; it usually took the hospital about a month to stabilise her with medication before sending her home but this time it had been just over two weeks. April was a bit apprehensive about this because she hadn't been invited to the discharge meeting and she was fully aware of the pressures on the mental health service. Beds were in short supply and units were under pressure to free them up as soon as possible.

Tina seemed a bit low in mood but was pleased to be back with her children, and Martha and Ben were clearly happy to be home with their mum. Although the home conditions were unwelcoming and sparse and bore no comparison with the foster carer's warm, homely and comfortable environment, the children were loved and happy enough, and this was where they wanted to be when their mum was well.

The outreach team were going to visit every day, and April arranged for a social work assistant to make daily visits for the first fortnight.

19

APRIL'S FATHER

April and Jed had met with Jenny for their individual sessions and the feedback she gave them was that she would be making a recommendation for them to be approved for up to two children. They were only planning to have one at this stage but Jenny had suggested that they should be approved for two just in case they changed their minds and were attracted to siblings. 'Just to keep your options open – you never know,' she said. Against her wishes, a rush of excitement soared through April's body. She hadn't considered siblings but she could suddenly visualise two little blond children, a baby girl and her toddler brother, in her front room, their new home. She pictured the baby wrapped in a soft pale pink blanket with flushed cheeks, sleeping peacefully whilst the little boy giggled with delight as Jed tousled on the floor with him. She pushed this from her mind, knowing there was a long way to go yet.

Jenny made a couple of recommendations, one of them being that April attended counselling to address the issue of her father. Jenny had been informed about the latest events concerning the conversation with Diana and agreed that the whole thing was a mystery. April had been honest with her and admitted her intentions to resume her attempt to trace her father. Jenny's advice was for April to try to resolve this matter before having a child placed with her, and April could understand why this made sense, although it was a bit frustrating to say the least. She couldn't bear the thought that there could possibly be some delay.

April was even more desperate to have a baby than she had ever been, and this was intensified by the hopes and dreams that developed following their adoption chats with Jenny. Although they had tried not to do it too much, they had looked through Be My Parent magazine at the various children waiting for adoptive parents to claim them. There were a number whose little faces jumped out at them, their sad eyes pleading for a mummy and daddy to love them. At least that's how April saw it. The adoption process could take a long time, which was no surprise to April but she would struggle to cope if it had to be put off for any length of time whilst she addressed issues to do with her father.

Jed was due to be working away for a couple of nights and April decided she would use the time on her own to do some investigations. Her father's name was Anthony Tuczemski which, being an unusual name in Britain, helped to narrow the search and gave her hope of success. Her paternal grandparents were Polish. If they were still alive, they were likely to be still living in Poland, but April had never met them. She didn't even know if there were any other relatives on that side of the family.

Following Jenny's advice, April arranged to see a counsellor, although she didn't relish the thought of opening up to a stranger. She frequently advised the parents she worked with to engage in counselling to address issues from their past and was very persuasive in convincing them that it would be worthwhile. Having been told to pursue this herself put a different perspective on it. She understood and agreed that benefits could be gained from counselling but was less than enthusiastic at the thought of doing it herself. She did it, though, because she was willing to do whatever she had to do to achieve her goal of becoming a mother.

The next step was to start the process of searching for her father. After talking to the counsellor and reflecting on the past it started to become clear to her that there had always been a deep longing to see him and to know him; she just had not allowed it to surface. The fear of further rejection would have been more than she could bear and she came to realise that this was what had always prevented her from taking it any further. It felt almost as though she was being driven by fate as she found herself being almost forced into something she had always wanted but not been able to do.

April had been looking at social media to see if there was anyone by the name of Tuczemski and found two people, both of them young girls who might have been sisters. She couldn't be sure, but there were clues as to where at least one of them lived. It was a long shot but April trolled through the electoral roll for that area and, after what seemed like ages scrolling through the pages of tiny writing and thousands of names, she saw Anthony Tuczemski. She followed this up with an enquiry in the telephone directory for that area and there he was with his address and telephone number. She clasped her hand over her mouth as she gasped out loud, 'Oh my God, that must be him.'

She inhaled and exhaled slowly and deeply, trying to get herself together whilst she looked at the number before her. She had always suspected it would not be difficult to find him if she really wanted to, but now she had the ability to do it and it was right in her grasp, she struggled to find the courage to take the next step. She just sat and stared at the number, thoughts racing through her mind. What if he became angry about her contacting him? What if he slammed the phone down? What if his wife answered, or his daughter; what would they say? What would she say? She quickly came to the conclusion that phoning was out of the question; it would need to be a letter. That way she would have to wait longer, but at least he would have a choice not to reply if he didn't want to. April lost no time; she sat down with a pen and paper and started to write.

Her blood was racing in a way she had never experienced before. She was shaken by the rush of emotions which overwhelmed her as years of suppressed feelings were suddenly unleashed.

Dear Mr Tuczemski,

I hope you don't mind me contacting you out of the blue in this way but I am wondering if you are the same Anthony Tuczemski who is my father. My mother is Diana and I was born on 12th September 1980 I also have a twin brother, Max.

I wonder if you would be kind enough to reply to the address above, whether you believe you are my father or not, so that, if necessary, I can make enquiries elsewhere. If you are my father and do not wish to have contact with me, I would be grateful if you could let me know this and you will not hear from me again.

I look forward to hearing from you.

Kind regards,

April Gardiner

April's hand trembled as she wrote the words, and with flushed cheeks, she stamped and sealed the envelope, then, wasting no time, went directly into the street to put it in the postbox. When she came back, she sat at her dining table with her head in her hands to try to stop the rush of blood to her head. 'Oh my God,' she said out loud. 'What have I done? I've started something now and there's no turning back.' She felt a pang of guilt about her mother, as though she had been disloyal in some way; but she had a right to find out about her father, she told herself, and her mother had not been fair in keeping things from her.

The next day April was back in the office and as usual work matters and other people's problems soon took over her thoughts. Sam was coming to the Family Centre today for contact and April was going to supervise it. She liked to observe contact sessions herself occasionally to assist with her evidence for court. So far the contact had been going quite well. Sam had turned up for every session and the children were always pleased to see their mum. Sam had also been attending her alcohol counselling and regular hair strand tests were clear, which was all very encouraging.

'April, I've been trying to catch up with you for weeks; we keep missing each other. We need a trip to the old Bow & Arrow this evening, don't you think? Life should not be all work without play, you know; it's not healthy and if you don't mind me saying so, you look a bit peaky.' This was Miles, who had sauntered over to her desk, looking gorgeous with his longish fair hair flopping over his eyes and his pale short-sleeved cotton shirt tight across his broad chest.

'You have tempted me, Miles; I would love that. Is Paula coming?'

'I knew you wouldn't be able to resist me. I'm just too attractive, aren't I, but yes, Paula is coming so you can't have me all to yourself, I'm afraid; well, unless you really insist of course. I might be able to arrange it.'

April felt a little flutter of excitement at the suggestion, but checked herself very quickly. 'Well, I'll just have to make do then, won't I, but I'm sure I will get over the disappointment.'

'If you say so.'

April needed to be at the Family Centre before 10am to observe the contact. 'I'll see you in the pub later then, probably be there about 5.30 to six,' she shouted to Miles as she dashed out of the office.

She arrived at the Family Centre just in time to see the foster carer lifting the children from their car seats. April walked over to give her a hand.

'Hello, April; we went to the seaside on Saturday and I can swim now,' Tayla said as she took hold of April's hand. 'I swam like this,' she dropped April's hand and started waving her arms back and forward whilst lifting her feet high off the ground one at a time, 'and I took my feet right off the ground like this.'

'Did you have both feet off the ground at the same time?'

'Yes, like this.' Tayla leant her body forward and flapping her arms with accelerating vigour she started running towards the family centre kicking her feet high behind her. April chuckled to herself but managed to look seriously at her when she waited for her response.

'That looks like very good swimming, Tayla. You can tell Mummy all about it when she comes.'

Sam arrived at ten on the dot and Tayla ran over to her as she walked into the Family Centre, followed closely by Lily Grace, who was never far away from her sister. April was willing Sam to pick the girls up and hug them, but all she did was look at them and smile before finding herself a seat to perch on. Tayla and Lily Grace just stood and watched as she sat herself down, which was heart-wrenching and very frustrating for April. Her experienced eye told her that Sam was delighted to see her girls, although a lot of people might have thought otherwise.

Sam turned to April. 'How have they been?'

'They've been very well. Tayla has got something to tell you, haven't you, Tayla?' April said, trying to encourage Sam to interact with her children.

'What have you got to tell me, Tayla?' Sam asked.

Tayla looked at April before answering as though she wanted reassurance.

'Tell Mummy what you told me, Tayla, about your swimming,' April encouraged her.

'I can swim now, Mummy,' Tayla said.

'That's good, Tayla; do you want some crisps?'

April's heart sank. 'Tayla has been to the seaside and has been swimming with both feet off the ground, haven't you, Tayla?'

Tayla looked solemnly at her mum. She may be only six years old but she was well aware that her being able to swim was not something that would capture her mother's interest. She took the bag of crisps that Sam offered her and skipped away towards the playhouse in the corner of the room, closely followed again by Lily Grace. Sam watched her children playing from her seat, clearly enjoying watching them but without a clue as to how to get involved with their play. April was aware that the social work assistant had been encouraging her and giving her tips on how to play with them, but judging by what April was seeing today there had been very little progress, if any.

She began thinking about parenting and how it is assumed that those skills are within us and come naturally to us all. If only that were true. We generally parent how we were parented, and how could Sam, who had never experienced affection or nurturing or indeed had anyone who was remotely interested in her, probably since the day she was born, be expected to know how to show love, affection and interest to her own children? She could be instructed on how to do it by a social work assistant but the responses that come naturally to mothers who have been loved and nurtured themselves and have the emotional capacity to pass this on to their own children, are just a blank void in mothers such as Sam. It doesn't mean these women love their children any less.

Paula and Miles were already sitting at a high table in the pub with their drinks in front of them when April arrived. She checked if they were ready for another drink, which they both declined, before going to the bar to get herself a large gin and tonic. 'I really need this,' she said as she sat down on the spare stool and took a long, slow drink from her glass. 'Heaven,' she said under her breath.

The three of them always made an effort not to discuss work in the pub but it did have a bad habit of sneaking into the conversation at times. April's mind was very much on Sam and her children and she felt the need to talk about her feelings. Paula had asked her how Sam was getting on. She had visited Sam a few times when she was duty social worker.

'I am starting to feel hopeful that the shock of having her children removed from her care may have been enough for Sam to shake herself up and think about what she could lose. I know she's a binge drinker and has been able to sustain periods without drinking, but then gone back to it. It's early days yet, I know, but it's looking quite positive at the moment. I just hope it stays that way.'

'Don't forget how much goes on behind our backs, and that our judgements are made based on the small amount of information that inadvertently comes to our notice. You would only really know if things were going downhill if there was a change in Sam's regular attendance at contact or at groups.'

April knew this to be true; it was the usual pattern of behaviour seen with alcoholic or drug-using parents, and of course if Sam stopped attending groups there would be no hair strand tests to provide absolute proof. Her non-attendance at contact or the groups would be a good indication that she was drinking again, though.

One of April's weaknesses was that she was inclined to be overly optimistic. Whilst social workers should always hope for the best, they should also prepare for the worst. April always desperately wanted everyone's lives, especially those of the families she worked with, to be happy. During her career there had been one or two mothers she hadn't liked, but mostly she felt sympathy and compassion for the hard lives they had endured.

'I know from experience that it's more likely Sam will fail, especially judging by the long period she has been having these problems, but I can't help hoping that she ends up being able to keep her two little girls.'

They both looked doubtfully at her.

'How is your love life, Paula? You haven't been keeping us up to date lately,' Miles asked.

'Well, I wasn't going to tell you yet because you know what it's like – as soon as I think things are going well something goes wrong – but I will tell you; I have been seeing someone for nearly a month now.'

'How many wives has he got at home?' asked Miles with a sarcastic gleam in his eye.

April nearly choked on her drink.

'If you must know, he has been married once, but he's been divorced for three years,' Paula said indignantly.

'That's great, Paula. What's he like, then?' April asked.

'Have you checked his criminal record on our system, just in case? I mean, you never know, do you?'

'Oh, shut up, Miles,' April said, giving his shoulder a slight push.

'If we are still together in a month, which I feel sure we will be, I will have a dinner party so that you can meet him. He's lovely; not as good-looking as you, Miles, but the difference is, he's a very nice person with it.'

'Oh, thanks!'

'Only joking.'

'Well, I think you need to set the date for the dinner party because it sounds like this is the one.'

All three of them simultaneously got their diaries out and a date was set.

'There we are; you have to stay with him now come what may, because I'm looking forward to this,' Miles said.

'Absolutely, I haven't been to a dinner party for ages,' April agreed.

'I think you should leave Jed at home, April. Me and you can get together then; I know you've always fancied me and I'll be all yours. Just imagine that.'

April couldn't disguise the flush that rose in her cheeks. She was alarmed by the excitement she felt at this comment. She still had no idea what Miles's marital situation was, and even now it was not discussed.

20

BECKY COMES CLEAN

April was in the office when her phone rang and she was told that Becky Simmons had arrived and was waiting in reception for her. April unfortunately had not had any time to think about or plan her meeting with Becky due to the amount of work she was trying to deal with. She quickly finished off the record she was typing up, which detailed the events at the contact session with Sam and her children, pressed the button to save it and then took herself off to meet Becky, notepad and pen in hand.

Becky smiled at her as she walked into the reception area as though she was meeting with an old friend.

'How are you, Becky?' April asked.

As usual Becky's hair was pulled back from her face in a ponytail and her foundation was thick and too dark for her skin. She also had the usual red lipstick and lime-green eyeshadow on, but it was even thicker than usual, making her look a bit like a pantomime dame. April wondered whether she actually ever looked in the mirror before she came out.

'I'm fine, thank you,' Becky replied, smiling; a curious response considering her little boy had been taken away from her and was in foster care.

April showed Becky into a small interview room and, much to her surprise, before Becky had properly sat herself down, she started talking animatedly about Freddie.

'I've been thinking about a lot of things lately,' she was saying. 'I want Freddie back with me. I cry myself to sleep every night because I miss him so much. All I can think about is, Is he OK; is he happy and being looked after? Does he get any cuddles, and how much does he miss me? I used to read him a story every night when he went to bed and he used to cuddle into me. I expect foster carers are too busy to read stories to children.

'I went to see his dad at the weekend and Hayley started really having a go at me. She said Colin was hitting Freddie and I should kick him out. She was shouting and yelling at me.' Whilst Becky described what Hayley had said to her, she demonstrated Hayley's actions by throwing her arms around. She was clearly very upset by what had happened, and April could tell that she was fighting back tears. 'Hayley told me I should be ashamed of myself for letting a man hit my boy; then Leon piped in…' She paused for a moment, watching for April's response. 'He said I'm a selfish bitch and I should go to prison for letting Colin hurt Freddie and not doing anything about it. What do you think, April?'

April was taken aback by her question. She had spent the last three months trying to get Becky to realise what needed to happen and now she was asking her what she thought. How very strange this woman was at times.

'Becky, all I know is that someone has been hurting Freddie and this started to happen after Colin moved in with you. Are you now saying that you know Colin has been deliberately hurting Freddie?'

'He disciplined him a lot because Freddie wouldn't do as he was told and I spoilt him. I know I should have been stricter with him. I tried, I kept trying but I didn't like it. I don't like it when he cries.'

'Could you give me an example of an occasion when Colin disciplined him for not behaving?' April was beginning to feel hopeful that at last there could be progress, but following this question Becky gave her customary blank look and April thought that was it. But after a short silence, Becky started talking again.

'There was the time when I brought him home from nursery and he threw up all over the carpet. Colin had just paid to have a new carpet laid and Freddie was sick on it.'

'What happened next?' April asked softly.

'He was slapped.'

'Where was he slapped, Becky?'

'He was slapped…' Becky avoided eye contact as the sentence she had started began to taper off.

'Take your time, Becky; tell me where he was slapped.'

'Across the face. Like that.' Becky demonstrated by opening her hand and slapping her own face.

April winced at this disclosure, imagining Colin's large hand striking Freddie's soft little cheek. She tried to remain calm in an attempt not to alarm Becky and to keep the conversation flowing.

'There was sick everywhere; I panicked. Colin was due home; I was scared he would shout at us again.'

For a moment April was confused. Becky had said Colin was due home. 'Are you saying Colin wasn't home when it happened?' Becky had said this so quietly April wasn't sure at first of what she had heard. 'Are you saying you slapped Freddie, Becky?' April tried hard to disguise her astonishment.

There was another short period of silence. 'Yes,' Becky almost whispered into her jacket. She was staring at the floor and April could see a deep scarlet colour rising from her neck and slowly spreading across her face. 'I didn't mean to. I was scared. I was scared Colin would see the sick on the carpet.'

'Have there been other times when you hurt Freddie because you were scared of what Colin might do, Becky?'

'Yes.' Becky was still looking at the floor.

'Can you tell me about it?'

'One time, he wet his pants at nursery. I tried to sneak his wet things into the washing machine but Colin caught me doing it. He

176

was really angry, shouting at me, saying I was turning Freddie into a wimp and he needed to be punished. He said it was for his own good because if I kept being soft with him, he would get laughed at when he went to school.'

She continued without taking a breath, and April could see that she was becoming increasingly agitated. 'He shouted at him and shut him in the bathroom. He said he couldn't come out until he learned to use the toilet.'

'Did Colin hit him?'

'Not really... well... sort of, I mean...' Becky's face had dropped even further and was now almost buried in the collar of her orange jacket whilst she struggled to continue.

'Where did he hit him?'

'I thought Colin was going to hit me and him. I thought he would really hurt Freddie if he hit him, so I hit him and told him off because I could tell that was what Colin wanted. If I hadn't done it, he would have and he might have really hurt him. I pushed Freddie to try to get him to go into the bathroom to stop Colin getting angrier, and he fell. He fell against the fireplace. He hurt his back and I was frightened he would cry, which Colin can't stand, so I pulled him into the bathroom and shut the door. I sat on the toilet with Freddie on my knee, trying to stop him crying. Colin was still shouting and banging things outside. He said we could stay in there until Freddie learned to use the toilet.'

'Was there anything else?' April realised that there were contradictions in Becky's description of what happened but she thought it best to leave that for now. It could be because of the stress she was under or it could be that she was still not telling the whole truth. Either way April felt it best to let her carry on without distraction for the moment.

Becky, embarrassed and distressed, tried to hide her guilt by continuing to bury her face in her jacket collar and avoiding eye contact with April.

'OK, you can tell me the rest another time, Becky, but can you tell me now what you have decided to do? It seems to me that you have come to realise that what has been happening to Freddie is not right and that's why you have come to see me. I presume you are asking for help, am I right?'

'I shouldn't have hit him. Honestly, April, I've never hit him before. I don't know what I was doing; I couldn't help it. I didn't mean it. I'm not a bad mother. Colin keeps telling me I'm a bad mother but I'm really not. It's true what Leon said: that it's only since he moved in that things have gone wrong.' Becky had a bunch of tissues in her hand, with which she was wiping the tears that had started to stream steadily down her face. Between loud sniffles she said, 'It was because of him; Colin. It was because I was so scared of him. I'm going to tell him to go. I didn't know how I was going to manage because I've got no money, but I managed before I let him move in so I'm sure I can do it again.'

She paused for a minute, and then for the first time looked into April's eyes. 'I'm scared of him.'

'Has he hit you, Becky?'

'No, he hasn't hit me, but he stands over me and shouts and his voice is really loud and angry. I think he might hit me if I tell him to go, though. I'm really scared.'

Becky had started to tremble. She was clearly petrified of Colin, and it was clear that the emotional abuse she had endured had been far worse than April had realised.

'You don't need to worry, Becky. I can get you some help. I will send a domestic abuse officer from the police round to see you, who will advise you on the best way to sort this out. They can change the locks for you and give you a special phone to use for emergencies.'

'When he's gone, I want Freddie back. He needs to be back with his mummy. I know I hit him, but I never hit him before Colin came. He made me do it. It won't happen again, April, I promise.' She looked directly at April again, eyes pleading.

'I'm afraid it is not going to be quite as straightforward as that. It's obvious that you love Freddie very much and he loves you, but even though you have been honest about what has happened and I can see that you have been seriously controlled by Colin, can anyone be sure that you won't meet someone else like him? And then there's the baby; what do you plan to do about the baby?'

'I don't want Colin to have anything to do with the baby.'

'I'm very sorry, Becky, but I can't allow Freddie to come back to you, and in any case, it is not my decision now. The court will make the final decision on that, and at this stage I am unable to tell you what that decision might be. I would like to be able to say to you that you will get him back but I'm afraid I can't.'

Tears continued to stream down Becky's cheeks, and by the time she left, her eyes were red and swollen. Although what had happened to little Freddie was unacceptable, April couldn't help feeling sorry for Becky. She was a vulnerable young woman who April believed had an undiagnosed learning difficulty. She had not been able to recognise that she was being completely controlled and manipulated by Colin Lyons. He was older and, she thought, wiser, and had a bit of money to spend on her and her home. She had never had spare money before and it had been lovely to be free of the constant worry and strain of stretching her limited budget to keep herself and Freddie fed and clothed and to buy the essentials for the home. When Colin bought her a car, although it was an old one, she felt a huge sense of freedom and pride. She could take Freddie to places they couldn't hope to get to before, and she could drive everywhere rather than waiting for buses. Before Colin came into her life, a car had been an unreachable dream.

Whilst this did not excuse her child being physically assaulted, April could feel some empathy towards her. Becky really wanted the relationship to work and for a time genuinely believed that Colin loved her. She didn't like being on her own and she didn't like having no money. She desperately wanted to believe the best of Colin, and her lack of belief in her own abilities was enough to convince her that he did know better than her about how to be a parent, and that she was not doing a good job of being a mother. Thankfully it appeared that she had now come to her senses, and it was interesting that it seemed to be Freddie's father and grandmother who had finally forced her to see the reality of what had been happening. April was reeling at Becky's disclosure that it was actually her who had harmed Freddie and not Colin after all, but it was clearly her circumstances and his treatment of her which had caused her to lose control. April suspected that it was unlikely that Becky had ever or would have harmed Freddie if it wasn't for the situation she was in. In her defence, it was a misguided attempt to protect him. Despite a few irregularities in her story, April felt inclined to believe what Becky had described on the whole.

Although Becky had disclosed two major incidents whereby Freddie was assaulted, it was obvious that there had been many more of these, but April hadn't felt the need to ask further yet. Freddie was safe in foster care and her main concern for this interview had been to assist Becky in getting Colin Lyons out of her house. It was most unfortunate that there was the added complication of the baby, but the court would deal with that. They were not due back in court for another month so there was time to see how things panned out and whether Becky really did mean to get Colin out of her life. April wondered what Becky's parents would make of the situation with Freddie now. They had been taken in by Becky's excuses for the frequent injuries Freddie had sustained, and astonishingly continued to believe Colin Lyons was a good man and that their daughter was lucky to have found him. If there was to be any chance of Freddie returning home to his mum it would be important to find out where his grandparents stood now and whether Becky had told them the truth about what had been going on.

April's next task for the day was to visit Bradley at his foster carers' home. He needed to be told that he was going to have to move again. Nothing April had tried could persuade the carers to change their minds about giving notice. It was such a shame that a young boy had been rejected by his family and blamed for the behaviour he had developed due to their treatment of him, and then suffered serial rejection by foster carers. Sadly, though, it wasn't uncommon. Each separate rejection takes its toll and confirms for a child what they already know about themselves: that they are unlovable, worthless, and nobody gives a damn about them.

Bradley was still in bed when April arrived at 11.15am. Jackie was pacing around the living room with an exasperated look on her face.

'He came home earlier last night, but obviously under the influence of some substance. He was acting strange, raiding the fridge and giggling at God knows what. When I tried to talk to him, he just stared at me with a stupid grin on his face. At least this time he wasn't aggressive or confrontational. I have given him a shout this morning and told him you were coming but he doesn't seem to have taken any notice. Is there any news of a new placement for him, April? I don't like to be pushy but he is disrupting our whole family now, and we need him to go as soon as possible.'

April was disappointed to hear Jackie speaking like this. She had looked after many difficult children in the past and didn't give up easily.

'I don't think I'm going to find another foster placement for Bradley. Once carers hear how many placements have already broken down they are not going to want him. I'm wondering whether he needs to be in a therapeutic residential setting for the time being.'

'I would definitely say so. He is constantly oppositional and seems to do things which he knows will cause arguments; he just wears me down. I feel bad that I haven't been able to help him but I'm afraid it's beyond me.'

April had referred Bradley to the child mental health service but he was still on the waiting list and was likely to be waiting at least another six months, much to her annoyance.

Bradley eventually came downstairs and grunted at April as he walked past the lounge where she was sitting, into the kitchen. He made himself a cup of tea before coming back into the lounge and perching on the edge of the sofa, holding his steaming cup in both hands. He was leaning his thin, gangly body forward with his elbows resting on his knees, his thin grey jacket zipped up and the hood over his head, covering part of his face.

'Hello, Bradley, how are you?' April asked.

'Yeah, good,' he replied without looking up.

April made small talk with him for a bit, to give him a chance to drink his tea and wake up properly. She told Bradley that she had visited his mother, and asked him if he had seen her at all.

'Have I shit. I've got better things to be doing than going to that shithole.' There was no eye contact when he said this.

'I'm so sorry that you've had such a difficult time, Bradley. I can understand why you're so angry with everything; anyone would be in your shoes.' With a heavy heart, April began to tell him that his carers were not going to be able to continue looking after him, and that she was going to have to find him another placement. She could almost feel the pain of this news herself.

'Good, this is a shithole as well. When can I go?' was his brave-faced response.

'Things haven't worked out for you, Bradley. You need a lot of support to help you deal with things that have happened to you in the past, and unfortunately it hasn't been forthcoming. It isn't your fault that the mental health service has not been able to help you, and I'm disappointed that the waiting list is so long. I am going to recommend that you go to a residential unit where they have therapists and can provide you with an education. It will be good for you to go back into education, and you've never really managed in mainstream school. You need to be taught in a special school where the teachers have more time to focus on your needs.'

Bradley continued to sit in the same position with his hood over his eyes so that there was no chance of April seeing his expression. 'Fine, school is always crap anyway, the teachers are crap. They're the ones that need help, not me.'

April left Jackie's house feeling quite deflated. It would be nice to see things work out for Bradley in the end but it was hard to see how that would be. Although she tried not to take her work home with her, the sadness and tragedy of the everyday lives of the families and children she worked with and the poor prognosis for young people such as Bradley, took their toll. She always hoped for a happy ending and it was her natural optimism that kept her going. Thankfully, every now and again things did work out well, and these occasions made her job worthwhile. She did not consider adoption to be a happy ending because although it was good that children were removed from abusive and neglectful situations, and also for the adopters who gained a child, adoption was always brought about by heartache and pain and was the tragic result of a family torn apart. What she considered to be a happy ending was for the parents to make dramatic changes in their lives by engaging with the support they were offered, and enable themselves to provide adequate care for their children, ultimately keeping the family together and the children where they should be: at home with their birth family.

It was the end of the week and Jed was due home. It had been six days since April had sent the letter to Anthony Tuczemski, and she found that with each day that passed, sorting through the post became more fretful and nerve-racking. She sifted through the junk mail, and in amongst cards from conservatory companies and magazines advertising holidays, she found two letters. One was addressed to both her and Jed, and the other (which looked like a business letter, tax or something of that nature) to just Jed. The letter to both of them had a Social Services stamp and she opened it, believing it was probably something to do with the adoption process, most likely confirming Jenny's recommendation to the panel.

It wasn't what she was expecting, and the shock almost threw her off balance. The letter was from Jenny, and was brief and to the point.

> *Dear Mr and Mrs Gardiner,*
> *Re. your application to become adopters*
> *I hope you are both well. I am sorry to have to tell you that a*

decision has been made to place your application on hold for the time being. I have been advised by the service manager that due to there being outstanding issues in your personal life, i.e. April's father, it would not be advisable to complete the adoption process at this stage.

I wish you luck with your search for your father, April, and strongly advise that you seek counselling whatever the outcome. I am happy to discuss this further if you feel it would help, but in the meantime I wish you well with your enquiries and hope to hear from you in the near future with the news that the matter has been resolved so that that we can proceed.

Jenny Burrows
Adoption social worker

April walked into the kitchen and threw the letter down on the table. She stared at it as it lay in front of her, then picked it up and read it again in disbelief. They had been led to believe that they were almost at the end of the process and would soon be matched with a child. The shock of this totally unexpected news was followed by an overpowering surge of anger. Jenny had not given any indication that this might happen; they had been completely misled. April had agreed to and started counselling. As for her father, what if she wasn't able to find out more about him; what more could she do? Could this mean the whole thing would fall through? She felt intensely frustrated and wanted to cry. Jenny should have told them in person; this was really bad practice in April's opinion.

By the time Jed came home, April was in floods of tears. She had focused all her hopes and dreams of having a child on this process and now it had come to a very abrupt halt. It seemed to her that they were doomed not to have a child.

Jed was equally disappointed and unhappy with the way they had been informed but he didn't let on to April, and as always tried to remain positive. 'Don't forget, April, we haven't been rejected; just put on hold,' he said.

This didn't stop April from feeling rejected. She wasn't really thinking straight because the shock had sent her brain spinning. To her it seemed as though they had been rejected. What she was being asked to do was to some extent out of her control. If her father didn't reply to her letter or the man she had located wasn't even him, what then?

April had not told Jed about the letter she had sent to Anthony Tuczemski. For some reason she kept this to herself, just as she had not told him earlier about the enquiries she had made. She could not explain why she found it so difficult to talk to Jed about her father, how the situation made her feel and her hopes regarding him. There was something deep inside her subconscious that stopped her opening up and admitting how much it actually consumed her. She knew that a conversation about that was inevitable following the letter from Jenny, but she would face that when it came.

21

SAM

When Sam was not having contact with her children or attending one of her groups, she spent most of her time searching for someone to be with because being on her own was unbearable. She had made it up with Charlie and had gone back to her usual habit of sitting in her house for hours, just smoking cigarettes and watching television.

Charlie tried to offer advice about what she needed to do to get her children back. 'If it was me, I would make an official complaint about that April Gardiner to Citizens Advice. You could sue her for defamation of character.' She had recently read this phrase in the paper and wasn't really sure what it meant, but thought it seemed to fit the circumstances and sounded impressive.

'My solicitor is going to try to get them back for me anyway. There's another lady called a guardian who seems nice. April pretends to be nice but she's a two-faced liar. She says nice things to my face and then lies out of her arse in court. You should see some of the things she said about me in her report; talk about dragging up the past.' Sam ferociously jabbed a cigarette butt into the ashtray as she spoke, ash spilling over onto the tabletop.

'You should go to the paper. I read before where a social worker took someone's kids away, she hadn't done anything wrong either.

Social Services didn't deny it and they had to give them back in the end.'

'They've stopped my benefits now as well because I haven't got the kids with me. I've been to the Job Centre; they're saying it will be up to six weeks before I get any money. I don't know what they expect me to do till then. I'm already in trouble for rent arrears.'

'You could ask for a crisis loan.'

'They won't let me have another one. I had one before when they stopped my money 'cause someone told them that Curtis was living with me, which was a load of shit. I haven't paid it back yet 'cause I haven't got the money.'

Eventually Sam left Charlie's and started to make her way home. She couldn't really think of anywhere else she could go. Her mum and Wayne were disgusted that her children were in foster care. They were so embarrassed that they didn't want her coming anywhere near their house until she got herself sorted out. Sam had sensed a bad atmosphere when she was there anyway and was sure they had been arguing again. She had noticed a large bruise on the top of one of her mother's thin arms, and a cut to the side of her face.

It was late afternoon by the time she unlocked the door to her flat and let herself in, treading on a pile of letters which lay on the floor untouched. Looking through into the bedrooms, the beds were depressingly tidy, exactly as they had been that morning when she left, and since the children were taken from her. The deathly stillness of the unchanged and untouched rooms was cold and accusing, like a punishment she had to endure. She had always disliked this flat, but now it felt cursed. She wanted to be away from here, but where could she go? She picked up the post and started to sift through it, throwing most of it aside. There was a brown envelope stamped Briar's Property Agents, which she looked at apprehensively. Without opening it she had a good idea what it would be; she had been expecting it for weeks. When she finally opened it, it was just as she had expected: a letter terminating her tenancy due to the rent arrears which had accumulated over the last year. She had one month to either pay the two thousand pounds in full, or hand the keys back and leave the premises. The letter threatened that if she failed to do either of these, legal action would be taken, which could result in considerable added costs to cover legal fees.

Sam left the flat, slamming the door behind her. As she walked, she was overcome by a feeling of helpless despair. She had lost control of everything in her life and she had nowhere and no one to turn to. There was a late-August chill in the air and goose bumps covered her bare arms and legs, but she was numb to the cold. She was too busy thinking; there were a million and one voices, all pushing their way forward at the same time. Unfortunately, not one of them was telling her what she could do to put things right. Her thoughts were dominated by what a complete failure she was and how badly she had screwed up her life and her children's lives. She felt like a walking disaster and was coming to the conclusion that her children would be better off without her. Not for the first time in her life, she contemplated ending it all. She loved the idea of being dead; no more grief, no more anger eating away at her from the inside. Death itself held no fear for her, but the fear of the process of dying was enough to keep her struggling on.

By the time she reached the park she had decided that there was no use trying any more; she felt weak and helpless against the might of the statutory authorities and could see no way forward. Her friends were already in their favourite spot and were clearly having a great time. She could see Damien playing a tune by banging two empty cans together, and Ronnie and Kate dancing. They were laughing so much they nearly fell over, causing cider to spill out of the can Kate was holding.

The next day, April was on her way to pick Bradley up to take him to see his residential placement, when she got the message from the social work assistant saying that Sam hadn't turned up for contact. She felt her heart sink.

At the residential unit, Bradley met some of the care workers and was shown the room which was going to be his: small and rectangular with a bed, a wardrobe and a little bedside table. The walls were painted pink and the thin, coarse carpet was orange.

'Don't worry, Bradley; I will arrange for you to have your own television, and when you have brought all your things over it will look quite cosy.'

Bradley made no comment; he rarely showed emotion and April could only guess what he must be feeling. A residential placement for a young person was always something that would only be considered when everything else had failed. The staff in such units generally did their best but were not able to provide anything that resembled a nurturing family environment. They were often young, lacked proper training, and staff turnover was high.

After dropping Bradley back at Jackie's, April drove straight around to Fairfield Rise. She rang the bell a few times but there was no answer. This wasn't unusual; Sam often took some time to answer the door. After a few attempts, she rang her number, which usually worked.

'Hi, this is Sam. Leave a message and I'll get back.'

April left a message asking Sam to phone her. She didn't want to just walk away from the flat without any idea where Sam could be. It was uncharacteristic for her not to turn up for contact, and April was worried about her. She strolled around a bit, wondering about trying Sam's mother's, but thought better of it, knowing the difficult relationship they had. She then made a decision to call at Charlie's house just on the off chance; it happened to be on April's route home.

It was never dull driving around Coronation Estate. There was always something going on. This evening it seemed that two women had fallen out over their children. April could see a scrawny woman with hardly any clothes on and dyed blonde hair pointing a finger at another, smaller woman who, judging by her expression, was shouting angrily back at the thin woman. There were three children of various ages also shouting at each other from behind their respective parents.

April knocked at Charlie's door and a young boy of about eight answered. She assumed this was Indigo, Charlie's son.

'Mum, there's an old lady at the door. I think it's that social worker,' he shouted.

April felt most indignant at being called an old lady, but thankfully when Charlie came to the door she told Indigo off, telling him not to be so cheeky and that the lady at the door was not old.

'Hello, Charlie, sorry to bother you but I'm trying to find Sam. I wondered if you have any idea where I might find her? I've been to her flat but couldn't get an answer.'

'No, sorry, I don't know where she is; she was here yesterday but I haven't seen her since. She was really fed up. I probably shouldn't tell you this but...' Charlie opened the door wide and, after looking over April's shoulder, possibly to make sure no one could see that she was inviting a social worker into her house, gestured for her to come in. 'I don't want to get her into trouble or anything, but I think you should know that she's going to lose her flat. I think she was pissed off with everything yesterday. When she's pissed off, what she does is go and get pissed.' This obviously amused Charlie, who laughed loudly. 'She'll be with those homeless people drinking in Princess Park. I bet that's where she is.'

April wasn't sure about Charlie's reason for telling her this; whether it was because she was genuinely concerned for her friend, or because she relished getting her into trouble. She wanted to believe that Charlie meant well. 'Thank you, Charlie; it's good that you told me about this. If she is drinking in the park, she needs help and keeping it a secret wouldn't help her would it? You did the right thing.'

April turned to leave and Charlie followed her to the front door, using what little time she had left to do her duty and report all she knew about Sam. 'That's why I thought I would tell you. She does it all the time; she used to do it when she had the kids with her. I don't think she can look after those girls, to tell you the truth.'

'Thank you very much, Charlie, you've been really helpful,' April said as she walked down the drive towards her car.

'I thought it best to let you know the truth because she's my friend and I feel really sorry for her,' Charlie persisted.

'Goodbye, and thanks again.'

April got in the car and drove round to Princess Park. She parked the car at the side of the road and walked through the iron gates onto the long winding pathway. Dark clouds raced across the sky and the air felt damp and cold. The park was quiet and still, and the only sound was the rustling of leaves as they moved with the wind. She could not hear any voices or see any sign of life, not even a dog walker. If Sam had been in the park she wasn't there now; all April could do was wait and see what happened on Thursday when she was due to have contact again.

As April was expecting, Sam never turned up for the next contact. April tried to ring her but her phone went straight to voicemail again. She had left a couple of messages asking Sam to phone but nothing came of it so she didn't bother leaving any more. It was sad watching the disappointment on the children's faces as they waited for their mum in the Family Centre, before being bundled back into the car to return to their foster placement.

Tayla was full of questions about where her mum might be, and some of the things she suggested were quite enlightening. 'Curtis might have hit Mummy and she's had to go to the 'ospital.'

'Don't worry, Tayla,' Karen said soothingly. 'I'm sure Mummy will be all right. If Mummy was in hospital April would have been told before now.'

'The policeman might have taken her to prison for being pissed.'

This amused April but as far as she was aware, Sam had never been in hospital as a result of a domestic abuse episode, and she didn't think Sam had ever been arrested for being drunk. There was always a lot more going on than a social worker would know about, but Tayla's worries more likely stemmed from her inner fears which had festered as a result of things she had witnessed whilst in the care of her mother. Social workers often found out a lot they wouldn't otherwise have known about by talking to the children.

22

TWIN BROTHER MAX

April and Jed were planning to visit their parents again at the weekend. April's brother Max was home. He was a psychiatrist and his wife, Joanna, was a paediatrician. They led extremely busy lives, and much to April's disgust their two children, who were only twelve and fourteen, were in boarding school. Joanna was not maternal and should never have had children, April thought, trying hard not to be bitter. Thankfully Joanna wouldn't be coming with Max this time.

As usual Diana was waiting by the door when they arrived, looking attractive and glamorous for her sixty-one years. She clenched each of them in a tight squeeze before letting them into the house. There was the usual delicious aroma of baking wafting from the kitchen, mingling with the welcoming smell of burning applewood from the wood burner in the lounge. It really wasn't cold enough to have the fire going but this would be Diana's idea of making them feel welcome.

It was lovely to see Max again. The twins rarely got the chance to get together these days, being caught up with their own respective lives. Jed and Max had always got on really well and they planned to go out for a round of golf whilst April and her mum did what they loved doing: window shopping in town. Diana served up sardine and tomato paninis, followed by homemade apple and cinnamon tartlets. It was too hot to sit in the lounge with the heat from the wood burner, even though the windows were open, so they sat in the conservatory to eat lunch. They chatted happily whilst they ate, but all April could think about was how she was going to get Max on his own. They had never spoken about their father as the taboo had permeated into their inner selves, becoming part of their make-up. April had always wondered how something that had never actually been voiced could have been so powerful in controlling this aspect of their lives, so that even as children they just knew that you didn't talk about Dad.

She was determined to find out what Max thought about it all and, crucially, whether he had any information she didn't have. She hadn't yet decided if she was going to tell him about the letter she had written in case he disapproved. She wasn't even certain that he would agree to talk about their father. He might be like Diana and just refuse to discuss the subject. She had decided to tread carefully, testing the water before jumping in. Finding out about her father had been somewhat on her mind for years, but it had now become potentially life-changing.

April and Diana had stopped to look in a shop window when April felt a hand touch her shoulder. She whirled round with a start and there before her was Catherine with her baby.

'Hi, April, it's so nice to see you again,' she gushed.

April's heart sank. Catherine really was the last person she wanted to see at this time, and she especially didn't want to have to look at her baby again. She somehow managed to smile. 'Hi, Catherine, lovely to see you. I can't believe we've bumped into each other again. We didn't see each other for years, and then twice within a couple of months. Isn't life strange? How is… um…' to her excruciating embarrassment, she had forgotten the baby's name, 'the baby?' She looked into the pushchair, and there before her was the sweetest little girl you could ever see. She had a cuddly rabbit tucked under one arm and the first two fingers of her other hand in her smiling mouth. She was making little chuckling noises as she looked up from her pillow at April with her large, pale blue eyes. She was covered in warm blankets but her little legs were kicking away gleefully underneath them, all because April was looking at her.

'Melody', Catherine reminded her, good naturedly.

April had to admit, Melody was the most endearing little girl, and looking at the pride on Catherine's face she was very aware that she was awaiting the gushing admiration for her beautiful child that she was accustomed to hearing. But instead of the expected praise, out of the blue, April found herself saying, 'I'm so glad I don't have to spend my days looking after a bundle of energy like she clearly is.' This was out of her mouth before she had time to think, and she noticed her mother looking at her, agape. At the same time, April noticed the look of enlightenment which had sprung up on Catherine's face. April's disappointment and pain around her childlessness were laid bare, as clearly as if she had told Catherine everything. As they said their goodbyes she could see the compassion in Catherine's eyes, and this was excruciating.

Nothing more was said between April and her mum about this incident. April was exasperated with herself, firstly for being nasty to her friend, but mainly for allowing her innermost pain to be so transparent. Her period was due, and she put it down to this. There was the familiar swelling in her stomach, along with the fluctuating moods.

Max and Jed returned from their round of golf, rosy-cheeked and windswept. They of course had stopped at the nineteenth hole for a swift half. April was always pleased and happy that her beloved twin brother and her husband got on so well, but this time all she could think about was that she needed to talk to Max. She suddenly had the flash of inspiration she had been craving. 'I've got an idea,' she said. 'Why don't we get a takeaway this evening? Max and I can go and collect it. It will save you cooking, Mum.'

'I wasn't thinking of cooking; I was thinking of taking you all out for dinner.'

'I was thinking of taking you all out for dinner too,' Max said.

April couldn't do much but go along with everyone else. She would need to devise another plan.

They agreed to go to the local Italian, which was within walking distance. It was a perfect evening for a walk. The leaves were starting to fall from the trees and the earlier rainfall had soaked them as they lay on the ground. They squelched underfoot as the family walked together, sweet autumnal fragrances filling the air. Although it was early evening, dusk was falling, reminding them that summer had ended. Diana was a regular at Giovanni's and they were made very welcome by Giovanni himself, who made a point of coming to their table to greet them all.

After a long, enjoyable evening, they were on their way home, and April finally saw her opportunity to talk to Max. She said to Jed, 'Why don't you and Mum walk ahead? I would love to have a chat with my brother. We haven't had any time together at all; do you mind?'

Jed didn't mind at all, especially as he guessed immediately what April was up to. He walked ahead quite happily, distracting Diana with his entertaining chatter.

'Right! I am going to come straight out with it, Max; I'm going to tell you everything.' April told him about her struggles to conceive, about the IVF and the adoption plan.

Max was genuinely surprised. 'I have to admit, April, I never had any inclination that all this was going on. I just thought you and Jed were enjoying your work too much to have babies at the moment. It's not too late is it? I mean…it could still happen couldn't it?'. He was looking quizzically at her.

'Yes, but because of the problems we have had and the years we have been trying with no success, we have been told we have unexplained infertility. We have been through too much and don't want to go down the path of trying again. We want to adopt, but there's a problem.' April went on to explain what had happened.

Max remained quiet as they carried on walking. Jed and Diana were chatting and laughing and April could see that Diana was perfectly oblivious to what was going on behind them. They were fast approaching home, and April took hold of Max's arm to hold him back.

'I'm not going in until you tell me everything you know.'

'I promise you, all I know is that he went off with another woman and Mum never saw or heard from him again, and never wanted to as far as I'm aware.'

'Has it never occurred to you that it's a bit odd, how she would never talk about him? I can understand how angry she must have been, but anger doesn't usually last for more than thirty years. I tried to talk about him when we went to France but she just blanked me. Have you ever wondered, Max; about him, I mean?'

'Of course. I wonder sometimes what he looks like and all that, but I haven't ever thought about trying to contact him or, even worse, asking Mum about him.'

'What do you think I should do?' Max had always had the most sensible ideas when they were young. He was only 20 minutes older than her but she looked up to him still. She desperately needed some good advice, and in this matter she could think of no one better to give it than Max.

Although they were twins, they looked nothing like each other, in terms of features or colouring; apart from their unusual eye colour which was a striking blue with flecks of green and yellow. Max focused his colourful, intelligent eyes on April as he gave serious thought to what she was asking.

'I'm really sorry, April. I just can't think of a way round this. I think you are just going to have to hope you get a reply to your letter, or if not, just keep trying to find him. You know as well as I do that I will get the same response as you if I try to bring it up with Mum.'

As Max said these words, April felt her head spin. She stood still for a moment with her feet firmly on the ground, trying to steady herself. All this was getting a bit too much for her.

23

TRAGEDY

Back in the office on Monday morning, as usual April's own troubles were forgotten as she absorbed herself in the more serious issues of her clients. If ever she started to feel sorry for herself, she would just remind herself that although she hadn't got everything she wished for, and life wasn't exactly perfect, she was extremely lucky compared to many, including the families she worked with. Even the disappointment of, after two weeks, not receiving a reply from the man she was sure was her father was wiped from her mind as she scrolled through her emails, selecting the ones she could see needed to be addressed. Luckily there was nothing that couldn't be left until later in the day, because she was planning to pay a visit to Becky. They were due back in court in a week's time and the court had asked for an update on Becky's circumstances. April was just about to shut her computer down, ready to be on her way, when an email pinged through from the district mental health crisis team. It was to do with Tina Jones, Martha and Ben's mum. Damn, she thought. This probably means that Martha and Ben are back in foster care. In which case, she would need to visit them today. This was most inconvenient because her day was already completely full.

April gasped loudly as she read the email. 'Oh my God, this is just terrible. Oh my God!' she repeated, clasping her hands to her mouth. The email reported that Tina had taken an overdose in the night and was currently in a coma. Her condition was described as critical. Ben and Martha were back with their foster carers.

Maria, who had been talking to Sarah at another desk, stopped what she was doing and came straight over to April. 'What is it, April?'

'It's Tina Jones,' April gasped, 'Martha and Ben's mum. She's taken an overdose. I knew she didn't look right when she was discharged. I should have questioned it. I wasn't happy with the way she looked. I didn't say anything. I had so much going on I lost sight of it, and now, oh my God, she could die.'

'April, it's not your fault. You're a social worker, not a mental health professional. If they discharged her and she wasn't well it's their fault, not yours,' Maria reassured her.

April was not convinced. She was thinking about little Ben and Martha and how frightened they must be for their mum. She couldn't help thinking she had let them down. She was keen to see Martha and Ben to talk to them about what had happened, but needed to contact the hospital to find out how their mum was first. Although it was a terrible shock and April was very worried about the children, this was coupled with frustration that once again her plans for the day had been disrupted. How lovely it would be if now and again her day went exactly as planned. She took a deep breath before picking up the phone and dialling the number of the intensive care ward which was included in the email. She waited patiently whilst the phone continued its prolonged and repetitive ringing. She eventually gave up and put the phone down, sighing as she placed her head in her hands. She could feel a headache coming on.

She went into the kitchen to make herself a strong cup of coffee and get herself together before giving it another try. There was still no answer. 'This is ridiculous!' she exclaimed as she thrust the phone back in its holder. 'I can't go to see the children if I don't know how their mum is.'

Maria heard her. 'Why don't you do your visit to Becky, then try again later? Ben and Martha are safe and they will have been told what has happened by the out-of-hours social worker.'

It was helpful for April to have someone think for her on this occasion because her head felt all over the shop. 'You're right. That's what I'll do. Thank you, Maria.'

'Have that coffee before you go, though,' Maria said bossily.

At Becky's house, April rang the bell. Whilst she waited, she looked around for signs of Colin Lyons as she half-expected him to be there. There was no dirty white van in the drive or in the road, which was a good sign, she thought to herself. She was taken by complete surprise when the door opened and there in front of her was Freddie's dad, Leon. It took April a few seconds to take in what she was seeing.

'Oh! Leon, I wasn't expecting to see you.'

Leon looked just as surprised to see April. Behind him stood Becky, and April watched her as a pink flush spread from the nape of her neck, over her chin and across her cheeks. She was clearly feeling caught out.

'I forgot you were coming,' Becky said.

'That's OK, don't worry. Is it all right for me to come in?'

Leon opened the door wider and stood aside to make room for her to enter.

Becky made April a cup of tea whilst the three of them chatted about Freddie and what he had been doing at his foster placement. During the course of their conversation, April couldn't help noticing how relaxed and at home Leon appeared. He was slouched in an armchair, dressed in baggy shorts, and his feet were bare.

'I'm glad to see you are friends again. Have you been visiting Becky often, Leon?'

Becky did her usual open-mouthed stare, but Leon said proudly, 'Me and Becky are back together. She kicked me out before 'cause I was drinking too much.' He leaned forward in the chair, and with strong hand gestures explained, 'It wasn't easy, I tell yer. I went through detox, had all the horrors; spiders crawling up the walls, scratching my skin till it bled, couldn't eat or sleep for weeks. I did it, though; I did it for my lad. He needs his dad. If it wasn't for him, I would be in the gutter now, or dead.'

'That's why I kicked him out before,' Becky said encouragingly.

It then occurred to April that there was a marked change in Becky. Whereas before she had seemed petrified of everyone and everything, cowering behind a thick, dark mask of make-up and never looking up from the floor when she talked, she was now giving direct eye contact and there was a spark of renewed confidence in her demeanour.

Whilst they talked, April observed the relationship between Becky and Leon and there was a clear mutual respect between them. Not only did Becky appear to have had a complete personality change; the atmosphere in the house seemed relaxed, a stark contrast to when Colin Lyons was there, despite his unremitting attempts to present himself as a caring partner and an overall decent human being. Leon was just himself, which April judged was honest, open and genuinely caring. She felt her natural optimism rising. She could envisage Freddie here with his parents; however, she reminded herself sharply of what Becky had done. She would have to make recommendations to the court and it was not going to be an easy decision to make, bearing in mind what had happened.

When April left Becky's, the first thing she did was telephone the hospital to find out about Tina Jones. To her annoyance, the person on the other end of the line refused to tell her anything over the phone. She had to attend the unit in person and show her ID. She gave a loud and deep sigh of frustration as she started the engine, released the handbrake and headed off towards the hospital.

Once there, she showed her ID card and was immediately directed into a small room to the rear of the specialist care unit. She was left waiting for at least ten minutes, increasing her pent-up annoyance and frustration. Effort had been made to make this room homely and comfortable, with a flecked green fitted carpet and cream curtains at the tiny window. There was a small settee and an armchair, both covered in loose floral throws. Apart from a tiny round coffee table at the side there was nothing else, not even a magazine.

Finally, a small, plump dark-haired woman in a white coat entered, shook April's hand and introduced herself as Dr Chopra. April had been impatiently pacing around the room and Dr Chopra asked if she would like to sit down. By the solemn expression on the doctor's face, April could guess that what she was about to be told would not be good news. The doctor sat down on the small armchair opposite April and looked directly into her eyes.

'I'm sorry to have to tell you, Mrs Gardiner, but Tina Jones passed away less than an hour ago. We have notified her next of kin, and someone who says she is her step-grandmother is on her way.'

April's hands flew to her face. All she could think about were the bubbly, happy little children who, at three and four were now in effect orphans, as nobody knew who their father was. It was a rare occurrence but just then April found herself wishing she was anything else but a social worker; sometimes the job was just too sad to bear. At least they had Gwen, who she hoped would offer them a permanent home. As she stood up, she felt her head spinning again. I need another holiday, she thought.

Thankfully April was accompanied by a tremendous bereavement counsellor when she broke the news to Martha and Ben. She was impressed by the way the counsellor dealt with this enormously difficult situation as she took over the task from April, and stunned by the calm way in which the children accepted what had happened. She herself had been struggling to hold back tears as they were told, but as she observed the skilful way in which they were told the news, and their calm responses, she felt more at ease. The counsellor explained that the first symptom of bereavement is usually disbelief and Ben and Martha would not have conceptualised what had happened. The process would be a long one and they would continue to need support and counselling for many years to come.

To April's further dismay, Gwen, the foster carer, wanted to let her know that the children would not be able to stay with her for the long term. Although she was fond of them, she was a respite carer and had no plans to change this. April would have to consider looking for adopters for them, but at the moment they needed to be given time to grieve and to start to come to terms with what had happened.

April was exhausted when she finally got home that evening, way after 6pm. As usual she sifted quickly through the post, searching for the letter she was longing to receive. Once again there was nothing. She had gone through various emotions whilst waiting for this letter, which began with hope, excitement and confidence that she would get a response. This gradually gave way to hope without the excitement, and now had become a strange mix of emotions including disappointment without any hope. As she put the last letter down on the small hall table without opening it, she wondered what she could do. She was starting to accept that either the man she had contacted was not her father, or he was her father but did not want to know her. She still hadn't told Jed about the letter she had sent, so couldn't talk about it with him.

She suddenly found herself overwhelmed by anger which rose from the pit of her stomach, taking her completely by surprise. How could a father walk out on his children and not even wonder how they are, or what kind of lives they have? The anger then focused on her mother who refused to talk about it. What hopeless parents I have been lumbered with. Why have I been so unlucky? She knew deep down that these thoughts were totally irrational and more to do with the daily disappointment she faced each time she opened the post, coupled with the premenstrual hormones surging around her body.

By the time Jed came home she had showered and got into her pyjamas. It had been another exhausting day which had taken its toll emotionally and physically. She was still feeling shaken up by the shock of Tina Jones's death and having to tell her children. As she walked into the kitchen to take the casserole out of the oven, she suddenly had another spell of dizziness.

Jed was walking behind her and noticed her sway. 'April, what's wrong?' he said, looking concerned.

'Oh, it's just exhaustion; work has been quite challenging lately. I've had a few dizzy spells. I've had a death today. Mother of two very young children, took an overdose.'

Jed placed his hands on her shoulders and turned her round to face him. He was looking at her with his warm, caring eyes.

'April, you don't look right. I know you have had a lot going on but I'm worried about you. Perhaps you should see the doctor.'

'I could do, I suppose. I'm wondering if I'm anaemic again. I have to admit I have been feeling really tired.'

'Well, it won't hurt to go, will it?' Jed said assertively.

'OK, I will. I can't go tomorrow because I'm too busy, but I will go to the drop-in session on Friday morning.'

Jed knew better than to argue with her.

24

FINAL CONTACT

On Tuesday, April planned to spend the morning catching up with her never-ending paperwork. She could see a list of emails as usual waiting to be read, and there was a message on her answerphone. She picked up the receiver and pressed the button to listen.

'I want to see my kids.' The voice sounded gravelly and was almost inaudible but April could tell immediately that it was Sam. 'I need to see them. I haven't seen them for ages 'cause of you lot. Phone me back or I'm going to the police.'

April couldn't help being slightly amused by the irony in this message. She returned the call, but once again it went straight to voicemail.

'Hello, Sam, it's April here. I have been trying to contact you for weeks. I need to see you to discuss how we can resume contact. Can you give me a ring, please? I will be in the office all morning if you can get yourself here.'

April started reading a report from Bradley's key worker which had come by email, updating her on how things were going for him. He had been registered with the special school and was due to start on Monday. The staff had been trying to encourage him to come out of his room and join in with the other young people but he was refusing to. He was only coming downstairs for his meals and then going straight back to his room to play on his PlayStation. There was no social interaction with anyone else in the home but it was early days and they were hoping this would change. April hoped it would improve for him; she couldn't bear to think of him alone and isolated.

There was a frenetic atmosphere in the office, with tap-tapping on keyboards, phones ringing and people talking. Paula's head was down as she typed away, completely absorbed in her work. April wanted to know how things were going with her new man but she knew better than to disturb her friend's concentration. She was probably trying to finish a statement for court which, knowing Paula, had been due in a week ago. Just as April was thinking about stopping for a sandwich, a call came through to say that Samantha Bushell was asking to see her.

April met her in reception and led her into the small interview room. Much as she tried, she couldn't stop staring at Sam. She was shocked at the change in her appearance. She had two new piercings on her upper lip with black spikes jutting from them. Her hair had been dyed and instead of charcoal black was now a mishmash of matted copper with burgundy streaks, which could have looked quite stunning on healthy hair and if it had been professionally done. Her face looked battered and weather-worn, with deep criss-crossing lines etched into her skin. Her appearance was startling and macabre in that she looked like an adolescent girl with an elderly woman's face. April did not need to be told what kind of lifestyle she had been leading since she had disengaged with the services; the evidence before her was loud and clear.

'When can I see my kids?' Sam demanded before she had even sat down.

'I'm afraid, Sam, that you can't just come back into their lives. They haven't seen you for three weeks and I need to be sure you intend to turn up regularly again before another session can take place.'

Sam fidgeted on her seat and was clearly becoming agitated. 'Are you saying I can't see my own kids? Who do you think you are? You haven't got any right to stop me. I want another social worker.' She was working herself up into quite a frenzy, and April was glad the table and chairs were fixed to the ground. She had never seen Sam lose her temper before, but she was becoming increasingly volatile. April felt certain that it wasn't just alcohol she had been using.

'Would you like to tell me what's been happening with you since I last saw you?'

'What the fuck has it got to do with you? I just want to see my kids,' Sam snarled.

'As I said, it's not as easy as that. I need to get a picture of what has been going on and why you have failed to turn up for the last three weeks.'

'I've had problems.'

'What kind of problems, Sam? You need to be honest with me. I would like to help you if I can but I can't do anything unless you tell me what's been going on.'

Like a child in a strop, Sam folded her arms tightly and turned her face away from April. 'I'm gonna be slung on the streets.'

'Oh, I'm sorry to hear that, Sam,' April said with genuine sympathy. So Charlie was telling the truth, about this anyway. 'How did that come about?'

Sam continued staring at the wall as she started to explain the problems she had been having with her benefits. April was not a bit surprised by what she heard because it wasn't the first time she had seen this kind of situation with her families, especially when their children had been removed from their care. All of a sudden, their financial situation changed and they found themselves in trouble through no real fault of their own. April scolded Sam appropriately for the way she had dealt with her problems, but offered to write a letter of support. She didn't expect that it would make any difference but she had no other suggestions to make. It might give Sam some hope and maybe just enough to stop her going off on another bender for a few weeks.

April told Sam that she must phone the office before 8.30 on Monday morning to confirm that she would be attending the contact, and that if she didn't phone first it wouldn't happen. She would begin by having contact once a week and they would take it from there.

Sam's initial aggression had waned and she was more submissive, agreeing with everything April suggested, desperate to see her two little girls again. 'Have they been missing me?' she asked tearfully.

'Of course they have; and you have to think about what it's like for them if they are waiting for you at the Family Centre and you don't turn up. Tayla was very worried, thinking that something terrible had happened to you.' April detected a small flicker of shame as it passed over Sam's face.

There wasn't much time to ponder over Sam's situation, although she did as she promised and sent a letter to the landlord asking if there was any way Sam could be helped to pay off the arrears and keep her flat. It was difficult because she couldn't give any information regarding Sam's circumstances which possibly could have helped. As it was, she felt certain it was a lost cause.

On Friday morning April dragged herself out of bed. She had slept really badly and consequently felt more tired than she had before going to bed. She felt a bit better after a nice hot shower, but looking in the mirror she could see what Jed meant when he'd said she looked pale. She pulled her short curly hair back from her face to have a closer look. She didn't look like herself; her skin, which was naturally fresh-looking with a touch of pink in her cheeks, had turned a pasty white. Instead of her usual healthy glow, her face was thin and drawn. She had questioned why she needed to go to the doctor's when all that was wrong with her was tiredness, but when she looked at herself in the mirror, her reflection, coupled with the dizzy spells she had been experiencing, convinced her that she needed to go.

It was always a pain waiting to see the duty doctor because you could never tell how long you were going to wait. She had brought her phone with her so that she could deal with emails as time was always precious. Surprisingly, she was called in after a short wait, although the person she was seeing was only a nurse practitioner, but to be fair, she seemed to be a competent young woman. Her blood pressure was taken and questions asked: 'Do you smoke? How much alcohol do you drink?' All the usual suspects for poor health. The nurse practitioner sat back at the desk and was facing April, awaiting her responses. The nurse then turned towards her computer and began moving the mouse around, clearly looking at April's medical history.

'I would guess your problem is that you're anaemic. I will do a blood test and send it for analysis. You may need a prescription for a low dose of iron. Then, 'When was your last period?'

April needed to think about this for some time. She never kept a record because her periods were so erratic it didn't mean anything. Ever since she was a young girl her periods had been all over the place.

'I would say it was probably around two months ago.' She tried to remember what she was doing when she had her last period.

'Could it be possible that you're pregnant?' the nurse asked, looking at her quizzically.

'Oh! No, of course not. I've got unexplained infertility. We were trying for years and nothing happened. I've had IVF and a miscarriage. I'm sure it can't be that.'

'I'm just saying, don't rule it out.'

It seemed unbelievable but this had not occurred to April at all. She looked back at the nurse in astonishment. A brief wave of excitement and hope passed over her, but red lights were flashing in her brain as she remembered the roller-coaster ride of hope, pain, disappointment, grief and anger from past experiences. She didn't want to go through that again. She had given up any hope of ever having her own child and had to some extent learned to live with it. She just could not cope with another bitter disappointment. She hurried out of the surgery fully intending to forget the suggestion that had been made. As far as she was concerned, it could not be true and if it was she would just be petrified that she would have another miscarriage.

By the time April pulled up outside her house she had already reasoned with herself that she was not pregnant. Why would she be pregnant now after all these years? She had never had regular periods in her life, so nothing had changed. She came to her senses and decided to ignore the nurse's unlikely suggestion, which after all was only speculation based on the fact that she was late with her period, which, April was aware, for her meant nothing.

25

FREDDIE'S FINAL HEARING

It was the final hearing for Freddie, and as always April arrived at the court in plenty of time. She had visited Becky and Leon a number of times and completed an assessment on their relationship and parenting capacity. She gave serious consideration to the positive facts including the couple's relationship with each other and with Freddie. They had previously been together for three years and had only ended the relationship because of Leon's alcohol misuse. He had sought support and counselling and had not drunk alcohol for over two years, so this was no longer an issue. They clearly got on really well and Becky seemed like someone reborn since Leon came back into her life. Taking these things into account, as well as the secure attachment Freddie continued to have with his mother and father, April had made the decision to recommend that Freddie was returned to his parents.

She was very much aware that there was still an element of risk and there was the potential for it to go wrong, particularly if Becky and Leon split up in the future. On balance April felt the risk was worth taking. Although one can never be certain about anything, she felt that Becky would not let herself get into the situation she had been in with Colin Lyons again. She had recognised that what had happened to Freddie was wrong, and even though it turned out to be Becky herself who was hitting him it was her fear and the control that Colin Lyons had over her that had led to that situation. She had been wrong but she had now put that right, and to April that was important. Leon had said he was happy to be a stepfather to the new baby and April fully believed he was a genuine, caring man. His limited cognitive ability would not be a barrier to him being a good father. The couple would likely require ongoing support and April intended to ask the court to make a Supervision Order, which authorises the Local Authority to stay involved for a year. With this order in place Freddie could be brought back into care at any time. Although April really hoped that would not be necessary, caution was always best when it came to a child's safety.

April, dressed in her dark grey court attire, was standing in the main waiting area looking out for the Local Authority barrister when she noticed the guardian, Angela, walk in. Angela was a tall, stout woman with a strong Nigerian accent which was sometimes difficult to understand. She could be quite overbearing with her loud voice and strong opinions. April acknowledged her and Angela came over to where she was standing.

'Do you fancy going upstairs for a coffee, April? We're a bit early. Knowing the barristers, they're not likely to appear for at least another hour. It's funny how their trains from London always seem to be late.'

April agreed, and together they walked up the stairs to the cafe.

'You go and get us a table while I get the coffees. There's one over there, look,' Angela bellowed, pointing to one of many empty tables with her large, colourfully clad arm. 'I'll get some croissants for us as well; do you prefer chocolate or plain?'

'Not for me, Angela. I don't really feel very hungry at the moment; just a coffee will be nice, thanks.'

'What's wrong? You've gone a funny colour,' Angela remarked.

'I'm just a bit off colour at the moment, not eating much.'

'OK, then I'll have two. I'll eat yours as well.'

April laughed at this as the croissants hadn't even been bought yet. 'Good idea,' she agreed.

Angela had hardly put the coffees on the table before launching in with her views about the case. 'I have seen what you're recommending, April, and I'm afraid to say I can't agree with you. I think it would be too much of a risk to put Freddie back with that mother and to leave the baby in her care. I was really surprised when I read your statement. Wouldn't it be better to be safe than sorry and have them both adopted?' Her voice was so loud, people at some of the other tables turned around to listen.

April was astonished by her attitude and the fact that she was discussing this confidential situation in the middle of a busy cafe. 'Don't you think we should wait until our legal people get here to discuss this, Angela?'

'I know we should really,' Angela said with a half-smile, 'but it's always nice if the guardian can agree with the social worker; it just makes life a lot easier. I was sure you would have the same view as me.'

'I suppose that's the nature of our work, isn't it? We'll just have to both present our evidence and let the magistrates decide. I'm sure the right decision will be made in the end.'

Their barristers arrived and the four of them, along with Becky's solicitor, spent the next hour in a little room trying to find some common ground. If April was to come around to the guardian's way of thinking and agree to a plan for adoption, the outcome would be more or less cut and dried. The magistrates would be highly unlikely to go against both the guardian and the social worker; however, April was not going to give in because she was convinced she was right. She had made her decision and she was going to stick to it.

When they finally came out of the room, April spotted Becky and Leon standing in a corner of the waiting area. With them were Becky's parents. Becky spotted April and called her over, but it was her father who spoke. He was a short, thin man, hardly taller than April, dressed in a shabby grey suit which looked a size too big for him. His wife Sue was also short but stout, and dressed in a wide grey coat which came below her knees, and white trainers.

'We've read your statement, April. I just can't tell you how grateful we are. We thought we were going to lose our grandson. We just couldn't bear that, could we, Sue?' he said, turning to his wife, who didn't speak but shook her head vigorously. It then occurred to April that she had hardly ever heard Sue speak.

'You need to understand,' she cautioned them, 'that nothing has been agreed yet. The final decision will be made by the magistrates, who will listen to what everyone has to say. The guardian has a different view as to what should happen. I sincerely hope that the magistrates agree with me, but I will warn you that magistrates place a lot of weight on the evidence of guardians because they are employed by the court to be independent advocates for the children in court proceedings.'

It was immediately clear to April by the stunned looks on all of their faces that they had not realised either that the guardian was opposing April's recommendations, or that her views were so important.

As April turned to leave, Becky caught hold of her arm. 'What do you think will happen, April? Will he come back to me, and will I be able to keep the baby?' She focused pleading eyes on April's face.

'I'm sorry, Becky, I really can't say. All we can do is wait and see.' With that she left them watching her in silence as she walked back to where the Local Authority barrister was standing.

The hearing was held in a small courtroom, which had rows of seats, enough for about thirty people; a platform for the magistrates and next to this, a witness stand. The only people present were Freddie's family, April, Angela, the barristers who took up the front row, and the court advisor who sat in front of the magistrates. As the three magistrates entered, everyone was asked to stand and the silence was broken by the sound of seats springing upright. The magistrate in the middle had a shocked expression on her face as she took her seat, and for a brief moment April, feeling a bit paranoid, thought it was to do with her recommendation. However, she soon realised that it was due to the lady's eyebrows being permanently high up on her forehead.

The Local Authority barrister began by outlining the case and the stage they had reached so far, followed by the recommendations of the Local Authority to return Freddie to his family. When she had finished her introductory statement, she called April to the stand. Although this was something April had done many times over the years, she always felt the grip of nervousness in her stomach as she waited for the questions. In this case it was particularly so due to the controversial nature of her recommendation.

The first part was easy because Sheva, the Local Authority barrister's questions were designed to give April the opportunity to put her case to the court and convince the magistrates that letting Freddie go home would be the best option for him. Becky's barrister's cross-examination was another easy ride as April was on their side, but the questions put to her by the barrister representing Angela were another story. He was a stern-looking man with an abundance of grey hair, and April thought he had a pompous and condescending attitude. From where he was sitting, she could see that he was of short stature, but as he stood up from his chair, he seemed to be stretching his neck and standing on tiptoes in an unsuccessful attempt to appear taller than he was. Although April had not been looking forward to this part of the day, she couldn't help finding some amusement in the sight of this man who she decided was suffering from a Napoleon complex. He had obviously scrutinised her statement closely, hoping to find ways of discrediting her evidence. She remained calm, thinking carefully before answering and formally addressing the magistrates each time with her answers.

'We have heard during the course of these proceedings that a three-year-old boy has suffered a series of physical injuries which the expert witness has declared were not accidental, and the evidence suggests were caused whilst in his mother's care. In actual fact, the mother herself has admitted to causing them.

'Yet…' This was said loudly and followed by a short pause, during which he cast his eyes around the courtroom to ensure he had captured everyone's full attention. 'And yet,' he repeated, even more loudly, 'the Local Authority is recommending' (loudly again) 'that this little boy is placed back in the very environment where he is believed to have come to such harm.' Another long pause, designed to give everyone in the room plenty of time to think about what a complete idiot April must be. 'I can only assume, Ms Gardiner,' he drawled, 'that you have become overly familiar, in an unprofessional manner, with the Simmons family and this has clouded your judgement, and in doing so you have lost focus on the child. What is your answer to that, please?'

This was a question that April had known was coming, and she was well prepared for it. She turned to address the magistrates before drawing their attention to her statement of evidence which clearly set out the reasons for her decision. 'I cannot in all honesty say that this was an easy decision to make, or that it is guaranteed risk free. Whilst we are always striving to keep children safe from harm, and that is and will always be my priority, however much I like the family concerned…' She looked back at the barrister and paused, and, using his own tactics for gaining maximum effect, she raised her head and spoke slowly and thoughtfully. 'The balance of risk against the needs of the child is sometimes a difficult one, but in this case, it is my opinion that the best outcome for Freddie in the long term would be for him to return to his birth family.' At the same time, she looked to the back row where the family were sitting, still and silent, staring ahead like statues; the intense emotions they were experiencing written all over their faces.

Her evidence was over at last and the court was adjourned for lunch. Becky would be the next one to give evidence and April hoped against hope that she wouldn't inadvertently say anything that would worry the magistrates. She couldn't say that she didn't have any reservations about what she was proposing, but she was still convinced it was the right thing to do. She wanted Becky to do well on the witness stand and wished she could chat to her about it beforehand. Becky's lawyer would be advising her and all April could do was hope that the advice was good, and clear enough for Becky to understand.

When they returned Becky was called to the stand. She sailed through the questions from the Local Authority self-assuredly. She appeared full of confidence as she addressed the court, making direct eye contact with the barrister as she answered the questions put to her. The questions she was being asked were designed to highlight to the court the positive aspects of her as a mother and the lovely relationship she had with her son.

'Would you say, Ms Simmons, that your contact sessions with Freddie have been a positive experience for him? Does he enjoy the time with you?'

Becky loved to be praised and seemed to be quite enjoying being up on the stand as she gave examples of Freddie having a nice time during the contact sessions.

'Can you tell the court, Ms Simmons, how Freddie behaves when he first sees you at contact, what you do with him whilst you are there, and how he is when you leave him?'

Becky was starting to visibly glow, telling the court all about the games she played with Freddie and the fun they had. She talked about making biscuits with him, and how he kept eating the chocolate. She had never had anything like this before, where a roomful of people sat listening intently whilst she talked about her mothering skills and her amazing little boy. 'He's only three but he is clever. We do counting together and he already knows some of his numbers.' With this she looked around the court, expecting gasps of admiration for her little boy's cleverness, her face radiating pride.

'And when you say goodbye to him at the end of the contact Ms Simmons, what happens?'

'He cries and clings to me. I hate it, I really do. I want to cry too but April said I mustn't cry in front of him so I wait until he's gone; but it's hard. It's really hard to leave him when he's crying.'

216

'Thank you, Ms Simmons, I have no further questions.'

Angela's barrister stood up and reminded Becky who he was. He gave his name and explained that he was there to represent the guardian. His first question was straight to the point. 'Ms Simmons, you are aware of the expert witness statement which reported on Freddie's non-accidental injuries which he sustained whilst in your care?'

In an instant, Becky's face drained of colour; for a moment she looked as though she was about to pass out. As usual when faced with a difficult, unwelcome question, she remained speechless and stared blankly at the questioner.

'Ms Simmons, I must insist that you answer my question,' the barrister said impatiently.

April looked again at the magistrate's eyebrows, which appeared to have risen even further up her forehead.

'Yes,' Becky murmured into her chest.

'You have admitted in your statement that you hit Freddie yourself due to your fear of Mr Lyons. Is that correct?'

'Yes,' she murmured again. She was now looking at the floor when she spoke.

The rest of the questions were harsh, unrelenting and direct, exactly as one would expect from an opposing barrister. April couldn't help feeling very sorry for Becky and was willing her to stand up for herself. The barrister had skilfully made sure the court was in no doubt about Becky's direct complicity in the harm Freddie had endured, and Becky did not have the confidence or intellectual capacity to defend herself.

In her evidence, Angela gave a convincing account of why it would be foolhardy to return Freddie to his mother. 'In my opinion there is no reason to believe that what happened to Freddie could not happen again. It is our duty to ensure this little boy is not put back into the vulnerable situation he has been removed from. The baby is also at risk for the same reasons. I have given credence to the evidence given by the social worker and the mother, but I remain of the view that both Freddie and the baby should be placed for adoption to ensure their future safety.'

April heard a gasp from the back of the court, and a chair seat swung into its upright position as Mr Simmons marched out of the room. As the door swung shut behind him all faces that had turned to see what was happening turned back to the magistrates to see what would happen next.

The barristers took their turns to sum up before the court was adjourned, whilst the magistrates left with the legal advisor to make their decision. It could go either way, but the one thing that was certain was that the guardian's recommendations were nearly always given more credence than the social worker's. The fact that there was a baby involved also made it more likely Angela would get her way, because the younger the child was, the higher the risk was likely to be. An older child can talk and will generally be seen by other professionals, whereas this isn't necessarily the case with a baby. The more April thought about it, the more she came to the conclusion that the court would agree with Angela and Becky's two children would be taken away from her permanently.

Mr and Mrs Simmons had gone outside for cigarettes, and Leon and Becky sat close together on chairs in the waiting area. April was back in the little room but she could see through the glass in the door that Leon was talking earnestly to Becky, who was leaning forward, looking at the floor. Leon's hand was on top of hers, clearly trying to comfort her. April turned away and took a seat at the table.

You could never tell how long a judgement would take, and she had been involved in cases where they had waited more than three hours. She would have liked to tackle some of her other work whilst waiting but she found care proceedings much too intense to be able to think of anything else. She did nothing but stand at the window, gazing out. From where she stood, she could see the comings and goings of the court – lawyers in suits, hurrying with their trolleys; young men, women and couples, some getting out of taxis, all with court-related issues. Suddenly a wave of exhaustion overwhelmed her and she had to take a seat. She had been taking iron tablets which had helped with the dizzy spells, but she still felt constantly tired.

It was quite a surprise when they were called back into the courtroom after only a short time. April had expected to have to wait much longer. She knew this didn't bode well for Becky.

Everyone returned to their seats and April noticed that Mr Simmons was back in the courtroom along with the rest of the family. When everyone was back and seated, the magistrates returned and took their seats on the podium. The woman in the middle with the shocked expression read from a sheet of paper which summarised the case. There was hardly a murmur from anyone else in the room.

'Our findings based on the evidence we have heard today, and the reports provided by the parties are that if Freddie and the unborn baby are placed in their mother's care there remains potential for further harm.'

April felt her heart sink. It's just as I thought. They have gone with the guardian. I should have known all along that's what they would do. All she could think about was how she would convince Freddie that he needed to have a new mummy.

The magistrate continued speaking. 'This has been a very difficult decision and we commend the social worker and the guardian for their thorough assessments which have been more than helpful to us in reaching our conclusion. We have considered case law and sought counsel from our legal advisor which has helped us to reach our final decision. Wherever possible children should be given the opportunity to be raised within their birth family, and this is a case where we believe that it is possible, given the mother's late but honest disclosure and change of circumstances. For that reason, our judgement is that Freddie should be returned to his mother's care and Ms Simmons should also be given the opportunity to care for the new baby. We recommend that Social Services continue to provide support and a Supervision Order will be made today, as requested by the social worker.'

There were raptures from the back row and April, looking round, saw that the family were all hugging each other in delight and disbelief. She could see Becky's broad smile and the tears streaming down her face.

Her job finished, April packed her papers away, picked up her bag and started to walk out of the court, but before she reached the door, she was pulled into the middle of the family group by Mr Simmons and found herself being hugged and thanked. Although this wasn't really appropriate and she had never experienced anything like it before, she couldn't help feeling moved by being included in the family's joy.

April left the court feeling very pleased about the outcome. It was lovely to see the family so ecstatically happy; a welcome change to the majority of cases she had taken to court. Whilst her instinct told her that on this occasion, the right decision had been made, there was a persistent niggle inside her head, especially now that little Freddie would be returned to his mother the following day. Social workers were not infallible and could only try to do what they thought was right, and whilst she hoped against hope that the decision was the right one and her reasons were carefully balanced, how could anyone be really sure?

Her journey home was a nightmare. It was the wrong time of day to be out on the road, with everyone doing the same thing, trying to get home after a day's work. She was sitting waiting for the traffic lights to change, which seemed to be taking an eternity, when her thoughts drifted back to the nurse's suggestion of possible pregnancy. She had tried hard to forget what had been said but just hadn't been able to push it from her mind. At last the lights changed but she found herself, instead of turning right towards home, going straight across the junction towards the town. She was responding to an overpowering need that had been slowly developing since the suggestion had been made that she could be pregnant, and was now heading to the chemist to purchase a pregnancy test.

At home she sat with the test kit on the table in front of her for quite some time, just staring at it. She picked it up a couple of times, ready to start the process, but then put it back down again. The apprehension was killing her. She didn't know what she was hoping for. If she was pregnant, she would have the terrible worry of another miscarriage, but if she wasn't, she would be upset. Either way, she couldn't win.

At last she found the courage to go to the bathroom and do what she had to do. She slowly pulled the wrapper off the tester which she screwed into a ball and placed on the side of the bath. There was no need to read the instructions because she knew exactly what to do. There being no other delaying tactics she could muster, she did the test and waited. Holding it up to the skylight, she saw with astonishment that it was positive. In total disbelief, she carefully carried the test closer to the window. She needed to make doubly sure. With the daylight shining directly on the test face, it still said positive. She placed it carefully on the table, wrung her hands and allowed a smile to spread slowly across her face. She then sat back down at the table, trying to calm herself and properly absorb what had just happened.

When she finally stopped reeling, she started to think about what to do next. Should she phone Jed now or wait until tonight? Should she not tell him until she reached the twelve-week stage? She had been here before, and recognised the need for caution. At the same time, she was acutely conscious that she would not be able to delay telling Jed, however strong her protective instinct. Still smiling in disbelief, she filled the kettle and made herself a cup of lemon tea in an attempt to settle the jitters in her stomach. Her earlier pang of foreboding had been wiped away by joy.

26

SLIPPERY SLOPE

After weeks of sleeping in the park or on a floor in someone's bedsit, anaesthetised by alcohol most of the time, Sam was back in her flat in Fairfield Rise. Things were looking up a bit for her; she had been given a reprieve on her tenancy and a new agreement had been signed giving her more time to pay off the rent arrears. The best thing was, she was no longer going to be on her own in the flat; she had a new boyfriend, Ryan from London, whom she met through the internet.

Ryan had moved around a lot, staying with various friends or sometimes sleeping on the streets, until he came into contact with Sam. They had been chatting online for two or three days when he suggested they meet, and within a few hours Sam was waiting at the station to take him back to her flat. She had seen photos of him, but the young man who stood in front of her didn't bear much resemblance to them, although she could tell it was the same person. She was surprised at how thin he was. He was tall with cropped ginger hair and freckles. He had piercings in both ears, a spike through one eyebrow and a heavily tattooed body. They stood on the platform, looking at each other awkwardly, not really knowing how to begin. Communicating on Facebook is a lot easier than standing face to face with someone you've never actually met before.

They set off together, heading for Fairfield Rise, leaving the station behind them and passing through a small, busy park which led into the town centre; walking side by side but feeling very much like the strangers they were. This was a Sunday and although it was a dull, drizzly day, families were out with their children, having picnics, feeding the ducks, playing on the swings and roundabouts. Various bicycles ridden by adults, children and young people weaved in and out as the two of them walked along the path. A skateboarder nearly knocked Ryan flying when he swerved to avoid a little dog that had been let off its leash. 'Fuckin' prat,' Ryan yelled aggressively.

As they turned into Coronation Estate, Ryan noticed the grocer's shop on the corner. 'Have you got any booze in your flat?' he asked.

'No, I haven't got any money. I don't get my money till Tuesday.'

'Shit, I haven't got any either. What shall we do?' he said, clearly agitated.

Sam felt a bit annoyed that he didn't have any money. She was wondering what he would do for food. She couldn't afford to keep him on her pitiful benefits. She was struggling to feed herself.

They turned the corner into Elder Road and then crossed the road to Fairfield Rise. Hardly any conversation had passed between them. As Sam opened the door to her flat, a strong smell of must and damp, mingled with the greasy smell of stale chips which she had eaten the day before, wafted over them. She shivered as the damp chill inside the flat settled on her skin. It was still early evening but there was a nip in the air which the Victorian sash windows and thirty-year-old boiler could not protect against. She tried to leave the heating off whenever she could because she got so fed up feeding the meter with all her money. It was never really warm in the flat, even with the heating on full.

'Is there anywhere you can score around here?' Ryan asked as they walked into the flat.

'Score what?' Sam asked, slightly alarmed.

Ryan laughed mockingly. 'What do you think? Anything, ketamine, crack, weed.'

223

'I don't take drugs, and anyway we haven't got any money.' Sam had smoked weed a few times and tried speed once but she was a little bit scared of drugs. At least she knew where she was with alcohol. She enjoyed it and knew what the consequences were going to be. Her social networks were made up of drinkers too, rather than drug users, although she was aware that some of them did both.

Ryan made himself at home by slumping into an armchair, throwing his legs over the arm and rolling a cigarette. Sam put a thick cardigan around her shoulders before sitting down and turning the television on. She wasn't really sure what Ryan was expecting of her but had continued to worry about the fact that he had no money. She looked at him slouched on her chair and was wondering whether she should have waited a bit longer before inviting him to stay.

'I'm starving,' he announced suddenly. 'What have you got to eat?'

Sam was a bit put out by this but answered meekly, 'I think I've got a packet of pasta in the cupboard.'

'That sounds good,' he said as he stubbed out the end of his roll-up in the already overflowing ashtray which sat on his lap.

'I'll go and make some then,' she said, getting up and going into the kitchen.

'Yeah, then I'll go and score.'

The pasta was cooked and eaten and then Ryan set off to wherever he was going to 'score' whilst Sam sat waiting nervously, not knowing what to expect. She was thinking that she would let him stay tonight since he had come all the way down from London, but she would ask him to leave tomorrow. She had decided it would be better to be on her own than with someone who didn't have any money and she wasn't even sure she liked very much.

It was nearly two hours before the bell rang and Ryan was back. Sam had been half-hoping he wouldn't come back.

'Sorted,' he said, looking pleased with himself as he walked back into the flat as though it was his own.

'What have you got?' she asked nervously.

'Ketamine, of course; only the best.'

'How did you get that when you've no money?'

'Never you mind; I got it and that's all you need to know. Just chill out, will you, and get off my case.'

Sam was reluctant about trying ketamine at first, worried by the unknown. Ryan was very persuasive, talking convincingly about how great it felt. He laughed loudly when she said she would rather have some beers.

'You wait, you'll be begging me for some more once you've tried it. Don't worry, you won't get hooked; you'll just like it.'

He rolled the ketamine into a joint and passed it to Sam. They sat together on the settee, and as she puffed at it, she slowly felt the enduring, low-level depression that was constantly with her start to dissipate and her spirits lift. The two of them moved closer, smiling and laughing together. Sam soon found herself drifting into her own sense of being. She was no longer sitting on the sofa in her cold, damp flat with a man she hardly knew. She was looking down from her position in the sky onto a crystal-blue ocean which rippled with sparkles of sunlight that bounced from the tips of the waves. She then felt herself gracefully and slowly enter the water, toes first, sinking blissfully down until her whole body was immersed in the delightful, comforting warmth. She was floating effortlessly with her head above the surface, her body swaying gently with the water's motion. She was a water nymph, at one with the elements; it was glorious. Sunlight sparkled all around her like diamonds which turned into prisms, and then colourful fireworks when she gently splashed the water with her hands. The power of being able to turn sunlight into firecrackers was exhilarating and she laughed and laughed, increasing the speed of her flapping hands, creating more and more colour and light which completely surrounded her.

She floated calmly on her back and watched whilst the firecrackers around her began to slow down, sizzling out before reaching their full height, dying in mid-air. The water was changing from crystal blue to grey and then shadowy black as the sunlight started to fade. The fireworks stopped completely and the water became still and cold, making her shiver. She thought she heard voices from a distance, but all she could see was water and darkness. There was no sky and no horizon. She heard the voices again, and then she recognised Tayla's. She was shouting, 'Mummy, Mummy.' Sam thought she could tell which direction the voice was coming from, but when she turned to swim in that direction, she realised the voice was behind her. She turned in the water, which was rapidly becoming dense and too thick to swim in. She heard the voice again shouting, 'Mummy, Mummy', and then it was Lily Grace shouting, 'Mummy, come back, I need you.' Sam was desperate to get to them. Her children needed her and she was stuck in this water which had now become a muddy swamp. The voices were coming from all directions and she didn't know which way to turn. She was trying to shout for someone to help her, but when she opened her mouth it filled up with mud, and the weight of it caused her to sink down into the mire. She was desperately trying to stay afloat and work out which direction the voices were coming from.

The rest of the night was spent in oblivion, and when Sam woke, she was scantily dressed and stretched out on her back across the settee. Ryan's head and shoulders were on the settee but his knees were on the floor, mouth wide open, completely dead to the world. A heavy and enduring melancholy was part of Sam's everyday existence but this morning it was too heavy to bear, the inevitable consequence of seeking temporary relief through illicit substances. She tried to drag herself off the settee but had no motivation to move. She lay there looking at the ceiling, thinking the blackest thoughts. She wiped at the constant stream of tears that ran down her face as she thought about everything that had happened to her, and every horrible experience was relived, from childhood to the present, like a film replaying itself. The pain felt so raw; it was as though it had all happened yesterday. She continued to lie on the settee as her thoughts became darker and more sinister, until she remembered with some relief that there was a way out of this misery.

The realisation that she had the power to end it all gave her the motivation to move off the settee and get herself dressed. She looked at Ryan, still lying there, and felt disgust at him and herself. Her mood was lifted by the thought that her disgusting self could be brought to an end.

It was still very early in the morning and the streets were empty and still as she made her way to the railway station. She had spent a considerable amount of time over the years pondering on the best way to kill herself. If she took an overdose there was a chance she could be found and saved, or she could end up being a vegetable, which would be even worse. The best way to ensure success was to throw herself under a train. The fear of pain had always been enough to stop her actually carrying out the plan, but this time she felt no fear. Living was worse and more painful than death could ever be.

Sam carried on walking, wiping at the drizzly rain on her face, until she turned into the open doors of the Victorian station building. There were a few early commuters milling around but no sign of any staff as she made her way over the concrete steps and then walked to the end of the platform. As she stood waiting, she gazed at the huge poster facing her from the opposite platform, which displayed a woman, slim and beautiful, in a white bikini with long dark hair tumbling down her back as she walked across white sands towards a crystal-blue sea. It was advertising luxury holidays in the Indian Ocean. This was not even within the scope of Sam's dreams.

She had been there for only a few minutes when she heard the distant rumbling of a train, which became increasingly loud as it approached. She walked to the edge of the platform in readiness and stood with her toes over the side. She almost felt euphoric as the end drew nearer and she watched the train approach from the tunnel.

Suddenly, from out of the darkness, she heard the voices of Lily Grace and Tayla, which seemed to be mingling with the rhythm of the train. They sounded just as they had during her drug-induced hallucination the previous night. She stepped back from the platform just as the train sped through. It was the fast train to London which didn't stop at this station.

She stood as though in a trance, staring at the railway track below where her mangled body should have been. She had not changed her mind; she just needed to see the children to say goodbye. As she started to think about what she would say to them it gradually dawned on her that it was Monday and she was supposed to have contact with them. A surge of desperation overcame her and, without hesitation, she turned away from the platform and headed back home to get ready.

She would probably be a bit late but she rushed around, trying unsuccessfully to find something clean to put on. She hadn't done any washing for weeks because she hadn't been at home. Searching through a pile of clothes on her bedroom floor, she managed to find some jeans that looked OK and a long jumper that was frayed around one of the elbows. It smelt clean, so would have to do. She pulled a brush through her matted hair and left the flat to walk to the Family Centre, not knowing or caring where Ryan was.

Although the weather had turned cold, she was still wearing sandals and her feet were blue. She walked as fast as she could, almost breaking into a run at times, despite her muzzy head, and managed to arrive at the Family Centre just after ten. She rushed into the reception, feeling pleased that she hadn't missed much time with her children. She stood waiting beside the reception desk, shuffling her feet back and forwards and tapping on the counter whilst the receptionist checked the appointment book. Sam was becoming frustrated because she had already missed ten minutes of her time – why couldn't this woman just let her in?

After what seemed like an eternity, the receptionist looked up. 'Are you sure you've got contact today, only there's nothing in the book?' she asked, looking at Sam over the top of her spectacles.

'Yes, of course I'm sure,' Sam said, really frustrated now. 'My kids will be in there waiting for me.'

'There are no children in there at the moment. Another session is due to start at eleven but that is not for you, I'm afraid. Would you like me to contact the social worker to find out what's going on?'

'Yes,' Sam said with a big sigh, 'thanks, that would be great!'

The receptionist put on ear phones and seemed to be clicking something on the computer. Sam didn't know what was going on until she heard the receptionist speaking, 'Oh, I see. OK, I will explain that to her.' Taking off her ear phones, she returned her attention to Sam. 'The social worker said contact was not arranged because you were supposed to phone first to confirm you were coming.'

Sam looked at her in disbelief. She knew it was true but she couldn't believe she had forgotten that. She wanted to see her children, she was desperate to see them, especially after the dreadful hallucination she'd had the previous night, which still seemed vividly real. She stood looking at the receptionist, hoping that something would change, that she would say she could sort it out. She then turned to walk away, head down, knowing she had lost, that there was nothing she could do, again. The only option was to go back to her flat and try to get through the rest of the day.

27

A BREAKTHROUGH FOR APRIL

April had been for her twelve-week antenatal appointment and she and Jed were walking back to the car, holding hands and ecstatic. Until they had seen the little body moving around inside her on the scan, neither of them had dared to believe they were really going to be parents. It was now sinking in, and this joint achievement and mutual joy brought them even closer together.

When they arrived home, April let herself in the front door whilst Jed put the car in the garage. It was due to get really cold and frosty overnight. After letting herself in, she picked up the pile of post which lay on the mat, sorting through the junk mail to find anything that might be remotely important. Two letters from the bank, one each for her and Jed, and another in a white envelope addressed to April Gardiner. Her heart missed a beat. She had given up hope of getting a reply from her father and hardly thought about it now, but staring wide-eyed at the envelope, she wondered if this could be it. She tried to avoid building her hopes up but opened it quickly and, looking straight to the bottom of the letter, saw the words, With much love, Dad. Her insides took a leap and she let out a squeal of astonishment just as Jed walked in the door.

'April, what's the matter, what is it?' he said, his eyes full of concern.

'I don't believe… I just can't… you read it for me, please; I can't read it. What does it say?' she said, handing him the letter with a trembling hand.

Jed started reading aloud.

> *Dear April,*
>
> *I cannot tell you how happy I was to receive your letter. I have never stopped thinking about you and wondering how you both are, longing to see you and Max and hoping that one day you would want to find me. I forgave your mother years ago for what she did to me and none of that matters any more. I wasn't sure what you knew about the past and didn't want to disrupt your lives in any way. You would never believe how much I have missed you.*
>
> *Unfortunately, I have been out of the country for some months, which is why I didn't reply sooner. Please let me know where and when we can meet; the sooner the better. Too many years have already been lost.*
>
> *With much love,*
>
> *Dad xxx*

April sat down heavily on a dining chair, and with her elbows resting on the table she held her head in both hands in an attempt to stop the whirling in her brain.

'You never told me that you had written to your dad. I wish you wouldn't keep me in the dark about these things, April.' Jed sat down next to her, took hold of her hands and looked intently into her eyes.

'But you read what he said?' April said breathlessly. 'He said he has forgiven Mum; what does he mean? He went off with someone else; why would he have to forgive Mum?'

There was a long silence, both of them trying to take in the startling revelation and think about what it could mean.

Eventually Jed spoke. 'Well, it could mean that your mum didn't tell the truth, I suppose. Maybe it wasn't him.' He was treading carefully with this suggestion, not knowing what April's reaction might be.

'That can't be possible. Mum would not have left him, and I'm absolutely sure she wouldn't have lied all these years, blaming him. She's not that kind of person; she's kind and honest. She could never have been that deceitful.'

There was another short silence; then Jed said, 'It could explain a lot of things, such as why she would never talk about it. Perhaps she couldn't cope with repeating the lies she told. Well, you know what you have to do now; you need to arrange to meet him and hear his side of the story. It seems to be the fairest way.'

'Do I tell Mum I'm meeting him or not? What do you think I should do?'

'I think you should, April; it would not be good to deceive her. She'll be upset and I know it was wrong of her to keep you in the dark all this time, but she doesn't deserve to be deceived in that way. We don't know anything yet so we shouldn't make judgements.'

'You're right as usual,' she said, standing up and placing a long kiss on his forehead.

Although April was exhausted, she just could not settle into sleep. There were so many mixed emotions running through her brain: her father, the baby, her mother, and amongst all of this she couldn't help thinking about Sam, who had not been seen since she had turned up at the Family Centre expecting to have contact with her children. She couldn't help worrying about her, particularly as she knew nobody else would be.

She tossed and turned for hours whilst Jed slept peacefully beside her. Luckily, she didn't have to worry about disturbing him; it didn't matter what she did, once he was asleep an earthquake wouldn't wake him. After lying there for some time, she became fed up and decided to go downstairs. She wanted to read the letter again to make sure she hadn't dreamt it, but also to reread the reference to her father forgiving her mum. Things can appear quite different late at night when all you are left with are your thoughts, and April had begun to wonder whether they had misunderstood something in the letter. She had not been thinking straight at first and she needed to check it all again. She put on her long, fluffy white bathrobe and made herself steaming hot chocolate before sitting down with the letter in front of her.

She was still there in the morning after the alarm had woken Jed up for work. He came downstairs to find her fast asleep in the armchair, head rolled back into the cushion and the letter still on her lap. He shook her gently to wake her up and placed the cup of green tea he had made in front of her.

'What time is it? I need to go to bed.' She sat up with a start.

'It's time to go to work now, April; you've slept all night in the chair.'

'Oh my God, I've got a really busy day today as well.' She leaned forward, ready to get up off the chair, but Jed stopped her with his hand.

'Stay where you are, April; you should take today off. You've had a lot going on these last few hours; you need to stay at home. I can phone and say you're sick.'

April laughed. 'You must be joking; I can't do that. I've got far too much to do,' she said, starting to get up again.

'Let someone else do it.'

'No one else will do it; it will all just be waiting for me when I go back. I will go in, I'm fine. I just need a shower and some orange juice. I don't want breakfast.'

Jed tutted as he walked into the kitchen to get himself another coffee. April made herself a kiwi and cucumber smoothie to take to the office. She was trying to make up for her lack of appetite and boost her energy by eating plenty of fruit and vegetables. She wouldn't be able to face it, though, until much later in the day.

That evening, April phoned her mum to make arrangements for her to come and spend some time with them. Diana was delighted;

she usually had to invite herself so it made a nice change to actually be asked, although Jed and April had always made it clear she was welcome any time. April had two important pieces of news to tell her, the first being the pregnancy. So far only she and Jed knew; she had been determined not to tell anyone else until she was out of the so-called danger zone of the first twelve weeks, and now that time had come, she was impatient to tell everyone the news. One person she was very keen to tell was Jenny, the adoption social worker. April had continued to feel angry about the way their case had been handled and she was looking forward to phoning and telling her to close the case completely because she was no longer needed.

The next morning, she was early to arrive at work and the only other social worker in was Paula, who was clearly dying to chat to someone.

'You seem to be dashing in and out so much these days; we don't get the chance to catch up.'

April sat down, turned on her laptop and waited for it to start up. She swivelled round in her chair to face Paula, who had sat down next to her. She had her usual smoothie to drink later and placed it on the table beside her laptop, ready to put in the fridge.

'No wonder you look so healthy, April. Is that why you've developed that glow?'

April was surprised to hear Paula say that since she hadn't been feeling her best and especially after a few consecutive nights of fretful sleep. 'Thanks, Paula. I have got an announcement to make but I won't say anything yet.' She hadn't meant to say anything but her mouth seemed to have a will of its own sometimes.

Paula put her finger to her mouth and tapped her lips, pondering. 'Hmm, you've had dizzy spells, you've looked pasty and now you're radiant, you're drinking superfood smoothies. April, you wouldn't be pregnant, I suppose?' She wore a knowing smile.

April couldn't prevent the broad smile forming on her face, and there was nothing else she could do but admit to Paula that she was right. 'I wasn't going to say but, yes, I am. I've had the twelve-week scan and everything is good.'

She waited for Paula's response. She could see that her eyes had glazed over with tears as she stood up from her chair, bent over and hugged April so hard she almost stopped breathing.

'I'm so pleased for you.' She beamed. 'How could you have kept it quiet?'

'I don't want everyone to know yet, Paula, if you don't mind. Our families don't know yet and I think they might be a little bit upset if they find out they are the last to know.'

'Of course, I won't say anything to anyone. I wouldn't dream of it, anyway; that's for your pleasure.'

'So how are things going with you, Paula? How is your relationship with… um, sorry, I've forgotten his name?' April looked sheepishly at her.

'It's Simon, and we are still together,' Paula said, looking really pleased with herself. 'I haven't forgotten the dinner party I promised; it's been over a month now but as Christmas is coming up, I think I will arrange something Christmassy. You'll be boring now, though, won't you? You won't be able to drink and you'll want to talk about mumsy things.'

They both laughed really loudly. Others had come into the office by now and started working, and April and Paula's mirth caused them to look up from their computers to see what the laughter was about.

'I must get on with arranging that dinner party I promised; I really want you to meet him now; he's just so lovely.'

'I'm really pleased to hear that all the effort hasn't been in vain, and I can't wait to meet him,' April said as they hugged again.

Paula went back to her desk and April turned around in her chair to face her computer. She was putting the finishing touches on the court report for Lily Grace and Tayla. Her conclusion had to be that Sam could not provide safe and adequate care for her children and that it would be in their best interests to be adopted. She wrote this with a heavy heart because she knew that somewhere deep inside

Sam was a caring, loving mother trying hard to emerge, and although she had really wanted to overcome her difficulties, she just couldn't do it; she was too emotionally frail. It could have been so different if only Sam had what other people took for granted: parents or family to support her. Someone she could turn to and trust when things became difficult; someone who cared about her.

April picked Diana up from the station late on Saturday afternoon. Back home, she got out of the car and walked round to the passenger side to help with the multiple bags and overnight case she'd piled on the back seat.

'What on earth have you got in all these bags?' April asked.

'Oh, just some bits and pieces; food and a little pot plant to put on your kitchen table.'

'You shouldn't bring things, Mum; it's a struggle on the train with all these bags. We've got plenty of food in the house and we can always buy a pot plant from down the road.'

'I know, dear, but you know I like to buy you things. Once I've got a grandchild, I will spend all my money on him or her instead of you, so you'd better make the most of it.'

April stopped in her tracks. How did she know already? She was just about to question this when it dawned on her that Diana was still thinking about adoption.

That evening, the three of them sat together in the lounge after finishing the lovely meal April had cooked of seared scallops, sea bass and crème caramel. They had a bottle of Touraine to wash it down with although, of course April had fizzy water instead. She hadn't been able to decide whether to tell her mother about the pregnancy first and then about the events with her father, or the other way around, but the problem resolved itself when Diana noticed Jed filling her glass and then his own with wine, leaving April without any. She had already noticed April did not eat the scallops and was far too astute to let this unusual behaviour go by without question.

'April, what's this? Are you not having any wine? I've never known that before; you must be unwell. What's going on?' She looked back and forth from April to Jed, then back to April, waiting impatiently for an answer.

Jed and April looked at each other and smiled.

'April!' Diana's eyes widened. 'I can't believe it – you're pregnant, aren't you?'

'Yes, Mum, I am.' April felt her cheeks begin to glow as she waited for her mother's response.

'I noticed you looked well. That was the first thing I thought when I got off the train. I thought, April has a healthy glow. I should have guessed.' She then asked with trepidation, 'How far gone?'

'I'm well past the twelve-week period; almost four months now, they tell me.'

Diana jumped up off her chair and clapped her hands in delight. 'Wonderful, wonderful; it's just so wonderful. I never dreamt of this after all you said about what you had been through.' She then looked seriously at each of them in turn. 'You won't be going ahead with the adoption now then?'

They both laughed at this; there was so much she didn't know.

'We might in the future, who knows, but we're going to have our own child first and see how that goes.'

The happiness on all their faces almost lit up the room.

As they sat down to get comfortable in the lounge, April said, 'Mum, I've got something else to tell you. I'm not sure you are going to be so happy about this, though.'

'What's that, dear?' Diana said with moderate interest. She didn't envisage that anything could dampen the surging joy she was still experiencing after April's news.

April paused. She was really not looking forward to this discussion, but there was no way out of it. It had to happen and she just hoped the lovely surprise of the pregnancy was enough to ward off any horrible fallout from this new revelation. She was still hesitant and found nothing was coming out of her mouth. She hadn't planned exactly how she was going to tell her, or what she was going to say.

Suddenly, Jed spoke. 'Diana, it's about April's dad.'

Diana's face turned a stony shade of grey. 'What about April's dad?' she asked diffidently.

Jed went on to explain in detail all that had happened, including the adoption being put on hold because of the unresolved issue. When he had finished, both he and April sat watching Diana with bated breath, April biting her bottom lip.

Diana suddenly stood up and left the room. She walked into the kitchen and then, as quick as she had left, she was back again, sitting bolt upright in the same chair, staring at the wall. To Jed and April's surprise, she started talking about the past, admitting that she was to blame for everything. Anthony had been working long hours and she was lonely at home with two babies. She started working part-time and met a man, whom she thought she was in love with. Anthony found out about it and left her. The affair turned out to be only an infatuation and she had tried to reconcile with Anthony, realising that he was the one she really loved, but he couldn't forgive her. They tried to get back together for a short time but Anthony was hurt and bitter and it kept coming between them, ultimately tearing them apart. As she spoke, Diana continued to stare at the wall, her body rigid.

Instead of being angry with her mum as she had expected, April felt a strong, deep compassion. She couldn't sit still any longer. She stood up and walked over to the window. 'That's not the worst thing anyone has ever done, Mum, and let's face it, Dad should have been able to find it in his heart to forgive you.'

By this time Diana had taken a tissue from her pocket and was wiping tears from her eyes. 'You don't know him, April, he's a very proud man.'

April sat on the arm of her mother's chair and put her arm around her shoulders. 'You were both to blame in your own ways; we all make mistakes, Mum. He might not have been able to forgive you but you need to forgive yourself.' April was thinking about Miles and how she might have been tempted by him if the situation had been similar. 'He forgives you now though, he said so in the letter'.

'I should have told you the truth. I was too ashamed.'

'If only you'd told me before. There was no need for you to suffer this guilt for all these years on your own. You should have told me,' April scolded.

28

THE UNFAIRNESS OF LIFE

April was back in the magistrates' court preparing the case with the Local Authority barrister. It was going to be straightforward and shouldn't take long because this time the guardian agreed with April, and Sam hadn't been seen or heard from for nearly six weeks. Adopters had already been identified for Tayla and Lily Grace and the introductory period would start as soon as it was agreed by the court. It was ironic that the couple who had been chosen to have the girls were similar in some ways to April and Jed: similar ages, professional, childless with unexplained infertility, nice comfortable home and a wide extended family who were very supportive of them. April could almost feel the emotions they would be experiencing at this time. She had explained to the couple that the court needed to agree with the adoption plan and unexpected things could happen in court, but nevertheless they were probably still brimming with hope and excitement. They had already prepared books for the children which contained photographs of themselves, their families, and Mimi, their spaniel. One of the books had photos of the family home, the bedrooms which had been decorated especially to suit the little girls' tastes, with princess bedding; the large garden with a summer house, patio and built-in barbecue at the bottom.

As April and the barrister chatted in the little meeting room, she glanced out of the window and was shocked to see, amongst the various people coming and going, Sam, looking a bit bedraggled, with her hands in her pockets, striding intently towards the main entrance. April moved closer to the window to make sure of what she was seeing, but Sam had already disappeared through the glass entrance. She was the last person April had expected to see; she had given no indication that she was coming, although it had still been assumed by the court that she contested the plan for adoption and continued to want her children returned to her care.

April left the room and quickly walked down the stairs to the entrance lobby where she could see Sam just coming through the bag check. She waited for her to come through.

'Sam, I didn't think you would come today. How are you?'

Sam stopped walking and looked, hollow-eyed, at April. 'What did you think, then; that you could just take my kids and I was gonna sit back and say, "Fine"? I've come to get my kids back; they need to be back with me. They're my kids!'

April was more than certain that Sam didn't have any chance of getting what she wanted, but at the same time she was pleased to see that she still had some fight left in her. It would be good for Lily Grace and Tayla as they got older to know that their mum had fought hard for them. They would know how much she loved them.

'Well, you have just as much right to be heard as anyone else, Sam, and I'm sure the magistrates will want to hear what you have to say. It's a shame you didn't manage to come to contact, though, because they won't be impressed with that.'

'I did come but you wouldn't let me see them. I didn't even feel very well but I came because I didn't want to let them down.'

'There's no point in us arguing about this now, where everyone can hear. You will have your chance to tell this to the magistrates.' With this, April left. She didn't want to get into an argument with Sam, who was clearly highly agitated. She had noticed that Sam's hands were trembling as she spoke and her speech was slightly slurred, leaving her in no doubt that alcohol and possibly Class A drugs were still being used as a prop.

April's evidence was short and soon over with, and it was Sam's turn to take the stand. It was perfectly obvious to April, as she listened to the garbled answers Sam gave to the questions she was asked, that even her own barrister was aware there was no hope of winning their case and was just doing what was right and giving Sam her chance to speak. When it was over and the barristers had given their submissions, the magistrates adjourned but were back within half an hour. The decision was exactly as most people had expected and an order was made which gave the Local Authority permission to place Lily Grace and Tayla for adoption.

April cleared her papers away and picked up her jacket before turning around to see if Sam was OK. She hadn't heard her go but by the time she looked round, there was just an empty seat where Sam had previously been sitting. She felt sad and disappointed because she would have liked the opportunity to have a last word with her and perhaps wish her luck, but that was how these things often ended. Sam had been in April's life for nearly a year and a lot had happened since their first meeting in the flat in Fairfield Rise which had initially appeared clean and homely. She was sure Lily Grace and Tayla would have a lovely life with their new family and would be safe and well cared for, but there was always a sense of failure for the social worker when a mother lost custody of her children. April's next job would be to start preparing Lily Grace and Tayla for the big change in their lives. Although it was very sad for Sam, she had no doubt that the right decision had been made.

April needed to go back to the little meeting room to tie up a few formal issues with the barrister. As she waited for her, she gazed out of the window onto the front of the court, and there she saw Sam walking away with her hands in her pockets and her head down against the bitter wind that puffed out her thin nylon jacket. April couldn't help wondering what would become of her now.

242

As she watched Sam striding away from the court, completely and utterly alone, she suddenly felt her insides flutter, as though she had swallowed a large butterfly. Her hands flew to her belly, and a slow smile spread across her face as it dawned on her that this was her baby making its presence known. How extraordinary, she thought, that her baby's first movement should happen at this time.

Mingled with the joy, April felt a sense of unfairness which reminded her of a phrase from Thomas Hardy's book, Mayor of Casterbridge, which read: -

'There are some people in this world who are born to be unhappy, and for many people happiness was but the occasional episode in a general drama of pain'.

April wasn't sure that this was exactly as it was written in the novel, but it seemed to be an excellent summary of many people's lives.

ABOUT THE AUTHOR

Teresa was brought up in a mining village and was the fourth of six children. She loved school and had great fun, but didn't take life seriously or start studying until she was in her thirties and had two children. She has been married for 32 years and has three lovely grandchildren. Apart from writing and being with the grandchildren Teresa likes to spend her spare time playing tennis, gardening or socialising with friends.

Teresa has a degree in Psychology and Social Policy and qualified as a social worker in 2001. After eight years of working on the front line of social work in a children and families team, she started working with disabled children, then went on to become a manager. She is now a full time writer and novelist.

Teresa is a political activist and a campaigner for social justice. She believes that political systems should be based on fairness and that every child, whatever their circumstances should be provided with the opportunity to reach their full potential, and that every family is entitled to receive the support to help them achieve this.